· T R O P H I E S ·

English-Language Learners
Teacher's Guide
Grade 4

Harcourt

Orlando   Boston   Dallas   Chicago   San Diego

Visit *The Learning Site!*
www.harcourtschool.com

Printed in the United States of America

ISBN 0-15-329337-3

5 6 7 8 9 10 082 10 09 08 07 06 05 04

Table of Contents

© Harcourt

ANT MASI

© Harcourt

English-Language Learners Resource Kit Teacher's Guide

TROPHIES *English-Language Learners Kit* is designed to provide teachers with the materials for 30–45 minutes of daily instruction to be used in addition and connected to the basic instruction in the mainstream English classroom. Materials are designed to help English-language learners (ELLs) read, write, comprehend, and speak at personally and academically proficient levels. These skills, coupled with the instruction in TROPHIES, will enable ELLs to become proficient in English.

The Kit includes the following components:

Grade Level	Components
Kindergarten	*Alphabet Books Collection, Teacher's Resource Book, English-Language Learners Big Book*
1	*English-Language Learners Books Collection, Teacher's Guide,* laminated lap boards
2–6	*English-Language Learners Books Collection, Teacher's Guide,* laminated lap boards

How to Use This Guide

Each 6-page lesson is tied directly to the corresponding lesson in TROPHIES. The *English-Language Learners Teacher's Guide* lessons provide opportunities to preteach and reteach the skills students must master. Pages vi–xxi provide additional information for utilizing the 30–45-minute period.

Following is a brief description of what appears on each lesson page. Pages are linked to specific sections of TROPHIES lessons cited in the **BEFORE** and **AFTER** boxes.

■ **Page 1**   BEFORE/AFTER   **Building Background and Vocabulary**

The teacher **accesses students' prior knowledge by building broad background concept(s)** important to both the TROPHIES selection and the *English-Language Learners Book*. This provides a foundation for the specific background building done for the TROPHIES selection (page 2) and for the *English-Language Learners Book* (page 3). The teacher **preteaches and reteaches selection vocabulary** using the TROPHIES Reteach Vocabulary Teaching Transparency and context sentences. The **Fluency Practice** feature suggests ways that students can demonstrate their reading and speaking fluency daily.

■ **Page 2**   BEFORE/AFTER   **Reading the TROPHIES selection**

After **building specific background for the TROPHIES selection**, the teacher **preteaches the focus skill**. Students are encouraged to use graphic organizers to apply to the selection what they have learned about the skill. The teacher uses the **directed reading** section to guide students through the TROPHIES selection. Scaffolded questions are used to monitor comprehension. The focus skill will be **retaught** after both the TROPHIES selection and the *English-Language Learners Book* have been read.

■ **Page 3**   BEFORE/AFTER   **Reading the *English-Language Learners Book***

After **building specific background for the *English-Language Learners Book***, the teacher introduces the concept words, 5–8 high-utility words from the *English-Language Learners Book*. The teacher uses the **directed reading** section to guide students through the *English-Language Learners Book*. The teacher **reteaches the focus skill** and asks students to apply it through the *English-Language Learners Book*.

■ **Pages 4–5**   BEFORE/AFTER   **Writing and Grammar**

The **writing lessons** in this *Teacher's Guide* parallel those in TROPHIES, but are scaffolded, beginning with shared writing and progressing to interactive writing and independent writing. The rate at which students move from one type of writing to the next varies with grade level. Student-generated writing is used for fluency practice and as working models for revising practice. The **grammar instruction** parallels that in TROPHIES. An initial emphasis on oral grammar helps students develop an ear for the English language. Students then apply knowledge of the grammar skill to their writing, noting how and when it was used and correcting errors.

■ **Page 6**   **Copying Master**

The activities on this reproducible page provide practice with various parts of the lesson. Notes to the teacher give suggestions and tips for use.

English-Language Development Fluency Stages

ELLs in any given classroom may span a range of fluency stages. In terms of comprehension, it is not necessary for every student to understand every word the teacher says. Considerable language acquisition will occur with even a modest percentage of comprehensible input. The following criteria are given for five identified stages of fluency. Students at each stage can be expected to continue behaviors from the previous stage.

1. Beginning English-Language Learners

Listening/Speaking

- respond nonverbally or with one or two words and short phrases
- ask simple questions
- participate in songs, chants, and rhymes
- use present-tense verbs and simple plurals correctly
- participate in group-generated stories

Reading

- decode but have difficulty with English phonemic awareness
- comprehend simple content
- begin to read single words and short phrases

Writing

- copy, label, and list
- write familiar words and phrases

The teacher should

- model, rephrase, and repeat sentence patterns and vocabulary
- use the Total Physical Response (TPR) method in which the teacher gives a command involving an overt physical response to which students respond. Initially, the teacher performs the action with students, but eventually the students perform it on their own.

2. Early Intermediate English-Language Learners

Listening/Speaking

- begin to model verb tenses, such as present participles
- ask and answer simple questions about familiar content
- participate in face-to-face conversations with peers
- begin to self-check and self-correct

Reading

- comprehend and recall main ideas of a simple story or other content
- improve pronunciation and phonemic awareness
- read student-generated text

Writing

- use graphic organizers and writing frames
- write simple questions and answers

The teacher should

- provide opportunities for students to negotiate for meaning (See page xiv.)
- use pictures, graphic organizers, and sentence frames
- use interactive writing

© Harcourt

3. Intermediate English-Language Learners

Listening/Speaking

- express creative thoughts and use original language
- use complete simple sentences
- produce sustained conversation on a variety of topics

Reading

- interact with a variety of print

Writing

- transfer reading and oral language to writing
- write for a variety of purposes
- participate fully in editing

The teacher should

- provide shared, paired, and independent reading opportunities
- model and provide practice for using expanded verb tenses

4. Early Advanced English-Language Learners

Listening/Speaking

- generally comprehend all usual English speech
- demonstrate adequate pronunciation and grammar usage

Reading

- use a variety of reading strategies
- use various study skills

Writing

- use extended written production in all content areas
- use adjectives, adverbs, and figurative language in writing

The teacher should

- teach, model, and allow for expanded discourse in writing and reading

5. Advanced English-Language Learners

Listening/Speaking

- comprehend concrete and abstract topics and concepts
- use effortless, fluent speech

Reading

- read grade-level materials with limited difficulty

Writing

- write to meet social needs and academic demands

The teacher should

- teach, model, and allow for practice of complex sentence structures

Learning to Read and Reading to Learn
Distinguishing Between ELD and SDAIE Instruction

Like students everywhere, ELLs move from learning to read to reading to learn. Tailoring instruction for students who are new to English involves moving from English Language Development (ELD) to Specially Designed Academic Instruction in English (SDAIE). The differences are as follows:

English Language Development (formerly known as ESL) refers to the beginning stages of fluency. It is characterized by beginning literacy and language development, not grade-level content. Though ELD is important for ELLs at all stages of language acquisition, it is crucial for those students in the Beginning and Early Intermediate stages.

The components of an **ELD** lesson are as follows:

Access Prior Knowledge

- Use primary language as necessary.

Provide Comprehensible Input

- Introduce vocabulary, concepts, and language patterns, using rich context.
- Speak slowly and clearly.
- Avoid idioms.
- Use cognates whenever possible.
- Chunk instruction for ten minutes, followed by two minutes of peer interaction in students' primary language as necessary.
- Use gestures, facial expressions, and dramatization.
- Use visuals such as realia, pictures, graphic organizers, and videos.

Check for Understanding

- Elicit responses in ways that do not require oral production.
- Paraphrase, repeat, and expand on what was taught before asking students for confirmation of understanding.
- Allow for extensive student-to-student interaction in students' primary language as necessary.
- Provide many opportunities for practice of new language patterns, concepts, and vocabulary.

Foster Beginning Literacy

- Link instruction to students' background knowledge.
- Make purposes clear.
- Scaffold activities by teacher modeling, cooperative group practice, and individual use.

Assessment

- Focus on language development.

The components of a **SDAIE** lesson are as follows:

Tap Prior Knowledge

- Access knowledge of content, vocabulary, and sentence structures.

Contextualize the Lesson

- Scaffold the instruction.
- Reuse vocabulary and key concepts in a variety of ways.
- Summarize the instruction after each lesson.

Modify the Text

- Develop background knowledge to initiate the lesson.
- Preview in primary language.
- Use read-alouds followed by group discussions.
- Provide a variety of high-interest, low-readability texts.
- Model reading and writing by thinking aloud strategies as you use them.
- Have students develop their own dictionaries. (See page xi.)
- Provide a variety of opportunities for student-generated writing.
- Use student-generated text for a variety of purposes, such as writing practice, grammar practice, and reading fluency.

Allow for Student-to-Student Negotiation for Meaning

- Have students work in cooperative groups.
- Encourage higher levels of student discourse, including stating point of view, giving opinions, and para-phrasing.

Teach Study Skills

- Provide graphic organizers and focused questions to help students set a purpose.
- Have students practice completing graphic organizers as they read or listen.
- Give instruction on multiple-meaning words.
- Use reference materials.

Assessment

- Check students' facial expressions and body language frequently for evidence of understanding.
- Have students demonstrate understanding by asking them to frequently paraphrase what they've just learned.

Making and Using Picture File Cards

A picture card file is a valuable instructional tool, particularly when students provide input and create the file.

First, gather magazines, catalogs, calendars, and the like. Then direct students to find pictures that are connected in some way to the content you will be studying. Students must provide some rationale to the class or small group for their choices. If the group agrees on a picture, the student who selected it glues it onto an index card. This process can generate as many as 100 cards in less than one hour. In addition to saving valuable teacher time, students are engaged in many higher-level thinking skills such as classifying, categorizing, evaluating, justifying, analyzing, making judgments, listening, and speaking. Following are a few of the ways you can use your picture card file:

- provide comprehensible input during background building and direct instruction
- stimulate discussion including questions, descriptions, and story-telling
- stimulate ideas for writing

Making and Using Big Books

It can be difficult to find a Big Book that emphasizes exactly the content, language patterning, and vocabulary for specific needs. By making your own Big Books, you can embed specific concepts and vocabulary with the right patterning in a comprehensible way to, for example, access prior knowledge and build background.

First, select and research a topic. Identify key concepts and vocabulary you want to cover. Then write some phrases to form the language pattern.

The following pattern models expository text—topic sentence/supporting details/closing sentence:

Key pattern phrase
  First key concept
  Second key concept
  Third key concept
Closing pattern phrase

Big Book illustrations run the gamut from a collage of magazine clippings to geometric patterns to hand-drawn artwork. First, read the text straight through without stopping for definitions or explanations. Students should feel the rhythm of the language patterns. After the first reading, ask students for their responses, and encourage questions. Then conduct a second reading with the emphasis on meaning. Encourage discussion. You may want to read a third time with students, asking them to read parts of the text, or as much as they can handle.

The Language-Functional Classroom: Using "Living Walls"

In a language-functional environment, every piece of text presented in class is posted on the walls to be read and reread, processed, discussed, and augmented daily. The walls are said to be alive because they grow in direct proportion with students' own language growth.

At the start of every thematic unit, perhaps six times per school year, the walls are blank. A thematic idea provides the seed that is germinated by its connection to students' backgrounds and prior knowledge. The walls become the home for completed graphic organizers, sentence patterning charts, and lists of words provided by and with students as they acquire the content of the subject at hand. The walls may also include student artwork and other pictorial representations of vocabulary and concepts. To fully utilize living walls, students must contribute to their growth and use them daily.

A living wall might begin with a large sketch of the setting of the next reading selection. During a discussion of concepts and content vocabulary, the teacher would add both pictures and words to the sketch. Throughout the theme or unit of instruction, students and the teacher add to the walls together.

Language Dictionary and Language Journal

ELLs will feel ownership of their vocabulary acquisition if they are able to capture words and phrases in a **Language Dictionary**. This is a notebook or stapled set of pages in which students record new vocabulary. Periodically they may reorganize their Language Dictionaries alphabetically by recasting pages or sections of pages.

Selection vocabulary and concept vocabulary are prime candidates for inclusion in a student's Language Dictionary. Familiarity with selection vocabulary will enable ELLs to participate in vocabulary activities in the mainstream classroom and to have more success with the core selection and attendant ancillary pages. Familiarity with concept vocabulary provides ELLs with high-utility words and phrases to use both in speaking and in writing.

Students may enter a vocabulary word in their Language Dictionaries followed by a picture, definition in their first language, or English definition. As they recast their Language Dictionary pages, they may want to amplify their definitions, adding definitions or changing drawings and first-language definitions to definitions written in English.

Language Dictionaries should be a useful tool for students' writing assignments.

Similarly, a **Language Journal** is a simple notebook in which a student can record anything from ideas for writing assignments to daily journal entries. It may provide a means for the teacher to conduct informal assessments of student progress throughout the school year. Students may use it as a tool for reviewing what they've learned and as a resource for completing various assignments.

Interactive Writing

Interactive writing is an excellent means of having students generate text under a teacher's supervision. This form of writing is most often used in kindergarten and first grade; however, beginning ELLs will benefit from this process:

1. Have students sit in a circle holding their lap boards. They should have an unobstructed view of the chart-paper stand or the board you are using.
2. Brainstorm a writing topic with students, ask them whether they have a question for observation about a content area, or provide a writing prompt.
3. Work with students to analyze the prompt and prewrite. Make sure students understand the writing objective. Write what students dictate to you.
4. Have students share with you the act of writing and the ideas of what to write. Allow students to come to the chart and write words and sentences. Prompt them with grammar and spelling tips as a review, and model grammar and spelling rules they have not yet learned. Use this student writing as a way to model correct letter formation, space between letters and words, spelling, punctuation, grammar, and writer's craft skills.
5. As you model correct grammar, spelling, and the like, have students practice writing the words and phrases correctly on their lap boards.
6. Think aloud about the structure and meaning of the text you are composing. Use explicit prompts to help students use the spelling and grammar they have learned.
7. Reread frequently with students during the composing of the text to monitor the message and to plan what to write next.
8. You may want to have students make a copy of the finished piece of writing either in their Language Journals or for publishing purposes.

Student-generated texts and frames are excellent reading and writing tools. Group Frames and Cooperative Strip Paragraphs are two techniques particularly useful in expository writing.

Group Frames This strategy is used to teach and model different writing forms. It can be used with students at most stages of language acquisition.

- Provide a topic sentence based on the writing form to be used.

- Students help plan the writing by brainstorming ideas, using graphic organizers, sketching their ideas, listing their ideas, and having substantive discussions.

- Gather ideas from as many students as possible to give even the most reluctant students some ownership of the final product.

Cooperative Strip Paragraphs This strategy is used to teach and model the writing process.

- Provide the topic sentence.

- Have students provide the supporting details from the graphic organizers or other brainstorming tools they developed.

- Students discuss what they will write and then write the sentences they have agreed upon. This strategy allows for a lot of negotiating for meaning and an anxiety-free environment for practice in developing any kind of text.

- Students revise and edit their own text.

- With modeling and practice, students will be able to generate their own topic sentences and supporting details.

Student-Generated Text This type of writing can and should be used for reading fluency practice.

- Students take a piece of text they have written and reread it together, highlighting what they find interesting or compelling.

- Students then read to see whether the writing makes sense and suggest revisions. For students at earlier stages of fluency, the teacher should suggest revisions based on ordering ideas, word substitution or sentence combining, adding, deleting, and so on.

- Model each change and discuss with students the reason for it. Then have students apply the changes to their work.

- Students should demonstrate their understanding of the benefits of the revision, noting in particular that the audience for whom the writing is intended will more readily understand the writer's message. They should also understand the revision process of reading and thinking about one's writing, rather than just physically writing, and the aggregate benefit of incorporating the suggestions of others.

- As students become increasingly comfortable with the revision process, teacher modeling should decrease as students move into more independent writing.

- After the revision, teach and model the editing process. As in the revision, students reread the writing and make suggestions to improve it in terms of spelling, punctuation, and so on. Students should never be expected to edit for a skill they have not yet been taught.

- Cooperative strip paragraphs can be used as authentic opportunities for modeling editing because there is less resistance to changing something of which no student has complete ownership.

- You may wish to create a final published copy of the text and distribute it for reading fluency practice either in a small group, with a partner, or silently.

Strategies for Effective Language Acquisition

Negotiating for Meaning

ELLs maximize comprehensible input when they **negotiate for meaning**. These student-to-student discussions at any point in the lesson provide opportunities to practice new vocabulary, including academic language, and help students achieve an understanding of concepts and language forms. This provides a risk-free environment for problem-solving and fosters positive interdependence. ELLs will have opportunities to internalize meaning, not just memorize vocabulary and facts.

An effective way to promote the strategy of negotiating for meaning is to allow at least two minutes of student processing (oral or written) after every ten minutes of instruction. Students may sit in first-language groups during the instruction. After a 10-minute chunk, students should briefly turn to their neighbors for discussion. This way, they can process new concepts in their primary language before doing so in English.

The prompts at the right can be used by teachers initially and then by students as they work with a partner or in a small group to negotiate for meaning.

Predicting

With a title like this, what do you think the story will be about? What will happen next? Why do you think so? Turn to your partner and talk to each other about what might happen next.

Monitoring and Adjusting

After reading, what do you still want to know? What do you still not understand? Turn to your neighbor and ask a question that you still have about the story. Find the part that you still don't understand. What can you do to understand it?

Paraphrasing and Summarizing

Explain to a partner what you have just read. List the main points. What was the most interesting thing you read about? What did you learn?

Assessment

Assessment should be authentic and performance-based. Teachers can use observation and informal chats with students to determine where they are and how much progress they have made.

As students work individually, in pairs, or in small groups, it is important to balance both promoting independence and providing support. This rubric and the accompanying Group Summary Record Form on page xvi can be used to record students' progress in oral fluency. You may want to tailor these tools to the needs of your students.

Oral Language Observation Rubric

	Beginning	Early Intermediate	Intermediate	Early Advanced	Advanced
Listening Comprehension	Does not understand simple conversation	Understands simple conversation with great difficulty	Understands most simple conversation spoken slowly with repetition	Understands nearly all simple conversation at normal speed with some repetition	Understands simple conversation and classroom discussion easily
Oral Fluency	Cannot carry on simple conversation	Carries on simple conversation very hesitantly	Carries on simple conversation and classroom discussion haltingly	Carries on simple conversation and classroom discussion nearly fluently	Carries on simple conversation and classroom discussion fluently and effortlessly
Vocabulary Skills	Cannot converse due to severe vocabulary limitations	Cannot make self understood due to considerable vocabulary limitations and misused words	Converses in a limited way due to inadequate vocabulary and misused words	Converses adequately by rephrasing often due to incomplete vocabulary	Converses fluently, using adequate vocabulary and idioms correctly
Pronunciation Mastery	Conversation is impossible due to severe pronunciation problems	Despite frequent repetition, conversation is severely limited by pronunciation difficulties	Conversation is often misunderstood due to pronunciation problems	Conversation is intelligible despite a detectable accent and intonation abnormalities	Conversation is natural and effortless due to accurate pronunciation and intonation
Oral Grammar	Conversation is impossible due to severe errors in grammar and word order	Conversation is limited to basic patterns of grammar and word order	Conversation is comprehensible despite frequent errors in grammar and word order	Conversation is understandable despite occasional errors in grammar and word order	Conversation is clear due to correct use of grammar and word order

Group Summary Record Form

Students' Names	Listening Comprehension	Oral Fluency	Vocabulary Skills	Pronunciation Mastery	Oral Grammar	Comments

Sounds and Features of the English Language

Similarities across languages can result in ELLs' confusion with reading and spelling. The information on pages xviii–xxi describes some of the most common difficulties ELLs experience in learning English. Understanding where the problems and contrasts lie will give you an opportunity to bridge the gap between students' knowledge of their first languages and their success in English.

Problem Contrast	Chinese	French	Greek	Italian	Japanese	Korean	Spanish	Urdu	Vietnamese
/ā/-/a/			x	x	x	x		x	
/ā/-/e/			x	x	x	x	x	x	x
/a/-/e/	x		x	x	x	x	x	x	x
/a/-/o/	x	x	x	x	x	x	x	x	x
/a/-/u/	x		x	x	x		x	x	
/ē/-/i/	x	x	x	x	x	x	x	x	x
/e/-/u/	x		x	x			x	x	
/ō/-/o/	x		x	x	x		x	x	x
/o/-/ô/	x			x	x	x	x	x	
/o/-/u/	x		x	x	x		x		x
/u/-/o͞o/	x	x	x	x			x	x	x
/u/-/ŏŏ/	x		x		x		x		x
/u/-/ô/	x		x	x	x	x	x	x	
/o͞o/-/ŏŏ/	x	x		x			x	x	x
/b/-/p/	x					x	x		x
/b/-/v/			x		x	x	x		
/ch/-/j/				x		x	x		x
/ch/-/sh/	x	x	x		x	x	x		x
/d/-/th/	x			x	x	x	x	x	x
/f/-/th/				x		x	x	x	x
/l/-/r/	x				x	x	x		x
/n/-/ng/	x	x	x	x	x		x	x	
/s/-/sh/		x		x	x	x	x		x
/s/-/th/	x	x		x	x	x	x	x	x
/s/-/z/	x		x	x		x	x		x
/sh/-/th/				x	x	x	x	x	x
/t/-/th/	x			x	x	x	x	x	x
/th/-/t̶h̶/	x	x		x	x	x	x	x	x
/th/-/z/	x	x	x	x	x	x	x	x	x

From *The ESL Teacher's Book of Lists*, © 1993 by The Center for Applied Research in Education

Decoding: Phonics Analysis

Consonants

Initial Correspondences /b/b, /d/d, /p/p
Some LEP students, including speakers of Chinese, Samoan, and Korean, may have difficulty differentiating the initial sound of *bat* from the initial sound of *pat* and *dad*.

Initial Correspondences /f/f, /p/p, /v/v
Some LEP students, including speakers of Tagalog and Vietnamese, have difficulty differentiating the initial sound of *fat* from the initial sound of *pat* or *vat*. Students must be able to hear and produce these different sounds in order to become successful readers of English.

Initial Correspondence /v/v, /b/b
Spanish-speaking students may have difficulty differentiating the initial sound of *bat* from the initial sound of *vat*, since they are used to pronouncing /b/ when the letter *v* appears at the beginning of a word. In pronouncing English words that begin with *v*, these students often substitute /b/ for /v/; thus *vest* becomes *best*, and *very* becomes *berry*.

Initial Correspondences /j/j, /y/y, /ch/ch
The sound /j/ in *jar* is difficult for LEP students who often confuse or interchange this sound with /ch/ or /y/, causing major comprehension difficulties. In addition, Spanish has a similar sound /y/ that is often substituted for the sound /j/, resulting in confusion when students try to differentiate between the words *jam* and *yam*.

Initial correspondence /s/c, s
The letter-sound association for *c* usually follows the same generalizations in both English and Spanish. When *c* is followed by the letter *e* or *i*, it stands for the sound /s/; when *c* is followed by the letter *a*, *o*, or *u*, it stands for the sound /k/. In some Spanish dialects, when the letter *c* is followed by the letter *e* or *i*, the *c* stands for the sound /th/. Therefore, some Spanish-speaking students might have difficulty with this sound.

Initial Correspondence /s/s, /z/z
The sound /z/ is difficult for many LEP students to master because often it is not found in their native language. It is especially difficult for students to differentiate this sound from the sound /s/.

Initial Correspondence /n/n, kn; /l/l
The sound /n/ at the beginning of a word seems to present no special difficulties for most LEP students. However, students whose native language is Chinese, sometimes have difficulty differentiating this sound from the sound /l/ at the beginning of *lot*.

Initial Correspondence /r/r, wr; /l/l
Some LEP students, including speakers of Chinese, Japanese, Korean, Vietnamese, and Thai, may have great difficulty differentiating /r/ as in *rip* from /l/ as in *lip* . These students often pronounce both *lip* and *rip* with the beginning sound /l/.

Initial Correspondence /kw/qu, /w/w
Some LEP students have difficulty differentiating the initial sound /kw/ as in *queen* from the initial sound /w/ as in *wet*.

Initial Correspondence /v/v, /w/w
Some LEP students, including speakers of Chinese, Arabic, German, Samoan, and Thai, have difficulty differentiating /w/ as in *wet* from /v/ as in *van* . These students need much practice producing the sound /w/ in order to avoid confusing it with the sound /v/.

Initial Correspondence /g/g; /k/k,c
Some LEP students, especially speakers of Korean, Samoan, Vietnamese, Thai, and Indonesian, have difficulty differentiating /k/ as in *cat* and *king* from /g/ as in *go*. Speakers of Vietnamese and Thai especially have difficulty with these two sounds when they appear at the end of a word.

Initial Correspondence /h/h, /j/j, /hw/wh
Students who already read in Spanish may have difficulty with these sound-symbol correspondences, because in Spanish the letter *h* is silent. Students may forget to pronounce this sound in trying to decode

English words, saying for example, /ot/ for *hot* and /at/ for *hat*. Because the sound /h/ is represented by the letter *j* in Spanish, this letter may be used in spelling English words that begin with *h*. Students may write *jat* for *hat*, *jot* for *hot*, *jouse* for *house*, and so on.

In addition, some LEP students may have difficulty differentiating the beginning sound of *hat* from the beginning sound of *what*. They will need practice in differentiating these two sounds.

Initial Correspondence /fr/fr, /fl/fl

The initial /fr/fr does not usually present difficulty for students who speak Spanish since these sounds are commonly found in Spanish. However, /fr/fr does present difficulty for students who speak Chinese or other Oriental languages, especially when differentiating /fr/fr from /fl/fl.

Initial Correspondences /gr/gr, /dr/dr, /br/br

Some LEP students, especially speakers of Chinese and Vietnamese, may have difficulty differentiating the initial sounds of *grass* from the initial sounds of *broom* and *dress*. Much practice is needed to help students hear and produce these sounds in English in order to avoid problems when they start to work with the written symbols that represent these sounds.

Initial Correspondences /th/th, /thr/thr, /t/t

Some LEP students, especially Spanish-speaking students, may have difficulty pronouncing words that begin with /th/ and /thr/, and differentiating these sounds from /t/. Much practice is needed to help students hear and produce these sounds in English in order to avoid problems when they start to work with the written symbols that represent these sounds.

Initial Correspondences /kr/cr, /kl/cl, /gl/gl

Some LEP students, especially speakers of Chinese or Vietnamese, may have difficulty with these clusters. These clusters do not present difficulty for Spanish-speaking students since they are commonly found in the Spanish language.

Initial Correspondences /skr/scr; /sk/sk,sc; /kr/cr

The intial consonant clusters /skr/scr and /sk/sk,sc may be difficult for LEP students of various language backgrounds. Spanish-speaking students have difficulty with the *s*-plus-consonant pronunciation. Speakers of other languages may have difficulty with the initial consonant cluster /kr/cr.

Initial Correspondences /st/st; /str/str; /sk/sk, sch, sc

The majority of LEP students, especially those who speak Spanish, have difficulty pronouncing these consonant clusters in the initial position. In Spanish, these clusters never appear at the beginning of a word. Thus students tend to add the /e/ sound in front of a word: *school* /sko͞ol/ becomes /esko͞ol/ and *street* is pronounced /estrēt/.

Initial Correspondences /tr/tr, /thr/thr, /t/t

The consonant clusters /tr/ and /thr/ are difficult for LEP students whose native languages do not have these sounds in combination. Some students have difficulty differentiating among /tr/, /thr/, /t/, and /t/ with the vowel *i*.

Initial Correspondences /sl/sl, /pl/pl

The consonant cluster *sl* presents some difficulty for Spanish-speaking students who are not used to encountering the *s*-plus-consonant sound at the beginning of words. These students often add the /e/ sound in front of a word; for example, *sleep* is pronounced /eslēp/. The /pl/ sound does not present difficulty for speakers of Spanish because it is common in Spanish. However, speakers of Chinese and Vietnamese, among others, may find it difficult to master.

Initial Correspondences /sp/sp, /sm/sm

The majority of LEP students have difficulty pronouncing the consonant clusters *sp* and *sm* in the initial position. In Spanish, these clusters never appear at the beginning of words. Often Spanish-speaking students add /e/ before the /s/; thus *spot* is pronounced /espot/.

Initial Correspondences /sh/sh, /ch/ch

The sound /sh/ presents difficulty for many LEP students because it is not found in most languages. The sound /ch/ seems to be more common. Therefore many students do not distinguish between /sh/ and /ch/ and tend to substitute one for the other, saying *cheep* for *sheep* and *chin* for *shin*. This is particularly true of Spanish-speaking students.

Final Correspondences /p/p, /b/b

Spanish-speaking students may have difficulty hearing the final sound /p/ and may confuse this sound with the final sound /b/, since the final sound /b/ and /p/ do not often occur in Spanish.

Final Correspondences /t/t, /d/d

Some LEP students may have difficulty differentiating the final sound of *bat* from the final sound of *dad*. Much practice is needed to help students hear and produce these sounds in English to avoid problems when starting to work with the written symbols that represent these sounds.

Final Correspondences /ks/x; /s/s, ss

Final consonants can present a problem, especially for students whose native languages do not emphasize these consonants as much as English does. In Spanish, for example, there are only a few consonants that appear at the ends of words (*n,s,z,d,l,j*). Many Spanish-speaking people tend to drop the final consonant sound in conversation; for example, *reloj* becomes *relo*.

Final Correspondences /z/z, zz; /s/s, ss

The sound /z/ is difficult for many LEP students to master because often it is not found in their native languages. It is especially difficult for students to differentiate this sound from the sound /s/.

Final Correspondences /k/k, ck; /g/g

The final sound /g/ may be difficult for Spanish-speaking students since this sound never occurs at the end of Spanish words. Students may have difficulty hearing this sound and may pronounce it as the sound /k/ or omit the sound completely.

Final Correspondences /f/f, ff; /p/p

Some LEP students may have difficulty differentiating the final sound of *wife* from the final sound of *wipe*. Much practice is needed to help students hear and produce these sounds in English in order to avoid problems when they start to work with the written symbols that represent these sounds.

Final Correspondences /p/p, /t/t

Some LEP students may have difficulty differentiating the final sound of *ape* from that of *ate*. Much practice is needed to help students hear and produce these sounds in English in order to avoid problems when they start to work with the written symbols that represent these sounds.

Final Correspondences /d/d, /b/b

Some LEP students may have difficulty differentiating the final sound of *lad* from the final sound of *lab*. Much practice is needed to help students hear and produce these sounds in English in order to avoid problems when they start to work with the written symbols that represent these sounds.

Final Correspondences /ld/ld, nt/nt, nd/nd

Some LEP students may have difficulty differentiating the final sounds of *old* from those of *lint* and *find*. Two final consonant sounds increase the difficulty. Much practice is needed to help students hear and produce these sounds in English in order to avoid problems when they start to work with the written symbols that represent these sounds.

Final Correspondences /ng/ng, /ngk/nk

Some LEP students may have difficulty differentiating the final sounds of *sink* from the final sounds of *sing*. Much practice is needed to help students hear and produce these sounds in English in order to avoid problems when they start to work with the written symbols that represent these sounds.

Final Correspondences /s/s, ss; /st/st

Some LEP students may have difficulty differentiating the final sound of *gas* from the final sounds of *last*. Much practice is needed to help students hear and produce these sounds in English in order to avoid problems when they start to work with the written symbols that represent these sounds.

Final Correspondences /sh/sh; /ch/ch, tch
Some LEP students may have difficulty differentiating the final sound of *mush* from the final sound of *much*. Much practice is needed to help students hear and produce these sounds in English in order to avoid problems when they start to work with the written symbols that represent these sounds.

Final Correspondences /th/th, /t/t
Some LEP students, especially speakers of Spanish, may have difficulty differentiating the final sound of *bat* from the final sound of *bath*. Much practice is needed to help students hear and produce these sounds in English in order to avoid problems when they start to work with the written symbols that represent these sounds.

Vowels

Vowel Correspondences /a/a, /e/e
Short vowel sounds are the most difficult for LEP students to master. These create problems when students try to learn and apply the concept of rhyming. LEP students have difficulty differentiating the short vowel sound in *bat* from the short vowel sound in *bet*. Much practice is needed to help students hear and produce these sounds in English in order to avoid problems when they start to work with the written symbols that represent these sounds.

Vowel Correspondences /o/o, /u/u
The vowel sounds in *cot* and *cut* often cause great difficulty for students who speak Spanish, Chinese, Vietnamese, Tagalog, and Thai. These sounds must be practiced frequently.

Vowel Correspondences /i/i, /ē/ee, ea, e_e
Words with the short *i* vowel sound are difficult for speakers of Spanish, Chinese, Vietnamese, and Tagalog, among others. LEP students in general have difficulty pronouncing this sound as they tend to confuse it with the long *e* vowel sound.

Spanish-speaking students in particular have the tendency to replace the short *i* sound with the long *e* sound.

Vowel Correspondences /u/u, /a/a, /e/e
The vowel sound in *up* is one of the most difficult for LEP students to master because it does not exist in many languages and yet is one of the most common sounds in English. LEP students often have difficulty differentiating this sound from the vowel sounds in *bat* and *bet*. Much practice is needed to help students hear and produce these sounds in English in order to avoid problems when they start to work with the written symbols that represent these sounds.

Vowel Correspondences /o/o; /ō/oa, o_e; /ô/au, aw
The vowel sound in *cot* often causes great difficulty for LEP students who speak Spanish, Chinese, Vietnamese, Tagalog, or Thai. This sound must be practiced frequently, especially to differentiate it from the vowel sound in *coat* and *caught*. In addition, when the letters *oa* come together in Spanish, they stand for two separate sounds. Therefore, many Spanish-speaking students may have difficulty understanding that the letters *oa* can stand for one sound in English.

Vowel Correspondences /ā/a_e, /e/e
It is difficult for LEP students who speak Vietnamese, Spanish, or Tagalog to differentiate between the vowel sound in *race* and the vowel sound in *pet*. Much practice is needed to help students hear and produce these sounds in English in order to avoid problems when they start to work with the written symbols that represent these sounds.

Vowel Correspondences /ī/i_e, /a/a
The vowel sound in *bike* may present a problem for some LEP students who have difficulty differentiating this sound from the vowel sound in *bat*. Much practice is needed to help students hear and produce these sounds in English in order to avoid problems when they start to work with the written symbols that represent these sounds.

Use with **"The Gardener"**

Build Background/Access Prior Knowledge

Have students look at the illustration on *Pupil Edition* pages 26–27.
Point to the girl and tell students that she is going to a new place to live.
Ask students how they think the girl might feel about this. Then ask

students to share their experiences
about moving. Ask: **How does
moving to a new place make you
feel? Why does it make you feel
this way?** Record their responses in
a chart like this one:

Moving to a new place makes me feel	because I
sad	miss my friends.
lonely	don't know anyone.
scared	have to go to a new school.

Selection Vocabulary

PRETEACH Display Teaching Transparency 9 and read the words aloud.
Then point to the pictures as you read the following sentences:

1. The girl feels **anxious**. She is worried and scared.
2. The girl will sit in the **vacant** seat. It is the empty seat.
3. The bus driver will **retire** soon. He will not drive the bus anymore.
4. "We **adore** the bus driver," say the children. "We like him so much!"
5. Mr. Green is **sprucing** up his bus. He is cleaning it.
6. The girl has no trouble **recognizing** the butterfly sticker on the bus.
   She has seen the butterfly sticker before.

Selection Vocabulary

RETEACH Revisit Teaching Transparency 9. Read the words with students.
Have students work in pairs to discuss the meanings of the words and to
answer questions such as: Does *vacant* mean "*occupied*" or "*empty*"? Does
anxious mean "*happy*" or "*nervous*"?

Write the following sentence frames on the board. Read each sentence
and ask students to choose a vocabulary word to complete it. Write
students' responses in the blanks.

1. Susana feels _____ because she cannot find her homework.
   (*anxious*)
2. Mr. Gomez is old enough to _____ , so he will quit his job. (*retire*)
3. No one lives in that house, so it is _____ . (*vacant*)
4. We are _____ up the house before my friend comes. (*sprucing*)
5. I _____ my new puppy Sam. (*adore*)
6. I never have a problem _____ my own bike because it has a red
   ribbon on it. (*recognizing*)

Have students write these words in their Language Dictionaries.

FLUENCY PRACTICE Have students read the sentence frames aloud.
Encourage them to describe the illustrations on Teaching Transparency 9, using
the vocabulary words and any other words they know.

Build Background: "The Gardener"

Revisit the picture on *Pupil Edition* pages 26–27. Tell students that the girl is Lydia Grace. Explain that Lydia Grace is going to live with her uncle. Discuss with students how someone might feel being far away from home. (sad, lonely, nervous, afraid)

LEAD THE WAY

 ## Narrative Elements

PRETEACH Tell students that stories have three narrative elements: a setting (when and where a story takes place), characters (the people or animals the story is about), and the plot (what happens in the story). Then draw a three-column chart on the board with the headings *Setting*, *Characters*, and *Plot*. Tell students that Lydia Grace is one of the characters in this story. Write her name in the chart.

Directed Reading: "The Gardener"

RETEACH Use these sentences to walk students through the story.

Pages 22–25
- This story is called "The Gardener." A gardener is someone who grows plants in a garden.
- Here is Lydia Grace. This is her grandma.
- Grandma is helping Lydia Grace pack.

Pages 26–29
- Lydia Grace is going to live with Uncle Jim in the city.
- This is Uncle Jim. He is another character in this story.
- Uncle Jim owns a bakery.

Pages 30–31
- Lydia Grace is in Uncle Jim's apartment in the city.
- Uncle Jim is reading a poem Lydia Grace wrote for him. Lydia Grace wants Uncle Jim to smile.

Pages 32–35
- Here are Ed and Emma Beech. They work in Uncle Jim's bakery.
- Lydia Grace is learning to make bread.

QUESTIONS: pages 22–35
- Does Lydia Grace arrive in the city by airplane? (*no*)
- Whom does Lydia Grace go to live with? (*Uncle Jim*)
- What does Lydia Grace want Uncle Jim to do? (*smile*)

Pages 36–39
- Lydia Grace is opening a letter from home. What is spilling from her letter? (*seeds, dirt, plants*)
- Lydia Grace is putting up signs to show Uncle Jim a big surprise.

Pages 40–43
- Lydia Grace's flower garden is on the roof. It is a big surprise for Uncle Jim.
- Uncle Jim has a surprise for Lydia Grace. He baked a cake with flowers on it.
- Uncle Jim has a letter for Lydia Grace. The letter says that it is time for Lydia Grace to go back home to her parents and her grandma.

QUESTIONS: pages 36–43
- Does Lydia Grace surprise Uncle Jim with her garden? (*yes*)
- What is Uncle Jim's surprise for Lydia Grace? (*a cake with flowers on it*)

FLUENCY PRACTICE Ask a volunteer to read a paragraph from page 30 aloud. Encourage students to describe the illustration on *Pupil Edition* pages 30–31, using as many vocabulary words as they can.

Build Background: "Dear Berta"

PRETEACH Remind students that "The Gardener" is about Lydia Grace, who goes to live with her uncle. "Dear Berta" is about Cristina, a girl who has moved to a new home. Both girls write letters. Ask students what they would write in a letter if they moved to a new place.

English-
Language
Learners
Book

Concept Words
miss
friend
lonely
home
visit
letter

Use the concept words in sentences to illustrate their meanings.
- I just moved to a new city and I **miss** my best **friend**.
- My new **home** is nice, but I feel sad.
- I feel **lonely** when I think about my best friend so far away.
- I will write a **letter** to my friend to tell him about my new home.
- I will ask my friend to **visit** me soon.

Have students add these words to their Language Dictionaries.

Directed Reading: "Dear Berta"

Summary *Cristina writes letters to her friend, Berta. She tells Berta how it feels to go to a new school. Cristina makes new friends. Berta sends Cristina a letter to tell her that she will visit.*

Use these sentences to walk students through the story.

Pages 2–3
- The story is called "Dear Berta."
- This is Cristina. She is writing a letter to her best friend, Berta. Cristina feels lonely because she has just moved to a new home.

Pages 4–5
- Cristina and her new friend Ling are eating lunch in the cafeteria.
- Berta sends Cristina pictures of a birthday party.

Pages 6–7
- Here is Cristina's mother.
- Cristina and Mami go shopping. Then they have lunch in a restaurant.

QUESTIONS:
pages 2–7
- Which character in the story has moved to a new home? *(Cristina)*
- With whom is Cristina eating lunch at school? *(her new friend Ling)*

Pages 8–9
- Here are Cristina's new friends, Ling, Maria, and Sarah. What are they doing? *(jumping rope)*
- What is the setting on this page? *(the school playground)*

Pages 10–13
- Berta has sent Cristina a drawing of her puppy, Canela.
- Cristina sends Berta two jump rope songs.

Pages 14–15
- Cristina goes to a science museum with her classmates.

Page 16
- Berta writes a letter to Cristina. Berta is coming to visit.

QUESTIONS:
pages 8–16
- Is Cristina happy to get a drawing of Berta's puppy, Canela? *(yes)*
- What happens at the end of the story? *(Berta says she will visit Cristina.)*

Narrative Elements

RETEACH Review the narrative elements, and draw a three-column narrative elements chart. Ask students to revisit "Dear Berta" to complete the chart.

FLUENCY PRACTICE Ask students to read one of Cristina's letters aloud. Have them use the illustration on pages 8–9 to retell part of "Dear Berta."

Shared Writing: Friendly Letter

PRETEACH Tell students that they are going to work with you to write a letter about moving to a new place. Generate a concept web. In the center circle, write the phrase *How I feel about moving to a new home.* In the surrounding circles, write the words *lonely, sad, anxious, nervous.* Then brainstorm with students additional words to add to the web.

Write the following sentence frames on the board or on chart paper. Read each sentence with students, and ask them to use a word from the web to complete each sentence. As you write the word in the blank, have students write it on their lap boards. Responses will vary.

Dear _____ ,

I like my new home, but I feel _____ . I miss _____ the most. When I make new friends, I will feel _____ .

Your friend,

_____

Grammar: Sentences

PRETEACH Discuss the definition of a sentence with students. Point out the following:

- A sentence is a group of words that tells a complete thought.
- The words in a sentence are in an order that makes sense.

Write the following sentences on the board and read them aloud:

- *Lydia Grace is a gardener.*
- *Lydia Grace moves to the city.*
- *Lydia Grace plants a garden in the city.*

Tell students that the three sentences name, or are about, Lydia Grace. The first sentence tells who she is; the second and third tell what she does.

Point out that every sentence begins with a capital letter. These sentences end with a period.

Read the following items aloud. Ask students to say whether each item is a sentence or not. If an item is not a sentence, discuss with students what they could add to make it a sentence.

1. Cristina and Berta (*no; Cristina and Berta are friends.*)
2. Ling is Cristina's new friend. (*yes*)
3. Berta has a new puppy. (*yes*)
4. mail the letters (*no; I mail the letters.*)
5. The girls sing songs. (*yes*)

FLUENCY PRACTICE Have volunteers read aloud the friendly letter they completed in the writing activity.

Shared Writing: Friendly Letter

RETEACH Display the completed letter from Preteach. Read it aloud with students. Ask them what they would like to change about it and why. Discuss students' suggestions for changing or adding to the letter. Write the revised letter, using students' suggestions. Then have students copy the revised letter into their Language Journals. Students should personalize their letters by using their own greeting and closing.

Grammar-Writing Connection

RETEACH Write these sentences on the board and read them aloud with students:

- *Lydia Grace moved far away from her family.*
- *Cristina moved far away from her best friend.*

Have students work in pairs or in small groups to discuss how it feels to move to a new place. Then have each student draw a picture to show his or her ideas. Encourage students to describe their pictures orally. Then work with them to write a sentence or two that describes their pictures. Remind students that a sentence expresses a complete thought and that it begins with a capital letter and ends with an end mark. Check students' writing and point out any corrections they need to make.

FLUENCY PRACTICE Have students choose a favorite letter or letters from "Dear Berta" to read aloud.

Name _____

Cut out these words and periods. Use them to make as many sentences as you can. Read your sentences aloud. Write your sentences in your Language Journal.

Berta	**eat**	**and**	**food**
Cristina	**friends**	**school**	**lunch**
are	**has**	**the**	**a**
visit	**will**	**anxious**	**is**
writes	**with**	**at**	**letter**
to	**students**	**good**	**home**
•	•	•	•

TO THE TEACHER Have students cut apart copies of these word and punctuation cards. Ask pairs of students to form sentences with the words. You may want to model forming a sentence such as *Berta and Cristina are friends.* Have students read their sentences aloud for sense.

Use with "Donavan's Word Jar"

Build Background/Access Prior Knowledge

Discuss with students their daily-life experiences with problem solving. Ask: **Have you ever had a problem in your daily life that you needed to solve? What was the problem? How did you solve it?** On the board, create a chart similar to the one shown and record students' responses.

Problem	Solution
bicycle with flat tire	used pump to inflate tire
didn't understand math homework	asked teacher for help

Selection Vocabulary

PRETEACH Display Teaching Transparency 19, and read the words aloud. Then point to the pictures as you read the following sentences:

1. The girl and her grandfather spend **leisure** time together. They relax and tell stories to each other.
2. The girl **chortles** at Grandpa's funny stories. She laughs out loud.
3. Grandpa feels **uneasy** about the rain. He is worried about getting wet.
4. The girl feels **disappointment**. She had hoped to hear more stories.
5. The girl and her grandfather reach a **compromise**. They agree to take the chairs inside and tell stories from there.
6. Grandpa says, "**Perseverance** is important when you want to solve a problem. You must keep trying to find a solution."

Selection Vocabulary

RETEACH Revisit Teaching Transparency 13. Have students answer questions such as: Does *leisure* mean "time for resting" or "time for working"?

Write the following sentence frames on the board. Read each sentence and ask students to choose a vocabulary word to complete it.

1. My friend would always _____ at my jokes. (*chortle*)
2. Mike felt _____ about going away to camp. (*uneasy*)
3. The students expressed their _____ that the field trip was canceled. (*disappointment*)
4. My grandpa does not work anymore and really enjoys his _____ time. (*leisure*)
5. The runner showed great _____ when he ran in the long race. (*perseverance*)
6. Tom and Wilma reached a _____ about what movie they would see. (*compromise*)

Have students write the vocabulary words in their Language Dictionaries.

FLUENCY PRACTICE Have students read the completed sentences aloud. Encourage them to describe the illustrations on Teaching Transparency 19 by using the vocabulary words and any other words they know.

Build Background: "Donavan's Word Jar"

Have students look at the picture on *Pupil Edition* pages 52–53. Explain that the boy in the picture is Donavan. Tell students that Donavan likes to collect words in a jar, but that he can't put any more words in the jar because it is too full. Ask students to predict how Donavan will solve the problem.

LEAD
THE
WAY

(Focus Skill) Prefixes, Suffixes, and Roots

PRETEACH Tell students that some words are made up of parts— prefixes, suffixes, and roots. Explain that a prefix is the word part that is added to the beginning of a root word and that a suffix is the word part added to the end of a root word. The root is the basic part of the word. It gives the word its meaning. Knowing the meanings of prefixes, suffixes, and roots can help students figure out the meanings of longer words.

On the board, draw a chart like the one shown to explain the concept. Have students add to the chart as they read the selection.

Prefix	Root Word	Suffix	New Word
	collect	ion	collection (a group of objects that are kept together)

Directed Reading: "Donavan's Word Jar"

RETEACH Use these sentences to walk students through the story.

■ This is Donavan. He has a problem. He can't fit any more words in his jar.

■ Donavan is taking his jar to his grandma's apartment. He hopes his grandma will be able to help him solve his problem.

Pages 52–57
■ Donavan is at his grandma's apartment.

Pages 58–61
■ Grandma is reading one of Donavan's words.

■ Grandma suggests that Donavan share his words with people. Donavan doesn't want to share his words.

■ Donavan is ready to go home. Grandma gives him a hug.

QUESTIONS: pages 52–61
■ Does Donavan collect words? (*yes*)

■ Where does Donavan take his word jar? (*to Grandma's apartment*)

Pages 62–67
■ These are Grandma's neighbors. Do they look happy or sad?

■ Donavan shows the word *compromise* to two people who are arguing. Donavan's word helps them reach an agreement.

■ Grandma's neighbors start taking Donavan's words.

Pages 68–70
■ Donavan's word jar is empty. The neighbors have taken all of his words.

■ Donavan finds the solution to his problem. He shares his words to make Grandma's neighbors happy.

QUESTIONS: pages 62–70
■ Is Donavan's word jar full at the end of the story? (*no*)

■ How does Donavan feel about sharing his words at the end of the story? (*happy*)

FLUENCY PRACTICE Encourage students to use vocabulary words to describe the illustration on *Pupil Edition* pages 66–67.

Build Background: "Science Fair!"

BEFORE
Making Connections
pages 74–75

PRETEACH Remind students that in "Donavan's Word Jar" Donavan had a problem he needed to solve. Tell them that in "Science Fair!" Colin has a problem—he has to do a project for a class science fair, but he doesn't know what to make. Ask students what they would make for a science fair.

English-Language Learners Book

Use the concept words in sentences that illustrate their meanings.

Concept Words
problem
solution
homework
science
project
idea

- Mike has a **problem**. He is always late.
- Our teacher gives us **homework** every night.
- In **science** class, we are working on a **project**.
- I have an **idea** for our next project.
- Mike thinks of a **solution**. He starts leaving five minutes earlier.

Have students add these words to their Language Dictionaries.

Directed Reading: "Science Fair!"

AFTER
Skill Review
pages 76–77

Summary *Colin has a bad day at school—he forgets his homework, spills juice on his sandwich, and doesn't know what to do for his science project. He finally comes up with an idea—he builds a box.*

Use these sentences to walk students through the story.

Pages 2–7
- The students are standing outside of a classroom. They are reading a sign. What does the sign say?
- This is Ms. Bale, the fourth-grade teacher.
- Here is Colin. He is looking in his backpack. He is looking for his homework. He has left it at home.
- Now the students are in the lunchroom. Colin spills his juice on his sandwich.

QUESTIONS: pages 2–7
- Is there a class science fair next week? (*yes*)
- What did Colin leave at home? (*his homework*)

Pages 8–16
- Colin is unhappy. He needs an idea for his science project.
- Look at the objects on Ms. Bale's desk. Which objects do you recognize?
- Colin and Alex are working on their science project.

QUESTIONS: pages 8–16
- Does Colin make a paper-cup scale? (*no*)
- What do Colin and Alex build? (*a box to make a bad day better*)

(Focus Skill) Prefixes, Suffixes, and Roots

RETEACH Review prefixes, suffixes, and roots with students. Have students revisit "Science Fair!" and look for words that have prefixes and suffixes. Have students add those words to the chart from the previous day.

FLUENCY PRACTICE Have students describe one of the science projects using vocabulary words and concept words.

Shared Writing: Character Sketch

PRETEACH Tell students that they are going to work with you to write a character sketch about their best friend. Explain that a character sketch is a piece of writing that describes a person.

Create a concept web like the one shown. Write *My Best Friend* in the center oval. Then brainstorm with students their best friend's traits and actions. Record students' responses in the outer circles.

Write the following sentence frames on the board. Read each frame with students and ask them to use words from the web to help them complete it. Responses will vary.

My best friend's name is _____. He/She is _____. He/She is also _____. His/Her favorite thing to do is _____. _____ is my best friend because _____.

Grammar: Declarative and Interrogative Sentences

PRETEACH Review declarative and interrogative sentences with students.

- A **declarative sentence** tells something. Use a period at the end of a declarative sentence.
- An **interrogative sentence** asks a question. Use a question mark at the end of an interrogative sentence.

Write the following sentences on the board.
1. All of the students did a science project.
2. Alex and Colin worked together.
3. What project did they do?
4. They made a box.
5. Did Ms. Bale like their project?

Read the sentences aloud, emphasizing the correct intonation at the end of each sentence. Then read aloud again the first, second, and fourth sentences and point out that they are all declarative sentences; they end with a period. Reread the third and fifth sentences and point out that they are interrogative sentences; they end with a question mark. Read the sentences once again and have students repeat them after you.

FLUENCY PRACTICE Have volunteers read aloud their character sketches.

Shared Writing: Character Sketch

RETEACH Display the completed character sketch from Preteach. Read it aloud with students. Ask students what they would like to change about it and why. Discuss students' suggestions for changing or adding to the character sketch. Work with students to add specific details to their writing. Write a revised character sketch using students' suggestions. Then have students copy the revised character sketch into their Language Journals.

Grammar-Writing Connection

RETEACH Review declarative and interrogative sentences with students. Then write the following sentences on the board, omitting the end punctuation.

1. Donavan likes to collect words
2. He puts the words in a jar
3. Is the jar full
4. How will Donavan solve his problem
5. Donavan goes to visit his grandma
6. He asks her to help him

Have students copy the sentences into their notebooks. Have them work in pairs to classify the sentences by putting a period at the end of the declarative sentences (1, 2, 5, 6) and a question mark at the end of the interrogative ones (3, 4). Monitor students' work as they complete it. Then have each student write two declarative sentences and two interrogative sentences. Encourage students to share their sentences by reading them aloud.

FLUENCY PRACTICE Have students read aloud their revised character sketches.

Name _____

A Read each sentence. Circle the period if it is a declarative sentence. Circle the question mark if it is an interrogative sentence.

1. I collect pennies   .   ?

2. What do you collect   .   ?

3. My friend Jose has a problem   .   ?

4. Can you help me solve this problem   .   ?

5. Alex has a good idea for a science project   .   ?

B Draw a picture of a problem and how you solved it. Write sentences to describe your picture.

_____

_____

_____

_____

_____

TO THE TEACHER Have pairs of students read the sentences together and choose the correct end punctuation. Discuss with students some problems they have solved. To model how to respond to Part B, you might write the following on the board: *A problem I once had was sharing a room with my brother. I solved it by writing a list of rules for both of us.*

Use with "My Name Is María Isabel"

Build Background/Access Prior Knowledge

Have students look at the illustrations on *Pupil Edition* pages 84–85. Point to the stars and the bell and ask students during which holidays they might see stars and bells. Then ask: **What do you already know about holidays? What would you like to learn?** Record their responses in a K-W-L chart. Have students add information to the third column as they read.

What I Already Know	What I Would Like to Learn	What I Learned
Many kinds	What is a menorah?	

Selection Vocabulary

PRETEACH Display Teaching Transparency 28 and read the words aloud. Then point to the pictures as you read the following sentences:

1. Mr. London's class is going to present a pageant. For scenery, some of the students have painted a **tropical** island in the ocean.
2. Quentin listens **attentively** to Mr. London's directions so he will know what to do.
3. Sue feels **restless.** She can't wait to start practicing.
4. During **rehearsals**, the students practice by reading their parts.
5. Nat finds some of his lines **troublesome.** They are hard for him to remember.
6. The students perform in the **pageant.** The show is a success.

Selection Vocabulary

RETEACH Revisit Teaching Transparency 28. Have students answer questions such as this: Does restless mean "unable to keep still" or "relaxed"?

Write the following sentence frames on the board. Read each sentence and ask students to choose a vocabulary word to complete it.

1. Pia listened _____ to the teacher. (*attentively*)
2. The _____ was about the first Thanksgiving. (*pageant*)
3. The _____ for the play is after school. (*rehearsal*)
4. Nan imagined lying on the beach of a _____ island. (*tropical*)
5. During the long car ride, Tim felt _____. (*restless*)
6. The holiday decorations were _____. They kept falling off the walls. (*troublesome*)

Have students write the vocabulary words in their Language Dictionaries.

FLUENCY PRACTICE Have students read the completed sentences aloud.

LEAD
THE
WAY

BEFORE

Reading "My Name
Is María Isabel"
pages 80–97

Build Background: "My Name Is María Isabel"

Revisit the picture on *Pupil Edition* page 87. Tell students that the girl is María Isabel. Explain that María Isabel did not get a part in the class play. Discuss with students how someone might feel about not getting a part in the class play.

(Focus Skill) Narrative Elements

PRETEACH Remind students that a story has three narrative elements: a setting, characters, and a plot. The plot includes the problem or conflict, the steps the characters take to solve it, and the resolution, or the way the problem is solved.

Draw on the board a flowchart with the headings *Problem*, *Problem-Solving Steps*, and *Resolution*. Tell students that María Isabel wants to be called by her whole name. Write this information under the heading *Problem*. Have students complete the flowchart when you reteach the skill after reading "School Holidays."

AFTER

Reading "My Name
Is María Isabel"

Directed Reading: "My Name Is María Isabel"

RETEACH Use these sentences to walk students through the story.

Pages 80–83
- This is María Isabel. Her teacher calls her Mary López. María Isabel wants to be called by her whole name.
- María Isabel wishes she had a part in the school play.
- This is a candle. María Isabel's class learns a song called "The Candles of Hanukkah."

Pages 84–87
- María Isabel helps her class make decorations. Point to the stars. Now point to the bell.
- María Isabel is reading *Charlotte's Web*. Charlotte is a spider.
- María Isabel does not want to tell her parents that she does not have a part in the play.

 QUESTIONS:
pages 80–87
- Does María Isabel have a part in the school play? (*no*)
- What book is María Isabel reading? (*Charlotte's Web*)
- How do you think María Isabel feels about not having a part in the school play? (*sad, disappointed*)

Pages 88–91
- María Isabel writes an essay about her greatest wish. María Isabel's wish is to be called by her whole name and to have a part in the play.

Pages 92–94
- María Isabel's teacher invites her to sing a song in the pageant.
- On the day of the show, María Isabel wears butterfly barrettes in her hair.

QUESTIONS:
pages 88–94
- Does María Isabel get her wish? (*yes*)
- What does María Isabel do in the play? (*sing a song*)

FLUENCY PRACTICE Ask volunteers to read aloud María Isabel's essay from page 90.

Build Background: "School Holidays"

PRETEACH Remind students that "My Name Is María Isabel" is about a girl who wants to be in a holiday play. In "School Holidays" they will read about several holidays. Discuss with students their favorite holidays.

English-
Language
Learners
Book

Concept Words
read
school
numbers
write
play
books

Use the concept words in sentences that illustrate their meanings.

- I am learning how to **read** at **school**.
- Catrina knows how to add **numbers**.
- Donnie will **write** his name on his paper.
- The class will **play** dodge ball at recess.
- We checked out **books** from the library.

Have students add these words to their Language Dictionaries.

Directed Reading: "School Holidays"

Summary *Children start a new school year and learn about many new things. They learn about holidays from many cultures.*

Use these sentences to walk students through the story.

Pages 2–7
- These boys and girls are starting a new school year.
- These students are learning about the holiday called Columbus Day. Christopher Columbus was the explorer who discovered America.
- Now they are learning about Thanksgiving. Thanksgiving celebrates the Pilgrims first successful year in America.

**QUESTIONS:
pages 2–7**
- Where are these children? (*at school*)
- Who is Christopher Columbus? (*the explorer who found America*)

Pages 8–9
- Kwanzaa is an African American holiday. Kwanzaa is celebrated for seven days and nights in December.

Pages 10–11
- People who come from Vietnam celebrate Tet. It is a new year holiday.

Pages 12–13
- Martin Luther King, Jr. Day celebrates Martin Luther King, Jr.'s birthday. Martin Luther King, Jr. wanted all people to be treated equally.
- Cinco de Mayo means "May 5." People who have come from Mexico celebrate this holiday.

Pages 14–16
- Memorial Day honors the men and women who fought for America.

**QUESTIONS:
pages 8–16**
- Are there many kinds of holidays? (*yes*)
- Which holiday did you enjoy learning about? (*Responses will vary.*)

(Focus Skill) Narrative Elements

RETEACH Review the narrative elements with students. Then return to the flowchart you began for "My Name is María Isabel" and work with students to complete it.

FLUENCY PRACTICE Have students use the illustrations on pages 6 and 7 to retell part of "School Holidays." Encourage students to use vocabulary words.

Shared Writing: Personal Narrative

PRETEACH Tell students that they are going to work with you to write a personal narrative. Explain that a personal narrative tells about an event or series of events the writer experienced.

Ask students to think about a time they learned to do something new. Write the title *Learning Something New* on the board. Then write on the board the sentence frames below. Read the sentences with students and ask them to add words and phrases about themselves to complete them. Model possible answers by filling in the blanks on the board. Responses will vary.

Learning Something New

Something new I have learned to do is _____. _____ taught me how to do it. At first it was _____. Then it got _____. Now I can teach other people how to _____.

Grammar: Imperative and Exclamatory Sentences

PRETEACH Discuss the definitions of imperative and exclamatory sentences with students. Point out the following:

- An **imperative sentence** gives a command, or tells others what to do. Use a **period** at the end of an imperative sentence.
- An **exclamatory sentence** expresses strong feeling, such as excitement. Use an **exclamation point** (!) at the end of an exclamatory sentence.

Write the following sentences on the board, leaving off the end punctuation, and read them aloud:

- I am so excited (*!*)
- Do research to learn more about holidays (.)
- Hurrah for María Isabel (*!*)
- I can't believe I got the leading role in the play (*!*)
- Do your homework every night (.)

Tell students that the five sentences on the board are complete sentences. Point out that each sentence needs an ending punctuation mark.

Reread each sentence, and ask: **Does this sentence give a command? Does this sentence express a strong emotion?**

Ask volunteers to tell whether each sentence is imperative or exclamatory and write the appropriate punctuation mark at the end of each sentence.

FLUENCY PRACTICE Have volunteers read aloud the personal narrative they completed in the writing activity.

Shared Writing: Personal Narrative

RETEACH Display the completed personal narrative from Preteach. Read it aloud with students. Ask them what they would like to change about it and why. Discuss students' suggestions for changing or adding to the personal narrative. Work with students to add an imperative or an exclamatory sentence to their writing. Write the revised personal narrative using students' suggestions.. Then have students copy the revised personal narrative into their Language Journals.

Grammar-Writing Connection

RETEACH Write these sentences on the board and read them aloud with students: *María Isabel took part in a holiday play. Students learn about holidays.*

Have students help you rewrite the sentences as imperative sentences or exclamatory sentences, using some of the same words.

Then have students work in pairs or in small groups to discuss how María Isabel felt before she got a part in the Winter Pageant and after she got a part in the Winter Pageant. Have each student draw pictures to show his or her ideas. Encourage students to describe their pictures orally. Then work with them to write a sentence or two that describes their pictures. Remind students that they can use imperative or exclamatory sentences. Check students' writing and point out any corrections they need to make.

FLUENCY PRACTICE Have students choose a favorite page from "School Holidays" to read aloud.

Name _____

Ⓐ Read each sentence and circle the correct end mark. Then write them in your Language Journal. Make sure you include the end mark for each.

1. Put up a New Year's tree for Tet   .   !

2. What a fantastic Cinco de Mayo celebration   .   !

3. Fly the American flag on Memorial Day   .   !

4. Hurrah for Kwanzaa   .   !

5. Start the music for the Thanksgiving parade.   .   !

Ⓑ On the lines below, write about a holiday that you know about. What is the name of the holiday? When is it celebrated? How is it celebrated?

_____

_____

_____

_____

Draw a picture that shows people celebrating this holiday.

_____

TO THE TEACHER Have pairs of students read the sentences together and choose the correct end punctuation. Have students draw a picture to show people celebrating the holiday they described. Ask students to share their pictures with the class.

My Name Is María Isabel/School Holidays • **Lesson 3**   **19**

© Harcourt

Use with "Lou Gehrig: The Luckiest Man"

BEFORE

Building Background and Vocabulary

Build Background/Access Prior Knowledge

Have students look at the illustrations on *Pupil Edition* pages 108–109. Ask what game the man in the picture is playing. (baseball) Then ask: **What sports do you play? Why do you like them?** Record their responses in a chart like this one.

Sports	
Sports I play	**Why I like them**
football	fun
soccer	good exercise
swimming	get to spend time with friends

Selection Vocabulary

PRETEACH Display Teaching Transparency 37 and read the words aloud. Then point to the pictures as you read the following sentences:

1. The **courageous** firefighter put out the fire. She was very brave.
2. The flames from the fire were **tremendous**. They were very big.
3. The mayor wanted to thank the firefighter. He showed his **appreciation** by giving her an award.
4. The firefighter got a raise in her **salary**. Now she earns more money.
5. Mr. Sanchez is an **immigrant**. He moved to the United States from Mexico.
6. The firefighter was **modest**. She did not boast about her award.
7. All of the players are **valuable** to the team. Each is important.
8. The girl shows good **sportsmanship**. She is fair and polite.

AFTER

Building Background and Vocabulary

Selection Vocabulary

RETEACH Revisit Teaching Transparency 37. Have students answer questions such as this: Does **courageous** mean *afraid* or *brave*?

Write the following sentence frames on the board. Read each frame and ask students to choose a vocabulary word to complete it.

1. The _____ firefighter entered the burning house. (*courageous*)
2. The fans showed their _____ by cheering loudly. (*appreciation*)
3. The coach asked the players to show good _____. (*sportsmanship*)
4. The _____ became a United States citizen. (*immigrant*)
5. Olivia has a job and earns a _____. (*salary*)
6. The boy looked tiny next to the _____ elephant. (*tremendous*)
7. Jen's teammates chose her as the most _____ player. (*valuable*)
8. Even though she was the best player on the team, Jen was a very _____ person. (*modest*)

Have students write these words in their Language Dictionaries.

FLUENCY PRACTICE Have students read the sentence frames aloud. Encourage them to describe the illustrations on Teaching Transparency 37 by using the vocabulary words and any other words they know.

Build Background: "Lou Gehrig: The Luckiest Man"

Revisit the picture on *Pupil Edition* pages 104–105. Tell students that the man is Lou Gehrig. Explain that Lou Gehrig was a famous baseball player. Ask students to share what they know about baseball or Lou Gehrig.

LEAD
THE
WAY

★ Focus Skill **Prefixes, Suffixes, and Roots**

PRETEACH Tell students that longer words are often made up of different parts—prefixes, roots or root words, and suffixes. Explain that a root is the basic part of the word that gives the word its meaning. A prefix is a word part that is added to the beginning of a root or root word, and a suffix is a word part that is added to the end of a root or root word. Point out that prefixes and suffixes add to the meaning of the root word. Then draw a four-column chart on the board with the headings *Story Word*, *Prefix*, *Root or Root Word*, and *Suffix*. Write the word *courageous* under the heading *Story Word*. Break the word into its separate parts by writing *courage* under the heading *Root or Root Word* and *-ous* under the heading *Suffix*. Discuss the meaning of the word *courageous*.

Directed Reading: "Lou Gehrig: The Luckiest Man"

RETEACH Use these bulleted sentences to walk students through the story.

- This is Lou Gehrig, a famous baseball player.
- He is at bat, or ready to hit the ball.
- Lou Gehrig is playing baseball for the New York Yankees.
- This is a baseball stadium where Lou Gehrig played. This is part of the baseball diamond.

- Was Lou Gehrig a famous football player? (*no*)
- Which professional team did Lou Gehrig play for? (*the New York Yankees*)

- The newspaper in this picture has a headline that says "Gehrig Slumps." This means that Lou was not playing well.
- In 1939, Lou Gehrig benched himself. This means that he stopped playing baseball because he wasn't playing well.

- Lou Gehrig found out that he was sick. The Yankees had a special day to honor him.
- Lou Gehrig told his fans that he considered himself the luckiest man alive.
- This is Lou's baseball uniform. The Yankees retired it. This means that no Yankee player will ever wear number 4.

- Did Lou stop playing baseball in 1939? (*yes*)
- Why did Lou stop playing? (*because he was sick*)
- Why did the Yankees have a special day for Lou? (*They wanted to show him how much they cared about him.*)

FLUENCY PRACTICE Ask a volunteer to read aloud a paragraph from page 113. Encourage students to describe the illustration on *Pupil Edition* pages 112–113 by using as many vocabulary words as they can.

Concept Words
team
goal
coach
players
score
time

Pages 2–5

Pages 6–7

 QUESTIONS:
pages 2–7

Pages 8–13

Pages 14–16

QUESTIONS:
pages 8–16

Build Background: "Coach"

PRETEACH Remind students that in "Lou Gehrig: The Luckiest Man" they read about a famous baseball player. In "Coach" they will read about different kinds of sports and coaches. Explain that a coach is a person who trains players on a sports team. Ask students which sport they would like to coach and why.

English-Language Learners Book

Write the concept words on the board. Use them in sentences.
- Ralf made the winning **goal** for his **team**.
- The **coach** told her **players** to keep their eyes on the ball.
- The team needs to **score** six points to win the game.
- The **time** the game starts is 2:00 P.M.

Have students add these words to their Language Dictionaries.

Directed Reading: "Coach"

📖 **Summary** *All sports have coaches. Coaches teach athletes how to best perform their sport.*

Use these bulleted sentences to walk students through the story.
- This is a soccer team. The coach tells the players what to do.
- The team scores two goals.
- Members of the winning team are very excited. The coach is excited, too.

- A baseball team has many coaches.
- Do baseball teams have coaches? (*yes*)
- How does a soccer team earn points? (*by scoring a goal*)

- This baseball player is at bat. That means it is this player's turn to hit the ball.
- The coach says encouraging words to the players such as, "You can do it!"
- This boy is running with a football. Another boy is chasing him.
- Football coaches stand at the side of the field.
- This girl is a diver. Some divers are part of a team.

- This coach is helping a basketball team.
- Can a diver have a coach? (*yes*)
- What are some of the sports that have coaches? (*Possible responses: basketball, football, diving, baseball*)

(Focus Skill) Prefixes, Suffixes, Roots

RETEACH Review prefixes, suffixes, and roots with students and redraw the chart you drew on Day 2. Ask students to revisit the story and to fill in the chart with words that have prefixes and suffixes.

FLUENCY PRACTICE Ask students to read aloud the information about a sport that interests them. Have students use the photographs on pages 4 and 5 to retell part of "Coach."

Interactive Writing: Story

PRETEACH Tell students that they are going to work with you to write a story about someone who is playing in his first baseball game. Explain to students that every story includes characters, a setting, and a plot. Draw on the board a three-column chart and begin a

Character	Setting	Plot
Kevin	baseball field	plays his first game
		is nervous
		steps up to the plate

list of plot events. Work with students to add additional feelings and events to the chart.

Then write the following sentence frames on the board. Read each sentence with students and ask them to use the chart to help them complete each sentence. As you write the word in the blank, have students write it on their lap boards. Responses may vary.

> Today is Kevin's first _____ game. He is excited and _____.
> Kevin steps up to the _____ and _____
> at the first ball. He misses. He swings at the second ball and
> _____ that one, too. Kevin doesn't think baseball is _____.
> Then, Kevin hits a home run! He decides that baseball is _____
> after all!

Grammar: Subjects and Predicates

PRETEACH Discuss the definitions of a subject and predicate. Point out that:
- The *subject* names the person or thing that the sentence is about.
- The *predicate* tells what the person or thing is or does.

Write the following subjects on the board and read them aloud: *Lou Gehrig, The baseball team.*

Tell students that these are subjects.

Write the following predicates on the board and read them aloud: *is a baseball player, won every game in the series.*

Tell students that these are predicates. Then combine the subjects and predicates into complete sentences and read them aloud. Tell students that a complete sentence must have a subject and a predicate.

Write on the board the words below, and read them aloud. Ask students to say whether each item is a subject or a predicate.
1. coaches (*subject*)
2. teach (*predicate*)
3. fans (*subject*)
4. cheered (*predicate*)

FLUENCY PRACTICE Have volunteers read aloud the completed story.

Interactive Writing: Story

RETEACH Display the completed story from Preteach. Read it aloud with students. Ask them what they would like to change about it and why. Discuss students' suggestions for changing or adding to the story. Write the revised story based on students' suggestions. Then have students copy the revised story into their Language Journals. Students may personalize the story by changing the character's name to one of their choice.

Grammar-Writing Connection

RETEACH Write these sentences on the board and read them aloud with students: *Lou Gehrig was a player on a baseball team. Different kinds of coaches help players in different kinds of sports.*

Have students work in pairs or in small groups to discuss how it feels to participate in sports. Then have each student draw a picture to show his or her ideas. Encourage students to describe their pictures orally. Then work with each student to write a sentence or two that describes his or her picture. Remind students that every sentence should have a subject and a predicate. Check students' writing and suggest any corrections they need to make.

FLUENCY PRACTICE Have students read aloud their revised stories from the writing activity.

Name _____

A **Draw a picture of a coach and her team. The team should have five players.**

B **Draw a picture of a player scoring a goal.**

C **Draw a picture of a clock. Show the time that school starts.**

TO THE TEACHER Read aloud the directions above each box. Point out the concept words that students are being asked to illustrate, and review their definitions as necessary. Have students orally describe their pictures.

Use with "Amelia and Eleanor Go for a Ride"

Build Background/Access Prior Knowledge

Have students look at the illustrations on *Pupil Edition* pages 128–129. Tell students that the woman on page 128 is Eleanor Roosevelt. She was a First Lady. This means that she was married to a President. The woman on page 129 is Amelia Earhart. She was a famous aviator. This means that she flew airplanes. Explain that these two women were friends. Ask students what kinds of things friends do together.

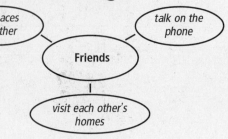

Record their responses in a web like the one shown.

Selection Vocabulary

PRETEACH Display Teaching Transparency 46 and read the words aloud. Then point to the pictures as you read the following sentences:

1. Mandy's aunt is **outspoken**. She says what is on her mind.
2. Mandy wears **practical** clothes. She likes her clothes to be useful.
3. Mandy's new dress is very **elegant**. It is very lovely.
4. The children reached high **elevations** on the swings.
5. It was a **brisk** day. It was cool outside.
6. It was a **starstruck** night. The sky was filled with stars.
7. Mandy **marveled** at the sky. She couldn't believe how beautiful it was.
8. Mandy made **miniatures**. She enjoyed making the tiny furniture.

Selection Vocabulary

RETEACH Revisit Teaching Transparency 46. Have students answer questions such as: Does *practical* mean "useful" or "useless"?

Write the following sentence frames on the board. Read each frame and ask students to choose a vocabulary word to complete it.

1. The _____ man clearly stated his opinions. (*outspoken*)
2. She wore an _____ dress to the party. (*elegant*)
3. The two mountains have different _____. (*elevations*)
4. On _____ days, you should wear a jacket. (*brisk*)
5. The _____ looked like real houses though they were much smaller. (*miniatures*)
6. Pack only _____ things for the trip. (*practical*)
7. We used a telescope to look at the _____ sky. (*starstruck*)
8. We _____ at the amazing sight. (*marveled*)

Have students write these words in their Language Dictionaries.

FLUENCY PRACTICE Have students read the sentence frames aloud.

BEFORE

Reading "Amelia and Eleanor Go for a Ride"
pages 126–141

Build Background: "Amelia and Eleanor Go for a Ride"

Revisit the pictures on *Pupil Edition* pages 128–129. Remind students that the woman on page 128 is Eleanor Roosevelt. The woman on page 129 is Amelia Earhart. Tell students that these women were adventurous. Discuss with students some exciting things they would like to do.

 ## Locate Information

PRETEACH Tell students that knowing the parts of a book and where they are located can help them find information in a book. Explain that the parts of a book may include the title, table of contents, preface, headings, glossary, appendix, and index. Use the *Pupil Edition* to point out book parts such as the table of contents, the glossary, and the index. As you point out each book part, model using it to locate information in the *Pupil Edition*.

AFTER

Reading "Amelia and Eleanor Go for a Ride"

Directed Reading: "Amelia and Eleanor Go for a Ride"

RETEACH Use these sentences to walk students through the story.

Pages 126–129

- This story is based on fact. This means that some of the things described in this story really happened, while others have been made up.
- Here is Amelia Earhart. She was a pilot. This means she flew airplanes. She was the first woman to fly, by herself, across the Atlantic Ocean.
- Eleanor Roosevelt was a First Lady. This means she was married to a President.
- Eleanor invites Amelia to come stay at the White House. The White House is where President Roosevelt and his wife Eleanor live.

Pages 130–131

 QUESTIONS:
pages 126–131

- Amelia and Eleanor are alike because they are both brave and independent.
- Was Amelia Earhart the First Lady? (*no*)
- Where does Eleanor live? (*the White House*)

Pages 132–135

- At the party, Amelia describes what it is like to be up in a plane when it is nighttime. Everyone imagines what the night sky would look like.
- Eleanor wants to take a ride in a plane with Amelia.

Pages 136–139

- Amelia takes Eleanor for a ride in a plane. They fly over Washington, D.C.
- The reporters ask Eleanor about the flight. They are interested because, during this time, there weren't many woman pilots or airplane passengers.
- When the women return, they decide to take a ride in Eleanor's car.

QUESTIONS:
pages 132–139

- Does Amelia take Eleanor for a ride on a plane? (*yes*)
- How would you describe Amelia and Eleanor? (*brave; independent*)

FLUENCY PRACTICE Have students describe the illustration on *Pupil Edition* pages 134–135.

Build Background: "Our Nation's Capital"

PRETEACH Tell students that "Our Nation's Capital" is about the capital city, Washington, D.C., which is where the President of the United States lives. In "Our Nation's Capital" they will read about some of the important buildings that are in Washington, D.C. Ask students to think about what they would like to see on a trip to Washington, D.C.

English-Language Learners Book

Use the concept words in sentences that illustrate their meanings.

Concept Words
city
states
buildings
laws
country
offices

- Washington, D.C., is the capital **city**.
- There are fifty **states** in the United States.
- People work and live in **buildings**.
- Congress is the part of the government that makes **laws** for our **country**.
- **Offices** are rooms in which people work.

Have students add these words to their Language Dictionaries.

Directed Reading: "Our Nation's Capital"

Summary *Washington, D.C., is the capital city of the United States. There are many important buildings and places in the capital city.*

Use these sentences to walk students through the story.

Pages 2–3
- Washington, D.C. is the nation's capital. It is the home of the United States government.

Pages 4–7
- The Capitol building is where Congress meets. Congress is a group of people who make the laws.
- This is the White House. This is where the President and First Family live.

QUESTIONS: *pages 2–7*
- Where is our nation's capital? (*Washington, D.C.*)
- Where does Congress meet? (*the Capitol building*)

Pages 8–9
- The Supreme Court makes sure the Constitution is being followed.
- The National Archives is the place where important papers are stored.

Pages 10–13
- Monuments and memorials are built to honor people or events. George Washington, Abraham Lincoln, and Thomas Jefferson have monuments in Washington, D.C.
- Some memorials are built to honor people who fought in wars.

Pages 14–16
- Washington, D.C. has many museums.

QUESTIONS: *pages 8–16*
- Are there nine judges on the Supreme Court? (*yes*)
- In which building are important papers kept? (*the National Archives*)

(Focus Skill) Locate Information

RETEACH Review book parts with students. Then ask students to find various book parts in one of their textbooks.

FLUENCY PRACTICE Ask students to read aloud the description of one building or monument in Washington, D.C.

Shared Writing: Personal Narrative

PRETEACH Tell students
that they are going to work
with you to write a personal
narrative, which is a story about an exciting
event that happened to them. Generate
a concept web with the phrase *It happened
to me* in the center circle. In the surrounding
circles, write the words: *flew on an airplane*, *got a baby sister*, *won a
prize*. Then brainstorm with students additional ideas to add to the web.
As a class, choose a topic from the web to write about.

Write the following sentence frames on the board or on chart paper. Read
each frame with students and work with them complete it. Responses will
vary.

> One day, I _____. (what happened) It was exciting because _____. I
> felt _____. This was a special day for me because _____. (why it was
> special)

Grammar: Complete and Simple Subjects

PRETEACH Discuss complete and simple subjects. Point out the following:

- The **complete subject** includes all the words that name the person or thing
  the sentence is about.
- The **simple subject** is the main word or words in the complete subject.

Write the following subjects on the board and read them aloud:

- *The <u>guests</u> at Eleanor's party*
- *<u>Amelia</u>*
- *The <u>city</u>*

Tell students that these are complete subjects because they include all the
words that name the person or thing each sentence is about. Point out
that *guests*, *Amelia*, and *city* are the simple subjects because they are the
main words in the complete subjects.

Read the following items aloud. Ask students to name the complete subject and the simple subject in each sentence.

1. The reporters asked Eleanor questions about her flight with Amelia.
   (*Complete subject: The reporters; Simple subject: reporters*)
2. The peaceful countryside was far below the plane. (*Complete subject:
   The peaceful countryside; Simple subject: countryside*)
3. George Washington was the first President. (*Complete subject: George
   Washington; Simple subject: George Washington*)

FLUENCY PRACTICE Have volunteers read aloud the personal narrative they
completed in the writing activity.

Shared Writing: Personal Narrative

RETEACH Display the completed personal narrative from Preteach. Read it aloud with students. Ask them what they would like to change about it and why. Discuss students' suggestions for changing or adding to the personal narrative. Work with them to add specific details to the narrative. Write a revised personal narrative using students' suggestions. Then have students copy the revised personal narrative into their Language Journals.

Grammar-Writing Connection

RETEACH Write these sentences on the board and read them aloud with students: *Eleanor Roosevelt was married to President Franklin D. Roosevelt. The President and the First Lady lived in the capital city, Washington, D.C.*

Ask students to identify the complete subjects in both sentences. (*Eleanor Roosevelt; The President and the First Lady*) Then ask students to identify the simple subjects in both. (*Eleanor Roosevelt; President, First Lady*)

Have students work in pairs or in small groups to discuss what it would be like to be President of the United States. Then have each student draw a picture to show his or her ideas. Encourage students to describe their pictures orally. Then work with them to write a sentence or two that describes their pictures. Have them underline the complete subject and circle the simple subject in each sentence that they write. Remind students that a complete subject includes all the words that name the person or thing described in the sentence; a simple subject is the main word or words in the complete subject. Check students' writing and point out any corrections they need to make.

FLUENCY PRACTICE Have students read aloud the sentences that describe their pictures.

Name _____

A Write a sentence for each simple subject. Underline the complete subject of each sentence you write.

1. city _____

_____

2. car _____

_____

3. building _____

_____

4. airplane _____

_____

B Choose one of the simple subjects from above. Then draw a picture of the subject.

TO THE TEACHER Read aloud the directions. Before students begin, review complete and simple subjects.

Amelia and Eleanor Go for a Ride/Our Nation's Capital • **Lesson 5**   **31**

Use with "The Baker's Neighbor"

Build Background/Access Prior Knowledge

Point to the man in the white hat on *Pupil Edition* page 153, and tell students that he is a baker. Explain that a baker makes cakes, pies, cookies, and breads. Ask: **What are your favorite foods?** Record their responses in a web.

Selection Vocabulary

PRETEACH Display Teaching Transparency 56 and read the words aloud. Then point to the pictures as you read the following sentences:

1. Sue is **elated** to be invited into the club. She is very happy because being a member is a **privilege**.
2. The members give their **assent** by clapping for the new member.
3. The vase is a **luxury**. It is beautiful, but it is not a necessity.
4. Two people **ad lib** a song by making up the words and tune.
5. One **shiftless** person is not singing. He is too lazy.
6. One member speaks **indignantly** to the people who aren't singing. He is upset.
7. The people look **shamefacedly** at the floor. They are sorry.

Selection Vocabulary

RETEACH Revisit Teaching Transparency 56. Read the words with students. Have students work in pairs to discuss the meanings of the words and to answer questions such as: Does *elated* mean "happy" or "sad"?

Write the following sentence frames on the board. Read each frame and ask students to choose a vocabulary word to complete it.

1. Sam's parents gave him the _____ of having a party. (*privilege*)
2. The boy looked down _____. He was sorry. (*shamefacedly*)
3. The baker was _____ because everyone liked his cakes. (*elated*)
4. The chef _____ answered questions about the food. He was angry that the customers did not like it. (*indignantly*)
5. The students decided to _____ their lines for the play. (*ad lib*)
6. The _____ dog lay on the porch. He was lazy. (*shiftless*)
7. My teacher gave her _____ for our class to put on a play. (*assent*)
8. The expensive necklace is a _____. (*luxury*)

Have students write these words in their Language Dictionaries.

FLUENCY PRACTICE Have students read the sentence frames aloud. Encourage them to describe the illustrations on Teaching Transparency 56 using the vocabulary words and any other words they know.

Build Background: "The Baker's Neighbor"

LEAD THE WAY

Display the illustration on *Pupil Edition* pages 154–155. Tell students that the man wearing the hat is the baker, whose name is Manuel. The other man is Pablo, the baker's neighbor. Discuss with students things they might see and smell in a bakery.

 ## Cause and Effect

PRETEACH Explain to students that the cause tells *why* something happened and the effect tells *what* happened. Then draw on the board a two-column chart with the headings *Cause* and *Effect*. Under *Cause*, write *Pablo smells the pastries but doesn't buy any*. Under *Effect*, write *so Manuel gets upset*. Explain to students that looking for signal words, such as *because*, *so*, and *since*, will help them recognize cause-and-effect relationships. Point to the chart on the board, and ask students which signal word was used in the chart. (*so*) Continue to fill in the chart as students read the story.

Directed Reading: "The Baker's Neighbor"

RETEACH Use these sentences to walk students through the story.

Pages 152–155
- This is the baker. His name is Manuel. He is putting out freshly-baked pies.
- This is Pablo. He is the baker's neighbor. He is smelling the pies.

Pages 156–159
- Manuel, the baker, is counting his money.
- Four children enter the bakery. They are Inez, Ramona, Carlos, and Isabel.
- The children buy some tarts to eat.

Pages 160–161
- Pablo whistles a happy tune.
- Carlos takes Manuel's hat. Manuel is angry.

 QUESTIONS: pages 152–161
- Is Pablo a baker? (*no*)
- Why does Pablo come to the bakery each day? (*to smell the baked goods*)

Pages 162–167
- Manuel goes to get the Judge because he wants Pablo to pay him for smelling his pastries.
- The Judge listens to Manuel and Pablo. He tells Pablo to bring ten gold pieces to Manuel.
- Manuel counts the gold pieces.
- The Judge tells Manuel to return the gold pieces to Pablo. He says that Pablo and Manuel are even because Pablo has smelled Manuel's pastries and Manuel has touched Pablo's gold.

Pages 168–169
- Manuel shares his pies and cakes with everyone.

QUESTIONS: pages 162–169
- Does Manuel think Pablo should pay him? (*yes*)
- Why is Manuel angry with Pablo? (*He thinks Pablo is stealing smells.*)

FLUENCY PRACTICE Ask volunteers to read aloud characters' parts from page 158. Encourage students to describe the illustration on *Pupil Edition* pages 158–159.

Build Background: "Tea with Jam"

PRETEACH Remind students that in "The Baker's Neighbor," Manuel learns to share his delicious pies and cakes. In "Tea with Jam" Natasha and her friends share delicious foods from their cultures. Ask students what foods from their culture they would bring to a party.

English-
Language
Learners
Book

Concept Words
Saturday
party
learn
surprise
something
can't

Write the concept words on the board and use them in sentences.
- On **Saturday**, we are going to my grandmother's house.
- She is having a **party** with ice cream and cake for my grandfather.
- I want to **learn** how to make a birthday cake.
- My grandmother wants to **surprise** my grandfather with a new watch.
- I want to give my grandfather **something**, too.
- I **can't** wait to see my grandfather's face when he sees all of us at his party.

Have students add these words to their Language Dictionaries.

AFTER

Skill Review
pages 172–173

Directed Reading: "Tea with Jam"

 Summary *Natasha invites her friends to a "tradition-sharing party." All of the guests bring a food from their culture to Natasha's party.*

Use these sentences to walk students through the story.

Pages 2–7
- This is Natasha and her friends Rita and Chun.
- This is Natasha at her old school in Russia.
- Natasha, Rita, and Chun make plans for Natasha's party.

 QUESTIONS: pages 2–7
- Did Natasha live in China before coming to America? (*no*)
- What is Natasha doing to celebrate being in the United States for one year? (*She is having a party.*)

Pages 8–11
- Natasha, Rita, and Chun invite three other friends to the party.
- Each friend is going to bring a special food to the party.

Pages 12–16
- Natasha, her mother, and her grandmother are greeting the guests.
- There is a teapot in the center of the dining room table.
- Natasha pours tea and hot water into her tea cup. Then she puts a spoonful of raspberry jam into her tea.

 Questions: pages 8–16
- Do each of Natasha's friends bring a special food to the party? (*yes*)
- What does Natasha add to the tea in her cup? (*hot water and a spoonful of jam*)

Focus Skill ## Cause and Effect

RETEACH Review cause and effect with students. Then draw on the board a two-column chart with the headings *Cause* and *Effect*. Work with students to complete the chart with examples of causes and effects from "Tea with Jam." Remind students to look for signal words like *because*, *so*, and *since*.

> **FLUENCY PRACTICE** Ask students to read aloud one page from the story. Have students use the illustrations on pages 12–13 to retell part of "Tea with Jam." Encourage them to use vocabulary words and concept words.

Shared Writing: Paragraph of Information

PRETEACH Tell students that they are going to work with you to write a paragraph of information about planning a party. Work with students to generate a concept web about planning a party. In the center circle, write the phrase *planning a party*. In the surrounding ovals, add words and phrases such as *send invitations, make a guest list, choose a time and place*, and *make food*. Work with students to decide in what order these steps should be completed. Brainstorm with them a list of sequence words to use in their paragraphs. (*first, next, then, before, finally*)

Write the following sentence frames on the board. Read each sentence with students and ask them to use sequence words or words from the web to complete each sentence. Responses will vary.

The first step in planning a party is to make a guest _____.
_____ choose a time and a place. Then, send out the _____.
Before the guests arrive, make the _____. Finally, relax and have a _____ time!

Grammar: Complete and Simple Predicates

PRETEACH Discuss with students the definitions of complete and simple predicates. Point out the following:

- The **complete predicate** includes all the words that tell what the subject of the sentence is or does.
- The **simple predicate** is the main word or words in the complete predicate.

Write the following sentences on the board and read them aloud:

- *Every day the baker makes many delicious things.*
- *Natasha's party is a lot of fun.*

Point out the complete predicate in each sentence. (*makes many delicious things; is a lot of fun*) Then underline the simple predicate in each sentence. (*makes, is*)

Read the following items aloud. Ask students to identify the complete and simple predicate in each sentence.

1. Each child promises to bring a special treat to Natasha's party. (*complete: promises to bring a special treat to Natasha's party; simple: promises*)
2. The judge listens to Manuel's complaint. (*complete: listens to Manuel's complaint; simple: listens*)
3. Carlos buys the tarts. (*complete: buys the tarts; simple: buys*)

FLUENCY PRACTICE Have volunteers read aloud the completed paragraph of information.

Interactive Writing: Effective Paragraphs

RETEACH Display the completed paragraph from Preteach. Read it aloud with students. Ask them what they would like to change about it and why. Discuss students' suggestions for changing or adding to the paragraph. Write the revised paragraph based on students' suggestions. Then have students copy the revised paragraph into their Language Journals.

Grammar-Writing Connection

RETEACH Write these sentences on the board, and read them aloud with students:

> *Manuel, the baker, bakes different kinds of foods for his bakery. Natasha and her friends make different kinds of foods for Natasha's party.*

Have students work in pairs or in small groups to discuss foods they like and dislike. Then have each student draw a picture to show his or her ideas. Encourage students to describe their pictures orally. Then work with each student to write a sentence or two that describes his or her picture. *Example: I like my mom's mashed potatoes.* Ask students to circle the simple predicate and to underline the complete predicate. Check students' writing and suggest any corrections they need to make.

FLUENCY PRACTICE Have students reread the part of "Tea with Jam" in which Natasha explains how to make tea the Russian way. (pages 14–16)

Name _____

Draw pictures on the Food Guide Pyramid to show some of the foods that go in each group.

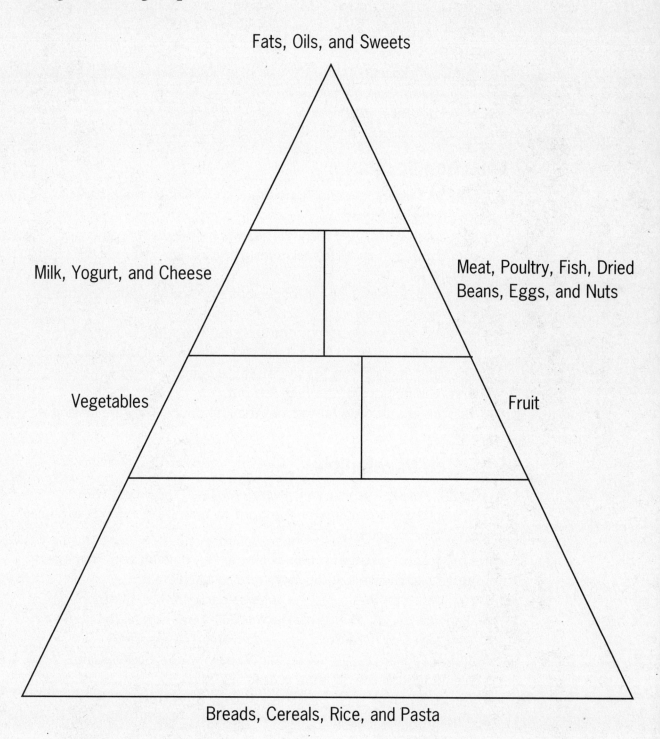

TO THE TEACHER Read the directions aloud. Brainstorm with students some foods that go in each section of the Food Guide Pyramid.

The Baker's Neighbor/Tea with Jam • **Lesson 6**   **37**

© Harcourt

Build Background/Access Prior Knowledge

Have students look at the illustration on *Pupil Edition* page 178. Point to the girl and explain that she is very special. Then ask them what makes them special. Record their responses in a web like this one.

am a good friend.

write good stories. — I am special because I . . . — draw funny pictures.

help my mom.

Selection Vocabulary

PRETEACH Display Teaching Transparency 65. Point to the pictures as you read these sentences:

1. Ann and Lee are **loyal** friends. They will be friends forever.
2. Ann thinks that the kite's tail is **insignificant**. She does not think it is important.
3. Lee wants to make the tail longer, but Ann is **unyielding**. She does not change the tail.
4. Lee ties some **steely** string onto the kite. This string is very strong.
5. Lee **twined** the string around the stick. She twisted it tightly.
6. The string is **encircling** Lee's wrist. It is around her right wrist.
7. Ann feels **neglected**. She feels left out.
8. The girls are **plotting** how to get the kite down. They are making a plan.

Selection Vocabulary

RETEACH Revisit Teaching Transparency 65. Read the words with students and have them answer questions such as: Does *insignificant* mean "important" or "unimportant"?

Write the following sentence frames on the board. Read each frame and ask students to choose a vocabulary word to complete it.

1. Mrs. Wu's class was _____ a surprise party for her. (*plotting*)
2. Grandma _____ the yarn around the knitting needle. (*twined*)
3. The plant died because I _____ to water it. (*neglected*)
4. The jar lid was _____ so we had to push it open. (*unyielding*)
5. We sat around the campfire so that we were _____ it. (*encircling*)
6. The athlete had _____ muscles. He was very strong. (*steely*)
7. A good friend is _____ and kind. (*loyal*)
8. The mistake is so _____ that no one will notice it. (*insignificant*)

Have students write these words in their Language Dictionaries.

FLUENCY PRACTICE Have students read the sentence frames aloud. Encourage them to describe the illustrations on Teaching Transparency 65 by using the vocabulary words and any other words they know.

LEAD
THE
WAY

Build Background: "The Emperor and the Kite"

Revisit the pictures on *Pupil Edition* pages 178–179. Remind students that the girl on page 178 is the emperor's youngest daughter, Djeow Seow. Explain that even though Djeow Seow is much smaller than her brothers and sisters, she is very special. Discuss with students what might make Djeow Seow special.

 ## Narrative Elements

PRETEACH Tell students that every story includes narrative elements—characters, setting, and plot. Explain that characters are the people or animals in a story; the setting is when and where the story takes place; and the plot is what happens in the story. Draw a three-column chart on the board with the headings *Characters*, *Setting*, and *Plot*. Tell students that Djeow Seow is the main character in this story. Write her name in the chart.

AFTER

Reading
"The Emperor and
the Kite"

Pages 176–179
Pages 180–181
Pages 182–185

Directed Reading: "The Emperor and the Kite"

RETEACH Use these sentences to walk students through the story.

- Here is Djeow Seow, the emperor's tiny daughter. She is making a kite.
- These are Djeow Seow's three sisters. They are bringing food to the table.
- Princess Djeow Seow likes to fly her kite high into the air.
- The monk stops to talk to Djeow Seow. A monk is a religious man.
- The man in the fancy robe is the emperor. He is the ruler of the country.
- Some evil men come and take the emperor away.
- Djeow Seow wants to rescue her father.
- The monk's poem helps Djeow Seow think of a way to save the emperor.

 QUESTIONS:
pages 179–185

- Is Djeow Seow the emperor's only daughter? (*no*)
- What does Djeow Seow like to do? (*fly her kite*)
- What happens to the emperor? (*He is taken away by evil men.*)

Pages 186–191

- Djeow Seow ties a rope to her kite and flies it up to her father.
- The emperor uses the rope to escape from the tower.
- When the emperor reaches the ground, he kneels before his tiny daughter.

Pages 192–195

- The emperor catches the evil men.
- Djeow Seow sits on a tiny throne next to her father.

 QUESTIONS:
pages 186–195

- Does the emperor escape? (*yes*)
- Who helps the emperor escape? (*Djeow Seow*)
- How do you think Djeow Seow feels sitting on a throne next to her father? (*Possible response: She feels proud and loved.*)

FLUENCY PRACTICE Ask a volunteer to read aloud a paragraph from page 194. Encourage students to describe the illustration on *Pupil Edition* pages 194–195 and to use as many vocabulary words as they can in their descriptions.

Build Background: "Inside and Outside Together"

PRETEACH Remind students that "The Emperor and the Kite" was about Djeow Seow, a tiny girl who was very special. In "Inside and Outside Together," they will read about Felipe, a boy who has a special talent. Invite students to share what is special about their friends or family members.

Concept Words
English
speak
idea
count
water
smiled

Use the concept words in sentences to illustrate their meanings.

- Felipe does not **speak** to his classmates. He does not know **English**.
- Do you have an **idea** for a game we could play?
- Can you **count** to ten?
- Fish live in the **water**.
- Felipe **smiled** because he was happy.

Have students add these words to their Language Dictionaries.

Directed Reading: "Inside and Outside Together"

 Summary *When the class sits outside under a tree, Felipe, the new student, sits alone making shadow puppets with his hands. Sandi sits next to him and tries to make a shadow rabbit. Before long, Sandi teaches Felipe how to play shadow tag.*

Use these sentences to walk students through the story.

Pages 2–7
- Ms. Lowe takes her fourth-grade class outside.
- This is Felipe, a new student in the class. He is last in line.
- The class sits under a tree, but Felipe sits alone.
- Sandi looks at Felipe. He is making a rabbit shadow.
- Sandi shows the class how to play shadow tag.

**QUESTIONS:
pages 2–7**
- Is Felipe a new student? (*yes*)
- Does Felipe sit with his class or does he sit alone? (*alone*)

Pages 8–11
- Sandi is sitting next to Felipe. She tries to make a shadow rabbit.
- Sandi and Felipe play shadow tag with their shadow rabbits.

Pages 12–16
- Felipe is playing shadow tag with the other children. He is having fun.
- The students write a shadow play. Then they perform it.

**QUESTIONS:
pages 8–16**
- Does Sandi try to make a shadow rabbit? (*yes*)
- What game does the class play? (*shadow tag*)

Narrative Elements

RETEACH Review the narrative elements with students. Then draw on the board a narrative elements chart, like the one you drew on page 39. Work with students to fill in the chart for "Inside and Outside Together."

FLUENCY PRACTICE Ask students to read aloud one page from "Inside and Outside Together." Have them use the illustrations on pages 8–9 to retell part of the story. Encourage them to use as many vocabulary words and concept words as possible.

Shared Writing: Written Directions

PRETEACH Tell students that they are going to work with you to write directions for playing shadow tag. On the board write the heading *Sequence Words*. Tell students that sequence words tell the order in which things should happen. Brainstorm with students a list of sequence words (*first, next, then, finally*) and write them under the heading.

Write these sentence frames on the board. Read each frame with students. Tell them to use words from the list to complete each sentence.

Sequence Words
first
next
then
finally
last

_____ , you set up the playing area. (First)

_____ , you pick someone to be "It." (Next)

_____ , the person who is "It" tries to tag someone else's shadow. The tagged person becomes "It."(Then)

_____ , the game ends when everyone is tired. (Finally)

Grammar: Compound Subjects and Predicates

PRETEACH Discuss with students the definition of a **compound subject**. Point out that: A compound subject is two or more subjects joined by the conjunction *and* or *or*. These subjects have the same predicate.

Write the following sentences on the board, underlining as shown.

- *The <u>emperor</u> and his <u>daughter</u> ruled the kingdom.*
- *<u>Sandi</u> or <u>Felipe</u> can make shadow rabbits.*

Tell students that these sentences have compound subjects. Point out the conjunction *and* in the first sentence and *or* in the second sentence.

Then discuss the definition of a **compound predicate** with students. Point out that: A compound predicate is two or more predicates joined by a coordinating conjunction such as *and* or *or*. These predicates have the same subject.

Write the following sentences on the board, underlining as shown.

- *Tina <u>runs</u> and <u>plays</u>.*
- *Ryan <u>reads</u> or <u>sleeps</u>.*

Point out the conjunction and predicates in each sentence. Ask students to name the subject in each sentence. (*Tina, Ryan*)

Write on the board these sentences. Have volunteers underline the compound subject or the compound predicate.

1. The boys and girls lived in the house. (*compound subject: The boys and girls*)
2. Ty waved and smiled. (*compound predicate: waved and smiled*)

FLUENCY PRACTICE Have volunteers read aloud their written directions.

Shared Writing: Written Directions

RETEACH Display the completed set of directions from page 41. Read it aloud with students. Ask them what they would like to change about it and why. Discuss students' suggestions for changing or adding to the directions. Write the revised directions based on students' suggestions. Then have students copy them into their Language Journals.

Grammar-Writing Connection

RETEACH Write these sentences on the board and read them aloud with students:

The emperor learns that Djeow Seow is special because she is loyal to him.

The children in Ms. Lowe's class learn that Felipe is special because he can make shadow rabbits.

Have students work in pairs or in small groups to discuss how they might make a new student feel special and welcome. Then have each student draw a picture to show his or her ideas. Encourage students to describe their pictures orally. Then work with each student to write a sentence or two that describes his or her picture. Remind students to write some sentences that have compound subjects and compound predicates. Check students' writing and suggest any corrections they need to make.

FLUENCY PRACTICE Have students reread the part of "Inside and Outside Together" in which the students write the shadow play. (pages 14–15).

Name _____

Cut out the sentences and put them in the correct order. Then glue the
sentences onto another sheet of paper. Be sure they are in the correct order
before you glue them down.

Then, I shine the bright light onto an empty wall.

**Finally, I put my hands in front of the light
and move them to make shadow animals.**

Next, I turn on a bright light.

First, I turn off the lights in the room.

TO THE TEACHER Read aloud the directions
and make sure students understand each step
of the activity. You may want to review the
sequence words before students begin.

Use with "Nights of the Pufflings"

Build Background/Access Prior Knowledge

Have students look at the photograph on *Pupil Edition* page 210. Point to the birds flying in the sky. Ask: **What do you know about birds?** Record their responses in a concept web like the one shown here.

Birds

most fly

lay eggs

Birds

have feathers

some swim

Selection Vocabulary

PRETEACH Display Teaching Transparency 75, and read the words aloud. Then point to the pictures as you read the following sentences:

1. The rabbits live on an **uninhabited** island. No people live there.
2. The rabbits nest in **burrows**, which are holes in the ground.
3. The rabbits do not **venture** far from their homes. They know it is dangerous to go too far from home.
4. The baby birds are **stranded**. They can't get off the island.
5. The rabbits **instinctively** close their eyes when the wind blows.
6. The baby **nestles** close to its mother so it feels safe.

Selection Vocabulary

RETEACH Revisit Teaching Transparency 75. Have students answer questions such as: Are *burrows* "holes in the ground" or "paths on the ground"?

Write the following sentence frames on the board. Read each frame and ask students to choose a vocabulary word to complete it.

1. The baby bird _____ next to its mother to stay warm. (*nestles*)
2. When we got off the boat, it felt strange to be the first people on an island that had been _____. (*uninhabited*)
3. Mr. Ortiz was _____ on the road when his car broke down. (*stranded*)
4. The ducks _____ follow their mother even though she does not teach them how to do this. (*instinctively*)
5. Some birds dig holes in the ground and then live in these _____. (*burrows*)
6. The baby birds do not _____ from the nest, because they do not know how to fly. (*venture*)

Have students write these words in their Language Dictionaries.

FLUENCY PRACTICE Have students read the completed sentences aloud. Encourage them to describe the illustrations on Teaching Transparency 75 by using the vocabulary words and any other words they know.

Build Background: "Nights of the Pufflings"

Have students look at the picture of the bird on *Pupil Edition* page 213. Tell students that this bird is a puffin. Ask students to point out the puffin's beak, wings, feathers, and feet.

LEAD
THE
WAY

 Summarize

PRETEACH Tell students that when they summarize a selection, they should retell the most important parts in their own words.

Write the following chart on the board.

Work with students to fill in the

Important Ideas to Include	Details Not to Include

chart as they read. Have them use the first column to help them summarize the selection.

Directed Reading: "Nights of the Pufflings"

RETEACH Use these sentences to walk students through the story.

- This is a puffin. Puffins are birds that live at sea most of the year.
- This is Halla. She lives on a small island in Iceland. Every year, the puffins come to Halla's island to lay eggs and raise chicks.

- This boy is watching and waiting. He wants to see the puffins' babies, the pufflings. He is waiting for the nights of the pufflings.

- Is a puffin a bird? (*yes*)
- What are baby puffins called? (*pufflings*)

- Look at the flowers. When these flowers bloom, the children will know it is time for the pufflings to take their first flight.
- These children are looking for pufflings that have landed in the village instead of in the sea. They have flashlights and boxes.
- Here is a lost puffling. A child finds the lost puffling and gently picks it up.
- It is the next day. Children send the pufflings that they have found into the air toward the ocean.
- This puffling is paddling away to sea. It will not return until next spring.

- Do the children keep pufflings as pets? (*no*)
- How do the children help lost pufflings? (*They take them to the ocean and set them free.*)

FLUENCY PRACTICE Ask students to describe the photographs on *Pupil Edition* page 216. Ask volunteers to read aloud the text on page 216.

Build Background: "Beaks and Wings"

PRETEACH Remind students that "Nights of the Pufflings" is about birds called puffins. In "Beaks and Wings" they will read about different kinds of birds. Point out that both selections are non-fiction. Discuss with students features birds have in common.

English-Language Learners Book

Use the concept words in sentences that illustrate their meanings.

Concept Words
fly
eggs
eyes
hungry
food
nest

- The crows **fly** across the sky and land in the branch of a tree.
- The baby birds hatched from the **eggs** yesterday.
- The eagle uses its **eyes** to see its prey.
- The **hungry** chicks need **food**.
- The woodpecker gathered twigs and grass to build its **nest**.

Have students add these words to their Language Dictionaries.

Directed Reading: "Beaks and Wings"

Summary *All birds have two wings, two legs, a beak, and feathers, and they lay eggs. In "Beaks and Wings," readers will learn about different kinds of birds.*

Use these sentences to walk students through the story.

Pages 2–5
- All birds have beaks, wings, legs, and feathers. All birds lay eggs.
- Penguins are different from most birds because they cannot fly.
- This bald eagle is the national bird of the United States. Eagles are protected by the United States government. The government has laws to help keep them safe.

Pages 6–7
- Barn owls hunt at night. This barn owl is perching, or sitting.

QUESTIONS:
pages 2–7
- Do all birds have feathers? (*yes*)
- How are penguins different from most other birds? (*They cannot fly.*)

Pages 8–9
- This is a crow. It is looking for insects to eat.

Pages 10–11
- Woodpeckers eat insects that live in trees. They get the insects by pounding their beaks into the bark of trees.

Pages 12–13
- Pelicans are water birds. They use their large bills to catch fish.

Pages 14–15
- Hummingbirds are very tiny. Their wings move very fast.
- The hummingbird uses its long beak to drink nectar, or juice, from flowers.

Page 16
- Many people enjoy learning about birds.

QUESTIONS:
pages 8–16
- Do all birds get food the same way? (*no*)
- How are woodpeckers and crows alike? (*They both eat insects.*)

(Focus Skill) Summarize

RETEACH Review the tips for summarizing. Have students write one or two sentences summarizing "Beaks and Wings."

FLUENCY PRACTICE Ask students to read aloud information about one type of bird.

Shared Writing: Summary

PRETEACH Tell students that they are going to work with you to write a summary of pages 4–5 of "Beaks and Wings." Explain that a written summary restates the most important information in a few words. Point out that students should restate the information in their own words. Brainstorm with students important information to include in their summaries of pages 4–5 of "Beaks and Wings."

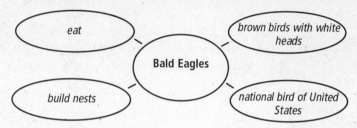

Write the following sentence frames on the board. Read each frame with students and ask them to use words and phrases from the web to complete it. Responses will vary.

The bald eagle is a large _____ bird with a _____ head. Eagles eat _____ and build _____. They are the _____ of the United States.

Grammar: Simple and Compound Sentences

PRETEACH Discuss simple and compound sentences with students.

- A **simple sentence** expresses only one complete thought.
- A **compound sentence** is made up of two or more simple sentences joined by a comma and a **conjunction**. *And*, *or*, and *but* are conjunctions.

Write the following sentences on the board and read them aloud:

- *Puffins spend the winter at sea.*
- *The eagle flies above the river, but it does not catch any fish.*

Tell students that the first sentence is a simple sentence. It expresses one complete thought. The second sentence is a compound sentence joined by a comma and the conjunction *but*.

Read the following items aloud. Ask students to say whether each item is a simple or compound sentence.

1. Crows build their nests from sticks, grass, and feathers. (*simple*)
2. The bird flies to her nest, and she feeds her babies. (*compound*)

FLUENCY PRACTICE Have volunteers read aloud their summaries.

Shared Writing: Summary

RETEACH Display the completed summary from Preteach. Read it aloud with students. Ask them what they would like to change about it and why. Discuss students' suggestions for changing or adding to the summary. Write a revised summary using students' suggestions. Then have students copy the revised summary into their Language Journals.

Grammar-Writing Connection

RETEACH Write these sentences on the board and read them aloud with students: *Puffins are one type of bird. Bald eagles, barn owls, crows, woodpeckers, pelicans, and hummingbirds are other types of birds.*

Ask students to identify whether the two sentences on the board are simple or compound sentences. (*simple*) Then ask students to rewrite the two sentences as one compound sentence, changing words where necessary. (*Possible response: Puffins are one type of bird, and bald eagles, barn owls, woodpeckers, pelicans and hummingbirds are other types of birds.*)

Have students work in pairs or in small groups to discuss different types of birds. Then have each student draw a picture to show his or her ideas. Encourage students to describe their pictures orally. Then work with them to write a sentence or two that describes their pictures. Encourage them to write one simple sentence and one compound sentence. Remind students that a simple sentence expresses a complete thought and that a compound sentence is made up of two or more simple sentences joined by a comma and a **conjunction**, or connecting word. Check students' writing and point out any corrections they need to make.

FLUENCY PRACTICE Have students choose a description of a bird from "Beaks and Wings" to read aloud.

Name _____

Pretend you are a bird. Answer each question. Then draw a picture to show what you look like.

1. What kind of bird are you? _____

_____

2. Where do you live? _____

_____

3. What do you eat? _____

_____

4. What do you look like? _____

_____

5. Can you fly? _____

_____

6. Can you swim? _____

_____

TO THE TEACHER Read aloud the directions. Have students answer the questions and draw their pictures. Allow time for students to share their work.

Nights of the Pufflings/Beaks and Wings • **Lesson 8**   **49**

Use with "The Garden of Happiness"

Build Background/Access Prior Knowledge

Have students look at the illustration on *Pupil Edition* pages 232–233. Point to the garden lot. Tell students this lot was once filled with garbage. Explain that the people who live near this lot decided to clean it up and make it into something prettier.

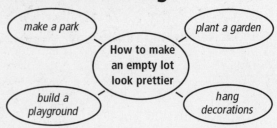

Ask: **If you wanted to make an empty lot look pretty, what would you do with it?** Record their responses in a concept web like the one above.

Selection Vocabulary

PRETEACH Display Teaching Transparency 84, and read the words aloud. Then point to the pictures as you read the following sentences:

1. The **haze** in the air made it hard for Bert to see across the street.
2. The delicious smells coming from the bakery filled the air. Bert **inhaled** a deep breath to enjoy the smells.
3. Bert looked at the **mural** painted on the wall.
4. The mural showed **lavender** flowers. Bert liked the pale purple flowers.
5. Connor saw Bert and **skidded** to a stop.

Selection Vocabulary

RETEACH Revisit Teaching Transparency 84. Have students answer questions such as: Does *inhaled* mean to "breathe in" or "to breathe out"?

Write the following sentence frames on the board. Read each frame, and ask students to choose a vocabulary word to complete it.

1. Patrice said _____ was her favorite shade of purple. (*lavender*)
2. Shameka painted a _____ on the hallway wall. (*mural*)
3. When Mr. Mendez tried to stop, the car _____ down the wet street. (*skidded*)
4. Tony _____ the sweet smell of the peach. (*inhaled*)
5. The _____ was so thick that we could not see the tops of the city buildings. (*haze*)

Have students write these words in their Language Dictionaries.

> **FLUENCY PRACTICE** Have students read the sentence frames aloud. Encourage them to describe the illustrations on Teaching Transparency 84 by using the vocabulary words and any other words they know.

Build Background: "The Garden of Happiness"

Revisit the picture on *Pupil Edition* pages 232–233. Tell students that the people in this neighborhood have decided to clean up the empty lot and change it into a garden. Discuss with students what kinds of plants they might grow in the garden. (*flowers, greenery, vegetables, fruits, etc.*)

LEAD
THE
WAY

Cause and Effect

PRETEACH Tell students that understanding cause-and-effect relationships will help them understand why characters in the story feel or act the way they do. Explain that the cause tells why something happened and the effect tells what happened. Then draw a two-column chart on the board with the headings *Cause* and *Effect*. Under the heading *Cause*, write *The empty lot is filled with garbage*. Under the heading *Effect*, write *People clean up the lot*. Point out that the people clean the lot because it is filled with garbage. Explain to students that signal words, such as *because*, *so*, and *since*, will help them recognize cause-and-effect relationships. Work with students to add to the chart as they read.

AFTER

Reading
"The Garden
of Happiness"

Pages 232–235

Pages 236–237
QUESTIONS:
pages 232–237

Pages 238–239

Pages 240–241

Pages 242–243

QUESTIONS:
pages 238–243

Directed Reading: "The Garden of Happiness"

RETEACH Use these sentences to walk students through the story.

- This is the Garden of Happiness, a garden that Marisol's neighbors are making in an empty lot. The garden is in the city.
- Marisol wants to plant something in the garden.
- She finds a patch of dirt in a crack in the sidewalk.
- Look across the street from the garden. Some teenagers are looking at a wall. They want to paint a mural on it. A mural is a picture.

- Marisol finds a seed. She plants it in her small patch of dirt.
- Does Marisol live on a farm? (*no*)
- Where do Marisol's neighbors plant their garden? (*in an empty lot*)

- Here is Marisol's sunflower. It is the giant sunflower that is growing from the crack in the sidewalk. Everyone likes the sunflower.

- Autumn is coming. The neighbors are picking their vegetables.
- Marisol's sunflower starts to droop. That makes Marisol sad.

- Marisol is sitting on the steps. She is very sad. She misses her sunflower.
- Now Marisol is standing in front of a mural that has been painted on the wall. The mural is filled with sunflowers. How do you think she feels?

- Do the teenagers paint sunflowers on their mural? (*yes*)
- What happens to the sunflower in autumn? (*It droops.*)

FLUENCY PRACTICE Have students describe the illustration on *Pupil Edition* pages 238–239 and use vocabulary words in their descriptions.

Build Background: "Sunshine Place"

PRETEACH Remind students that in "The Garden of Happiness" some people make an empty lot look prettier by cleaning out the garbage and planting a garden. In "Sunshine Place" students will read about four students who make an old building look prettier by painting a mural on it. Ask students what they could do to make their neighborhood look prettier.

Use the concept words in sentences that illustrate their meanings.

Concept Words
green
red
orange
yellow
brown
blue

- **Green** grass covered the hills.
- The strawberries were a beautiful shade of **red**.
- **Orange** is a color and the name of a fruit.
- The bananas are **yellow**.
- The farmer sifted the **brown** dirt through his fingers.
- There were no clouds in the **blue** sky.

Have students add these words to their Language Dictionaries.

Directed Reading: "Sunshine Place"

📖 **Summary** *Alberto lives in an old town called Milford. Alberto and his friend Leslie give the town a lift by painting a brightly colored mural.*

Use these sentences to walk students through the story.

Pages 2–3
- This is Alberto. He lives in a town called Milford. Milford looks old and empty.

Pages 4–7
- Alberto and his friend Leslie have an idea. They want to paint a mural on the sign on the Baker building. A mural is a big wall painting.
- Alberto and Leslie tell their art teacher, Mr. Stone, about their idea.

❓ **QUESTIONS: pages 2–7**
- Does Alberto want to paint a mural? (*yes*)
- Who is Mr. Stone? (*Alberto and Leslie's art teacher*)

Pages 8–9
- Alberto, Leslie, Martin, and Nina plan to paint the mural.

Pages 10–13
- Mr. Hollis owns the building. He says it's okay to paint the mural.

Pages 14–16
- Alberto and his friends paint a mural of people enjoying a park. At the bottom of the mural the street sign says "Sunshine Place."
- The town holds a party to celebrate the mural.

❓ **QUESTIONS: pages 8–16**
- Did the people of Milford like the mural? (*yes*)
- What did the students use the paint for? (*to paint a mural*)

★
Focus Skill **Cause and Effect**

RETEACH Review cause and effect with students. Then draw on the board a two-column chart with the headings *Cause* and *Effect*. Work with students to complete the chart with causes and effects from "Sunshine Place."

FLUENCY PRACTICE Ask students to describe the mural.

Shared Writing: How-to Paragraph

PRETEACH Tell students
that they are going to
work with you to write a
paragraph that explains to others
how to make a peanut
butter and jelly sandwich.
Brainstorm with students

gather the ingredients

How To Make a Peanut Butter and Jelly Sandwich

spread one slice of bread with peanut butter

spread another slice with jelly

put the two slices together

the steps for making a peanut butter and jelly sandwich. Organize their responses in a web. Then help students put the steps in order.

Write the following sentence frames on the board. Read each frame with students and ask them to use words from the web to complete it.

> Making a Peanut Butter and Jelly Sandwich.
> Making a peanut butter and jelly sandwich is easy if you follow these steps. First, you _____.Then, you _____.Next, you _____. Finally, you _____. Enjoy!

Grammar: Independent and Dependent Clauses

PRETEACH Discuss with students the definitions of a clause, an independent clause, and a dependent clause. Point out the following:

- A **clause** is a group of words that has both a subject and a predicate.
- Clauses that can stand alone as sentences are called **independent clauses**.
- **Dependent clauses** cannot stand alone as sentences. They begin with connecting words, such as *before*, *when*, and *after*.

Write the following sentences on the board and read them aloud:

- *After the children paint the mural, all of the townspeople have a party.*
- *Alberto wants to make a mural, but he does not have any paint.*

For each sentence, point out the clauses. Explain that sentence I has a dependent clause, which means the clause cannot stand alone. Call students' attention to the connecting word *after* that starts the dependent clause. Next point out that sentence 2 has two independent clauses, which means each clause can stand alone as a sentence.

Read the following items aloud. Ask students to say whether each item has a dependent clause or only independent clauses. Then ask them to underline the dependent clause.

1. On East Houston Street there is an empty lot. (*dependent; On East Houston Street*)
2. The plant grew tall, and it had a flower at the top. (*independent*)

FLUENCY PRACTICE Have volunteers read aloud their how-to essays.

Shared Writing: How-to Paragraph

RETEACH Display the completed how-to paragraph from Preteach. Read it aloud with students. Ask them what they would like to change about it and why. Discuss students' suggestions for changing or adding to the paragraph. Write the revised paragraph using students' suggestions. Then have students copy the revised how-to paragraph into their Language Journals. Students should personalize their how-to paragraphs by adding descriptive adjectives.

Grammar-Writing Connection

Write these sentences on the board, and read them aloud with students: *Marisol and her neighbors make an empty lot look prettier by planting a garden. After they painted the wall white, Alberto and his friends made an old building look prettier by painting a mural on it.*

Ask students to identify the dependent clause in the second sentence.

Have students work in pairs or in small groups to discuss what kinds of things they could do to make their neighborhood look prettier. Then have each student draw a picture to show his or her ideas. Encourage students to describe their pictures orally. Then work with each student to write a sentence or two that describes his or her picture. Remind students to use dependent and independent clauses in their sentences. Check students' writing, and point out any corrections they need to make.

FLUENCY PRACTICE Have students choose a favorite page from "Sunshine Place" to read aloud.

Name _____

Complete the following sentences to tell how Marisol grew a sunflower.

1. First, Marisol _____

2. Next, Marisol _____

3. Then, Marisol _____

4. Finally, Marisol _____

Draw pictures to show the four steps you listed above.

Step 1	Step 2

Step 3	Step 4

TO THE TEACHER Have students write four steps that Marisol did to grow her sunflower. You may want to model how to write a sentence—for example, *First, Marisol found a place to plant her seed.* Next, invite students to illustrate the four steps that they wrote. Ask students to share their illustrations with the class.

The Garden of Happiness/Sunshine Place • **Lesson 9**   **55**

© Harcourt

Use with "How to Babysit an Orangutan"

Build Background/Access Prior Knowledge

Have students look at the photographs on *Pupil Edition* page 259. Point to the baby orangutans. Tell students that, like people, baby animals grow and change as they get older. Then ask students to share how they have grown and changed. Record their responses in a concept web like the one shown here.

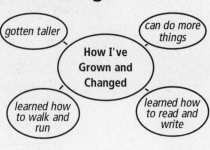

Selection Vocabulary

PRETEACH Display Teaching Transparency 93 and read the words aloud. Then point to the pictures as you read the following sentences:

1. Nancy **smuggled** the cat into the house. She hid it under a blanket.
2. Mom's **facial** expression is not a smile. It is a frown.
3. Mom tells Nancy about her **displeasure.** Mom does not want the cat in the house.
4. The cat is healthy and has good **coordination**. It can easily jump to the counter in the kitchen.
5. Nancy says the cat is **endangered**, but her mother knows she's joking.
6. The dog is **jealous** of the cat. He wants Nancy's attention.

Selection Vocabulary

RETEACH Revisit Teaching Transparency 93. Read the words with students. Have students work in pairs to discuss the meanings of the words and to answer questions such as: Does *displeasure* mean "dissatisfied" or "satisfied"?

Write the following sentence frames on the board. Read each frame, and ask students to choose a vocabulary word to complete it. Write students' responses in the blanks.

1. Ella showed her _____ by frowning. *(displeasure)*
2. It takes _____ to hit a baseball. *(coordination)*
3. A smile is a _____ expression. *(facial)*
4. Pierre was _____ of Nina because she got a higher grade on the test than he did. *(jealous)*
5. Some bad people _____ orangutans out of the rain forest. *(smuggled)*
6. Animals on an _____ species list must be protected. *(endangered)*

Have students write the words in their Language Dictionaries.

FLUENCY PRACTICE Have students read the sentence frames aloud. Encourage them to describe the illustrations on Teaching Transparency 93 by using the vocabulary words and any other words they know.

Build Background: "How to Babysit an Orangutan"

Revisit the photographs on *Pupil Edition* page 259. Tell students that these animals are orangutans. Explain that orangutans grow and change as they get older. Point out that young orangutans that are orphaned, or without their mother or father, cannot survive without help. Discuss with students what kinds of help the orangutans might need. *(getting food; finding shelter)*

LEAD THE WAY

⭐ Focus Skill **Summarize**

PRETEACH Tell students that when they summarize a selection, they should retell the most important information in a few words.

Write the following chart on the board.

Tips for Summarizing		
The Most Important Ideas	Other Important Information That Supports the Most Important Ideas	Information That Is Not as Important

As students read the selection, work with them to fill in the chart. Then help them summarize the selection in one or two sentences.

Directed Reading "How to Babysit an Orangutan"

RETEACH Use these sentences to walk students through the story.

Pages 254–257

- This is a baby orangutan. Orangutans are a kind of ape. They live in rain forests.
- This orangutan is holding hands with its human babysitter. The babysitters take care of baby orangutans that don't have mothers.
- These baby orangutans need to learn to survive.

Pages 258–261

- The babysitters have to feed the orphaned orangutans. Young orangutans drink milk.
- Point to the orangutan that is eating bananas.

QUESTIONS:
pages 254–261

- Do people babysit orangutans? *(yes)*
- Where do orangutans live? *(the rain forest)*

Pages 262–263

- Baby orangutans like to play. They have "best friends."
- This baby orangutan is learning to be more comfortable in trees.

Pages 264–265

- Orangutans nest in trees. They make nests from leaves and branches.
- Here is a baby orangutan, Nanang, playing hide-and-seek. He covers his face with his hands.
- The baby orangutan has built a nest on the ground.

QUESTIONS:
pages 262–265

- Do orangutans make nests in trees? *(yes)*
- Where do orangutans like to play? *(in trees)*
- What would you like best about babysitting an orangutan? *(Responses will vary.)*

FLUENCY PRACTICE Ask students to choose a paragraph from "How to Babysit an Orangutan" to read aloud.

Build Background: "Kid Care"

PRETEACH Remind students that "How to Babysit an Orangutan" is about how people care for orangutans. In "Kid Care" students will learn more about taking care of themselves. Ask students to point to their nose, mouth, eyes, and ears.

English-Language Learners Book

Concept Words
work
protect
smile
remember
jobs
healthy

Use the concept words in sentences that illustrate their meanings.

- The students **work** on improving their soccer skills by practicing every day.
- The mother dog will **protect** its babies from other animals.
- The happy child gave her mother a big **smile**.
- It is important to **remember** to brush your teeth every day.
- Your heart and your lungs have different **jobs** in your body.
- If you take care of yourself, you will have a **healthy** body.

Have students add these words to their Language Dictionaries.

Directed Reading: "Kid Care"

Summary *Different body parts do different jobs. It is important to care for all of your body parts.*

Use these sentences to walk students through the story.

Pages 2–3
- This story is called "Kid Care." You will learn about the parts of your body.
- Look at the picture of the boy. Point to his ear. Now point to his nose.

Pages 4–7
- You use your eyes to see. How are these students protecting their eyes?
- You use your ears to hear. What does an alarm clock sound like?
- You use your nose to smell. Your teeth help you eat and talk.

QUESTIONS: pages 2–7
- Does your nose help you smell? *(yes)*
- Which body part allows you to hear? *(ears)*

Pages 8–9
- Your tongue helps you taste and eat food.
- Your bones give your body shape. Protect them by wearing helmets and knee and elbow pads.

Pages 10–13
- Take care of your hair, skin, and nails by keeping them clean.
- These boys and girls wear hats and sunglasses to protect their skin and eyes from the sun.
- This is the Food Pyramid, which divides foods into different groups. Eat a variety of healthy foods every day.

Pages 14–16
- Exercise helps your body get stronger and healthier.

QUESTIONS: pages 8–16
- Is exercise important to your body? *(yes)*
- Which food group do apples belong to? *(fruit)*

Focus Skill ## Summarize

RETEACH Review the tips for summarizing. Have students orally summarize the story in one or two sentences.

FLUENCY PRACTICE Ask students to choose a section of "Kid Care" to read aloud.

Shared Writing: Summary

PRETEACH Tell students that they are going to work with you to write a summary of "How to Babysit an Orangutan." Remind students that a summary of a selection contains only the most important ideas and details from the selection. Use a web like the one shown here to brainstorm with students information to include in their summaries.

Write the following sentence frames on the board. Read each sentence frame with students, and ask them to use words from the web to complete each sentence. Responses will vary.

> "How to Babysit an Orangutan" is about people who _____. These people care for orangutans by _____. The babysitters _____ their job.

Grammar: Complex Sentences

PRETEACH Discuss with students the definitions of a complex sentence, a dependent clause, and an independent clause. Point out the following:

- A **complex sentence** is made up of an independent clause and at least one dependent clause.
- An **independent clause** can stand alone as a complete sentence.
- A **dependent clause** cannot stand alone as a complete sentence and often begins with a connecting word such as *after, because,* or *if.*

Write the following sentences on the board, and read them aloud:

- *If your eyes need to be cleaned, tears do the work.*
- *When you eat food, your tongue tastes it.*
- *Camp Leakey is unusual because it is an orphanage for orangutans.*

Tell students that the three sentences are complex sentences. Call students' attention to the connecting words that signal the dependent clauses. (*If; When; because*)

Read the following complex sentence aloud. Ask students to say which part is the independent clause and which part is the dependent clause.

> **You should take care of your bones because they protect your organs.** (independent: *You should take care of your bones;* dependent: *because they protect your organs*)

> **FLUENCY PRACTICE** Have volunteers read aloud the summary they completed in the writing activity.

Shared Writing: Summary

RETEACH Display the completed summary from Preteach. Read it aloud with students. Ask them what they would like to change about it and why. Discuss students' suggestions for revising the summary. Ask if there are any places where they would like to add or delete information. Write the revised summary using students' suggestions. Then have students copy the revised summary into their Language Journals.

Grammar-Writing Connection

RETEACH Write these sentences on the board and read them aloud with students:

Orangutans grow and change as they get older. People grow and change as they get older.

Ask students to identify the independent and dependent clauses in the sentences on the board. (independent—*Orangutans grow and change; People grow and change*; dependent—*as they get older; as they get older.*)

Have students work in pairs or in small groups to discuss how they grow and change as they get older. Then have each student draw a picture to show his or her ideas. Encourage students to describe their pictures orally. Then work with each student to write a sentence or two that describes his or her picture. Remind students that a complex sentence has an independent clause and at least one dependent clause. Check students' writing, and point out any corrections they need to make.

FLUENCY PRACTICE Have students read aloud their revised summaries.

Look at the Food Guide Pyramid on page 12 of "Kid Care." Use the Food Guide Pyramid to plan a lunch. Draw a picture to show the lunch you have planned. Label each food in your picture.

TO THE TEACHER Discuss the Food Guide Pyramid with students. Talk about the importance of eating balanced meals. Ask students to plan a lunch using information from the Food Guide Pyramid. Tell them to draw pictures to show the lunch they have planned. Encourage students to share their pictures with the class.

Use with "**Sarah, Plain and Tall**"

Build Background/Access Prior Knowledge

Write the word *homesick* on the board and read it aloud to the class. Tell students that people often miss their home when they are far away from it. Ask: **If**

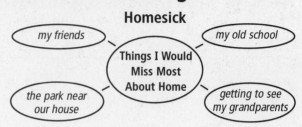

you moved away from your home, what would you miss most? Why? Record students' responses in a web like the one above.

Selection Vocabulary

PRETEACH Display Teaching Transparency 103, and read the words aloud. Then point to the pictures as you read the following sentences:

1. We keep all the horses in the **paddock** during the day. It is fenced in, so the horses can't get out.
2. The farmer planted the trees as a **windbreak**. The row of trees helped block the wind.
3. The wind blew the leaves of the tree. Brian liked listening to the **rustle** of the leaves.
4. Brian has a **conch** shell. When he puts it against his ear, he can hear the sound of the ocean.
5. Brian was not **alarmed** by the animals on the farm. He knew there was nothing to be frightened about.

Selection Vocabulary

RETEACH Revisit Teaching Transparency 103. Read the words with students. Have students work in pairs to discuss the meanings of the words and to answer questions such as these: Is a *paddock* a "fenced-in area" or "an open pasture"? Is a *rustle* a "sound" or a "taste"?

Write the following sentence frames on the board. Read each frame, and ask students to choose a vocabulary word to complete it. Write students' responses in the blanks.

1. The rancher built a new _____ for his horses. (*paddock*)
2. Ginger was _____ when she heard the fire truck sirens. (*alarmed*)
3. Keeno found a _____ shell on the beach. (*conch*)
4. The fan caused the papers to _____ on the desk. (*rustle*)
5. The farmer used a line of oak trees as a _____. (*windbreak*)

Have students write these words in their Language Dictionaries.

FLUENCY PRACTICE Have students read the sentence frames aloud. Encourage them to describe the illustrations on Teaching Transparency 103 by using the vocabulary words.

Build Background: "Sarah, Plain and Tall"

Have students look at the picture on *Pupil Edition* page 281. Tell students that the story they are going to read is about a woman named Sarah who has come from the seashore in Maine to live on a prairie farm. Ask students how they think they would feel if they moved far away from home.

LEAD
THE
WAY

Draw Conclusions

PRETEACH Explain to students that authors do not always give information in a direct way. Tell students that they can draw conclusions about what the author is saying by combining information from the story with their own knowledge.

On the board, draw a chart like the one below. After you have read through the story, help students complete the chart.

Story Details	My Own Knowledge	Conclusion
Papa and Sarah travel in a wagon.	Today people usually travel in a car or truck.	The story takes place long ago.

Directed Reading: "Sarah, Plain and Tall"

RETEACH Use these sentences to walk students through the story.

Pages 276–277
- Papa and Sarah are in a wagon. The wagon is traveling across the prairie.
- Look at Sarah's clothes. You can tell that this story takes place long ago.

Pages 278–279
- This gopher is standing up. It is listening and watching for the wagon.
- Anna and Caleb do their chores. They are waiting for the wagon, too.

Pages 280–281
- A bonnet is a type of hat. Sarah is wearing a bonnet when she arrives.
- Sarah gives Caleb a present. It is a moon snail shell. It comes from Maine, by the seashore, just like Sarah. Sarah's cat, Seal, sits next to Sarah.

QUESTIONS: pages 276–281
- Is Sarah from the prairie? (*no*)
- What pet does Sarah bring with her? (*Sarah brings her cat, Seal.*)

Pages 282–283
- Sarah describes the seashore in Maine to Anna and Caleb.
- This is a conch shell, and Sarah says that it sounds like the ocean when you hold it to your ear.

Pages 284–285
- Sarah, Papa, and the children are getting ready for dinner.
- Everyone is happy. Anna and Caleb hope Sarah will be their new mother.

Pages 286–287
- Sarah cuts Caleb's hair and Papa's hair.
- Sara sings a song about the summer. Anna and Caleb know that she is planning to stay.

QUESTIONS: pages 282–287
- Do Papa and the children live near the seashore? (*no*)
- Where does Sarah come from? (*Maine*)

FLUENCY PRACTICE Ask a volunteer to read aloud a paragraph from his or her favorite page in the story. Encourage students to describe their favorite illustration in the story. Tell students to use as many vocabulary words as they can.

Build Background: "Under One Roof"

PRETEACH Remind students that "Sarah, Plain and Tall" is about a woman who gets homesick because she is far away from her home in Maine. "Under One Roof" is about a girl who gets homesick when she moves from Vietnam to America.

Write these words on the board and use them in sentences to illustrate their meanings.

Concept Words
class
help
instructions
age
date
lunch

- The teacher gave every student in the **class** a form to fill out.
- Kate needed **help** with part of the form. She could not do it by herself.
- She did not understand the **instructions**. She did not know what to do.
- The teacher told Kate to write her name and **age** on the paper.
- Kate wrote on the form the **date** she was born.
- Kate gave her form to the teacher before she went to eat **lunch**.

Have students add these words to their Language Dictionaries.

Directed Reading: "Under One Roof"

 Summary *Bian and her family move from Vietnam to the United States. They live with relatives while they look for a house of their own.*

Use these sentences to walk students through the story.

Pages 2–3
- This is the main character. She lives in the United States.
- Her cousin Bian lives in Vietnam.

Pages 4–5
- The main character is talking with her parents. They tell her that her cousin Bian's family is coming to live with them for a while.
- The main character's family greets Bian's family at the airport.

Pages 6–7
- The main character and her cousin Bian are at school. They walk down the hallway together. At lunch time, they go to the cafeteria to eat.

**QUESTIONS:
pages 2–7**
- Is Bian from the United States? (*no*)
- Where does the main character greet Bian's family? (*at the airport*)

Pages 8–9
- Bian and her cousin are in a classroom. The teacher is talking to the class. Bian leans over to ask her cousin for help.

Pages 10–11
- The main character looks in her brother's room for a pencil. She sees her cousin Chim is there.
- Bian describes the photographs in her photo album.

Pages 12–13
- Bian has been asked to play the flute in the school band.
- Bian is practicing the flute in the bedroom, but her cousin wants to study.

Pages 14–16
- Bian and the main character work out the problem.
- Bian's family is moving. They have finally found a house of their own.

**QUESTIONS:
pages 8–16**
- Does the main character share a bedroom with her cousin Bian? (*yes*)
- What makes Bian's cousin frustrated? (*She misses having her own space.*)

(Focus Skill) Draw Conclusions

RETEACH Review drawing conclusions with students. Draw a three-column chart with the headings *Story Details*, *My Own Knowledge*, and *Conclusion*. Ask students to revisit the story to complete the chart.

FLUENCY PRACTICE Have students use the illustration on pages 4–5 to retell part of "Under One Roof." Encourage them to use as many vocabulary words and concept words as possible.

Interactive Writing: Cause-and-Effect Paragraph

PRETEACH Tell students that they are going to work with you to write a cause-and-effect paragraph. Draw a two-column chart on the board with the headings *Cause* and *Effect*. Remind students that a cause is what makes something happen, and an effect is what happens. Then brainstorm with students cause-and-effect relationships in "Under One Roof." (*For example:* Effect—*the main character feels frustrated.* Cause—*She is sharing her space with her cousin Bian.*)

Cause	Effect

Write the following sentence frames on the board or on chart paper. Read each frame with students. Have volunteers suggest words from the chart to complete the sentences. Work with students to write a draft of the paragraph, based on the sentences below.

> The main character and Bian have not seen each other in three years because _____. The main character and her family go to the airport so they can _____. Since Bian is from Vietnam, she does not know _____. Bian feels homesick because _____.

Grammar: Common and Proper Nouns

PRETEACH Discuss with students the definitions of common and proper nouns. Point out the following:

- A **noun** is a word that names a person, a place, a thing, or an idea.
- A **common noun** names any person, place, thing, or idea.
- A **proper noun** names a particular person, place, thing, or idea. Names of magazines, newspapers, works of art, musical compositions, and organizations are also proper nouns.
- Proper nouns begin with capital letters. A common noun is not capitalized unless it begins a sentence.

Write the following sentences on the board, and underline the nouns.

1. Sarah moved from the seashore.
2. The dogs were happy to see Caleb.
3. The family from Vietnam must learn to speak English.
4. The girls share a bedroom.
5. The two families live in the same house.

Read each sentence aloud. Call students' attention to the nouns in each sentence. Point out that *seashore, dogs, family, girls, bedroom, families,* and *house* are all common nouns. Point out that *Sarah, Caleb, Vietnam,* and *English* are all proper nouns. Remind students that proper nouns start with capital letters.

> **FLUENCY PRACTICE** Have volunteers read aloud the paragraph they completed in the writing activity.

Shared Writing: Cause-and-Effect Paragraph

RETEACH Display the completed cause-and-effect paragraph from Preteach. Read it aloud with students. Ask them what they would like to change about it and why. Discuss students' suggestions for changing or adding to the paragraph. Write the revised paragraph based on students' suggestions. Then have students copy the revised paragraph into their Language Journals.

Grammar-Writing Connection

RETEACH Review with students what common and proper nouns are. Then write these sentences on the board, and read them aloud with students.

Sarah moved to the prairie from Maine.
The girl from Vietnam made new friends.

Have students work in pairs or small groups to discuss how it feels to be homesick. Then have each student draw a picture to show his or her ideas. Encourage students to describe their pictures for the class. Then work with each student to write two sentences that describe his or her picture. Remind students that proper nouns should be capitalized and common nouns usually should not. Suggest that students try to include examples of common and proper nouns in their sentences. Monitor students' work as they complete the sentences.

FLUENCY PRACTICE Have volunteers describe their pictures and read their sentences aloud for the class. Point out any common or proper nouns that appear in students' sentences.

Name _____

Read each question. Then write a complete sentence to answer it.

1. What is your **age**? _____

_____

2. What is today's **date**? _____

3. What do you like to eat for **lunch**? _____

_____

4. What is your favorite **class** in school? _____

_____

5. How could you **help** a friend? _____

_____

Draw a picture of some foods you like to eat for lunch. Write the name of each food you draw.

_____

Draw a picture of yourself helping a friend.

TO THE TEACHER Read aloud the directions. Review with students the meanings of the concept words.

Sarah, Plain and Tall/Under One Roof • **Lesson 11** **67**

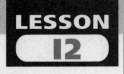
Use with "Stealing Home"

Build Background/Access Prior Knowledge

Write the word *change* on the board. Discuss with students some of the different changes that occur in life. Ask: **What kinds of changes have happened in your life? How did those changes make you feel?** Record students' responses in a chart.

Facing Changes	
Changes I've Faced	**How I Felt**
I went to a new school.	scared and nervous

Selection Vocabulary

PRETEACH Display Teaching Transparency 112, and read the words aloud. Then point to the pictures as you read the following sentences:

1. Rob looked **glumly** at his mother. He felt sad and gloomy.
2. Mom was grumpy, and spoke **irritably** to Rob.
3. Mom said, "Don't **impose** on Vic. He should not do your chores."
4. Vic and Rob **bicker**. They argue over doing different chores.
5. At first, Rob holds a **grudge** against Vic. Then Rob realizes that it is wrong to have bad feelings toward his brother.
6. Rob offers to **tutor** Vic at basketball. Rob will teach Vic how to play.
7. Rob is usually nice, and has a friendly **disposition**.
8. The boys would rather play basketball than do chores. Basketball is one of their favorite **pastimes**.

Selection Vocabulary

RETEACH Revisit Teaching Transparency 112. Have students discuss the words and answer questions such as these: Are *pastimes* things you do "for fun" or "things you do for work"? Does *tutor* mean "to teach" or "to learn"?

Write these sentences on the board, and ask students to choose a vocabulary word to complete each one.

1. The girls _____ over which game to play. (*bicker*)
2. Nathan never holds a _____ against people. (*grudge*)
3. My cat has a friendly _____. (*disposition*)
4. Sports and hobbies are fun _____. (*pastimes*)
5. Mr. Hastings will _____ Kate in math. (*tutor*)
6. When Nancy was sick, she had to _____ on her friends to get her homework. (*impose*)
7. Ms. Jones grumbled _____ when she got up. She was not in a good mood. (*irritably*)
8. The children looked _____ at the rain. They were sad they could not play outside. (*glumly*)

Have students write these words in their Language Dictionaries.

FLUENCY PRACTICE Have students read the sentence frames aloud. Encourage them to describe the illustrations on Teaching Transparency 112 by using the vocabulary words and any other words they know.

Build Background: "Stealing Home"

Have students look at the picture on *Pupil Edition* pages 304–305. Tell students that the boy on the left is Thomas. Explain that Thomas is unhappy because his great-aunt has come to live with him and his grandfather. Have students share different ways of dealing with change.

LEAD
THE
WAY

 Focus Skill

Compare and Contrast

PRETEACH Explain to students that to **compare** means to tell how things are alike, or the same, and to **contrast** means to tell how things are different. On the board, draw a chart like the

Before Aunt Linzy Visits	After Aunt Linzy Visits
Thomas lives with his grandfather, a cat, and a duck.	Thomas lives with his grandfather, a cat, a duck, and Aunt Linzy.

one above to explain the concept. After you have read the selection, work with students to fill in the chart with information from the story.

Directed Reading: "Stealing Home"

RETEACH Use these sentences to walk students through the story.

- This is Aunt Linzy. She is visiting Thomas and his grandfather.
- This is Ringo, the cat.

- Thomas and his friend Donny are eating cones. They are talking about why Thomas is unhappy that Aunt Linzy is visiting.
- Thomas tells Donny that his Aunt Linzy is "cleaning the whole place." She even puts away the checkers and the dominoes.

- Is Thomas unhappy? (*yes*)
- Who comes to live with Thomas and his grandfather? (*Aunt Linzy*)

- Thomas and his grandfather are watching a baseball game.
- Aunt Linzy comes in and talks during the most exciting part.
- Thomas hears Grandfather and Aunt Linzy talking. Aunt Linzy says she wants to share their interest in sports.

- Aunt Linzy makes changes around the house. She cleans. She makes curtains.
- Aunt Linzy is a good cook. She makes dinner for Thomas and Grandfather.

- Grandfather tells Thomas that Aunt Linzy is a cheerful person and that they can't tell her to leave.
- Thomas and his grandfather together play a game called Scrabble®.
- Thomas decides to try harder to get along with Aunt Linzy.

- Does Aunt Linzy leave because Thomas is unhappy? (*no*)
- Why is Thomas upset that Aunt Linzy is visiting? (*He is upset because Aunt Linzy is changing everything.*)

FLUENCY PRACTICE Ask a volunteer to read aloud a paragraph from his or her favorite part of the story. Encourage students to describe the illustration on *Pupil Edition* pages 310–311.

Build Background: "At Summer's End"

PRETEACH Remind students that "Stealing Home" is about a boy who has to deal with the change of having his great-aunt live with him. "At Summer's End" is about Maria, who goes to live in the country rather than the city. Ask students how they would handle moving to a new place.

English-
Language
Learners
Book

Concept Words
different
hears
smells
cries
watches
laughing

Use the concept words in sentences to illustrate their meanings.

- Gina thinks living in the country is very **different** from living in the city.
- She **hears** the cows moo.
- She **smells** the animals in the barn.
- At first, she **cries** because she misses the city.
- Then Gina **watches** the kittens play in the barn.
- Soon she is **laughing** at the silly kittens.

Have students add these words to their Language Dictionaries.

Directed Reading: "At Summer's End"

 Summary *Maria and her mother leave their apartment in the city. At first Maria is sad. Then she realizes there are many interesting things to do in the country.*

Use these bulleted sentences to walk students through the story.

Pages 2–3
- This is Maria. She is looking out the car window.

Pages 4–5
- Maria is going to stay at a farmhouse with her aunt, her uncle, and her two cousins.
- Look at all the farm animals. Name the farm animals that you see.

Pages 6–7
- Maria's cousins Elaine and Eddie take Maria to see the barn.

QUESTIONS: pages 2–7
- Does Maria go to a farmhouse? (*yes*)
- Who lives at the farmhouse? (*Maria's aunt, uncle, and cousins*)

Pages 8–9
- One of the cats has just had kittens. How many do you see?
- When it is time for lunch, Maria sits next to Elaine at a long dining table.

Pages 10–11
- After lunch, Maria's mother leaves. Maria is sad to see her go, but excited about being on the farm. Maria and her cousins pick peas for dinner.

Pages 12–13
- Elaine carries a large bucket. The girls are going to feed the pigs.

Pages 14–15
- Maria is on the porch. She sees the garden, the fields, and the woods.

Page 16
- Maria hopes that one day her cousins will come visit her in the city.

QUESTIONS: pages 8–16
- Does Maria like farm life? (*yes*)
- How does Maria feel after her first day in the country? (*She is happy.*)

Compare and Contrast

RETEACH Review the definitions of *compare* and *contrast*. Draw a two-column chart on the board with the headings *City Life* and *Country Life*. Ask students to revisit "At Summer's End" to complete the chart.

> **FLUENCY PRACTICE** Have students use the illustration on pages 4–5 to retell part of "At Summer's End." Encourage them to use several vocabulary words.

Interactive Writing: Explain a Process

PRETEACH Tell students that they are going to work with you to write a paragraph that explains a process. Create a flow chart with the title *How to Pack for a Trip*. In the boxes, write the words *First*, *Next*, *Then*, and *Finally*. Then brainstorm with students the steps they would use to pack for a trip.

How to Pack for a Trip

First

Next

Then

Finally

Write the following sentence frames on the board or on chart paper. Read each sentence with students, and have them suggest phrases from the flowchart to fill in the blanks. Responses will vary.

How to Pack for a Trip

To pack for a trip, the first thing you have to do is _____. Next, you should _____. Then, you _____. Finally, you should _____.

Grammar: Singular and Plural Nouns

Discuss with students singular and plural nouns. Point out the following:

- A **singular noun** names one person, place, thing, or idea.
- A **plural noun** names more than one person, place, thing, or idea.
- Most nouns are made plural by adding *-s* or *-es*.
- Nouns that end in a consonant and *y* are made plural by changing the *y* to *ies*.

Write the following words on the board:
boxes
shirt
flowers
ladies
dress

Read each word aloud. Ask students to say which nouns are singular (*shirt, dress*) and which are plural. (*boxes, flowers, ladies*) Circle the *-es* and *-s* endings on *boxes* and *flowers* to show what was added to make those nouns plural. Then circle the letters *ies* on *ladies*. Write *lady* on the board next to *ladies*. Point out that the singular noun *lady* ends with the letter *y*. Tell students that to make *lady* plural, they must change *y* to *ies*. Remind students that the word *dress* is singular and that the *s* is part of the word, not an ending that has been added.

FLUENCY PRACTICE Have volunteers read aloud the paragraph they completed in the writing activity.

Interactive Writing: Explain a Process

RETEACH Display the completed paragraph from Preteach. Read it aloud with students. Ask them what they would like to change about it and why. Discuss students' suggestions for changing or adding to the paragraph. Write the revised paragraph based on students' suggestions. Then have students copy the revised paragraph into their Language Journals.

Grammar-Writing Connection

RETEACH Review with students the difference between singular and plural nouns. Then write the following nouns on the board:

job
beaches
sheets
fields
road
stories
fence
pigs
babies
branches

Create a two-column chart with the headings *Singular (one)* and *Plural (More than one)*. Have students copy the chart into their notebooks. Then have them complete the chart by writing each noun in the appropriate column. (Singular: *job, road, fence;* Plural: *beaches, sheets, fields, stories, pigs, babies, branches*) Monitor students' work as they complete the chart. Then have students choose two nouns from each column and use each noun in a sentence. Check students' sentences for subject-verb agreement.

FLUENCY PRACTICE Have students choose a page from "At Summer's End" to read aloud.

Name _____

Draw a picture of your family. Label each person. Underneath your picture, write one sentence telling how you are like someone in your family and one sentence telling how you are different from someone in your family.

_____

_____

_____

_____

_____

TO THE TEACHER Read aloud the directions. Write on the board
a list of words for family members, such as *aunt, uncle,* etc. Review
with students the meaning of each word.

Stealing Home/At Summer's End • **Lesson 12** **73**

LESSON 13

Use with "The Cricket in Times Square"

Building Background and Vocabulary

Build Background/Access Prior Knowledge

Show students pictures of different kinds of transportation. Ask students to share information about different kinds of transportation they have taken. Record students' responses in a web.

Selection Vocabulary

PRETEACH Display Teaching Transparency 121 and read the words aloud. Then point to the pictures as you read the following sentences:

1. Abe is new in town. He makes the **acquaintance** of three children.
2. The children understand Abe's sadness. They listen **sympathetically**.
3. Abe looks **wistfully** at Martin. Abe sadly remembers his old friends.
4. Martin tells Abe that the **logical** thing to do is to make new friends. Making new friends is a sensible solution.
5. Penny is **eavesdropping** on the boys to hear what they say.
6. Abe is an **excitable** boy. When he finds a box, he can't wait to open it.
7. Abe is **scrounging** in the box. He is looking for rare baseball cards.

AFTER

Building Background and Vocabulary

Selection Vocabulary

RETEACH Revisit Teaching Transparency 121. Read the words aloud. Have students discuss the meanings of the words and answer questions such as this: If something is **logical**, is it *reasonable* or *unreasonable*?

Write the following sentence frames on the board. Read each sentence, and ask students to choose a vocabulary word to complete it.

1. Paula was _____ at the door. She wanted to hear what her mother was saying. (*eavesdropping*)
2. Paula listened _____ as her mom said it was hard to move. (*sympathetically*)
3. Paula thought _____ about her old friends. (*wistfully*)
4. Then Paula heard another girl's voice. Paula became _____. (*excitable*)
5. Mom knew the _____ thing to do was to take Nita to meet Paula. (*logical*)
6. Paula pretended to be _____ through a box of old magazines. (*scrounging*)
7. However, Paula was glad to make the _____ of her new friend, Nita. (*acquaintance*)

Have students write these words in their Language Dictionaries.

FLUENCY PRACTICE Have students read the sentence frames aloud. Encourage them to describe the illustrations on Teaching Transparency 121, using the vocabulary words and any other words they know.

Build Background: "The Cricket in Times Square"

Have students look at the picture on *Pupil Edition* page 343. Tell students that Chester Cricket traveled from the country to the city, where Tucker Mouse and Harry Cat live. Ask students to predict how Chester got to the city.

LEAD
THE
WAY

 Draw Conclusions

PRETEACH Tell students that authors do not always tell everything in the story. Explain to students that they can use information from the story and

Story Information	Your Own Knowledge	Conclusion
Tucker Mouse lives in the subway station.	I know people do not like mice.	Tucker must hide from the people.

their own knowledge to draw conclusions. Draw a chart on the board to explain the concept. Give students an example from the story. As you move through the story, help students fill in the chart.

Directed Reading: "The Cricket in Times Square"

RETEACH Use these sentences to walk students through the story.

Pages 328–329
- Here is Tucker Mouse, Chester Cricket, and Harry Cat.
- Tucker and Harry live in Times Square in New York City. Chester is from the country. He has never been in a city before.

Pages 330–331
- Tucker is on a stool. He is talking to Chester who is in a matchbox on the counter. Tucker wants to find out who Chester is.

Pages 332–333
- Tucker finds out that Chester is from Connecticut. Connecticut is a state.
- Tucker goes inside a drain pipe. This is his home.

Pages 334–335
- Chester and Tucker are eating liverwurst. Liverwurst is a type of sausage.
- Chester tells Tucker how he ended up in New York. Chester fell asleep in a picnic basket and was carried away.

QUESTIONS: pages 328–335
- Does Chester Cricket come from the city? (*no*)
- How did Chester get to the city? (*He fell asleep in a picnic basket.*)

Pages 336–339
- Chester sees Harry Cat. At first, he is frightened and hides.
- Chester learns that Harry is Tucker's friend and comes out of the matchbox.

Pages 340–341
- Chester, Tucker, and Harry eat together to celebrate their new friendship.

Pages 342–344
- Tucker, Harry, and Chester are on a street. They are looking at Times Square.
- There are crowds of people, lots of noise, and bright lights everywhere. Chester has never seen these things before. He is a little frightened.
- Then Chester looks up at the sky. He sees a familiar star, the same one he sees in Connecticut. Chester feels better.

QUESTIONS: pages 336–344
- Is Harry a mouse? (*no*)
- What does Chester celebrate with Tucker and Harry? (*their new friendship*)

FLUENCY PRACTICE Ask a volunteer to read aloud a paragraph from the story. Ask students to describe the illustration on *Pupil Edition* page 343. Encourage them to use vocabulary words in their descriptions.

Build Background: "Going Places"

Remind students that "The Cricket in Times Square" is about a cricket that travels to the city. Tell students that in "Going Places," they will read about different kinds of transportation.

English-
Language
Learners
Book

Use the concept words in sentences to illustrate their meanings.

Concept Words
travel
car
bus
airplane
train
ride

- Carlos loves to **travel**. He has visited many places.
- Mom drives the **car** to work every day.
- I ride the **bus** to school in the morning.
- Lucy flew to Texas in an **airplane**.
- The conductor told everyone to board the **train**.
- We like to **ride** our bicycles around the neighborhood.

Have students add these words to their Language Dictionaries.

Directed Reading: "Going Places"

📖 **Summary** *Different kinds of transportation help people get to places that are close and to places that are far away.*

Use these sentences to walk students through the story.

Pages 2–3
- Traveling helps you learn about the world. There are many ways to travel.
- There are lots of cars and buses on this street. The city is very busy.
- A taxicab is a car that will take people to the places they want to go.
- Look in the sky. An airplane is flying over the buildings.

Pages 4–5
- These people are on a subway. A subway is a train that runs underground.
- This girl rides a horse to get where she wants to go.

Pages 6–7
- This is how the land looks from an airplane that is high in the sky.
- This is a different kind of train. It does not travel underground.

❓ QUESTIONS: pages 2–7
- Do taxicabs fly in the sky? (*no*)
- Where does a subway run? (*under the ground*)

Pages 8–9
- Many people travel by bus. Bus drivers often tell interesting stories.
- A ferry boat carries cars and people across the water to the island.

Pages 10–11
- Helicopters use a propeller to fly. Point to the propeller.
- The person wearing a helmet is riding a motorcycle.

Pages 12–13
- Some people like to travel by cruise ship.
- Some people would rather paddle their own boat.

Pages 14–16
- This is a monorail. It is a ride at an amusement park.
- This girl is on a bicycle. She is riding through her neighborhood.

❓ QUESTIONS: pages 8–16
- Does a helicopter have a propeller? (*yes*)
- How do motorcycle riders and bike riders protect their heads? (*with a helmet*)

(Focus Skill) Draw Conclusions

RETEACH Review with students how to draw conclusions. Draw a three-column chart with the headings *Story Information*, *Your Own Knowledge*, and *Conclusion*. Ask students to help you fill in the chart.

> **FLUENCY PRACTICE** Have students look at the illustration on pages 2–3 of "Going Places." Ask students to describe what they see. Encourage them to use as many vocabulary words and concept words as possible.

Interactive Writing: Explanatory Paragraph

How to Get from Our
Classroom to the
Cafeteria

PRETEACH Tell students that they are going to work with you to write a paragraph. Draw a flow-chart on the board with the title *How to Get from Our Classroom to the Cafeteria*. In the next four boxes, write the words: *First, Next, Then,* and *Finally*. Then brainstorm with students the steps they would use to go from the classroom to the cafeteria.

First

Next

Then

Finally

Write the following sentence frames on the board or on chart paper. Read each sentence with students, and have them suggest phrases from the flowchart to complete the paragraph.

How to Get from Our Classroom to the Cafeteria

To get from our classroom to the cafeteria, the first thing you have to do is _____. Next, you should _____. Then, you _____. Finally, you should _____.

Grammar: Possessive Nouns

PRETEACH Discuss the definition of possessive nouns with students. Point out the following:

- A **possessive noun** tells who or what something belongs to.
- An **apostrophe** (') is used to form a possessive noun.
- A **singular possessive noun** shows ownership by one person or thing.
- To form the possessive of most singular nouns, add an apostrophe and an *s*. (*'s*)
- A **plural possessive noun** shows ownership by more than one person or thing.
- To form the possessive of a plural noun that ends with *s*, add only an apostrophe.

Write the following sentences on the board:

1. Chester Cricket's house is a matchbox.
2. The mouse's eyes are shiny and black.
3. The three friends' adventures take place in Times Square.
4. The bus's horn is loud.
5. The men's luggage was at the airport.

Read each sentence aloud. Ask volunteers to circle the possessive nouns in each sentence. Point out the singular possessive nouns. (*Chester Cricket's, mouse's, bus's*) Remind students that an apostrophe plus *s* is added to make the singular nouns possessive. Point out the plural possessive nouns. (*friends', men's*) Explain how each was formed.

FLUENCY PRACTICE Ask volunteers to read aloud the paragraph they completed in the writing activity.

Interactive Writing: Explanatory Paragraph

RETEACH Display the completed the paragraph from Preteach. Read it aloud with students. Ask them what they would like to change about it and why. Discuss students' suggestions for changing or adding to the paragraph. Write the revised paragraph based on students' suggestions. Then have students copy the revised paragraph into their Language Journals.

Grammar-Writing Connection

RETEACH Review possessive nouns with students. Then write the following sentences on the board, underlining as shown.

1. <u>Tucker</u> favorite food is liverwurst. (*Tucker's*)
2. The <u>mouse</u> home is in a drain pipe. (*mouse's*)
3. Chester wondered if all <u>cities</u> traffic was this noisy. (*cities'*)
4. The <u>author</u> story is about three friends. (*author's*)
5. All <u>helicopters</u> windows are large. (*helicopters'*)
6. This <u>train</u> tracks are clean. (*train's*)
7. The two <u>women</u> bus was late. (*women's*)
8. The <u>ferry</u> decks are filled with people and cars. (*ferry's*)

Have students copy the sentences into their notebooks. Tell students to make each underlined noun possessive. Remind students to pay close attention to the underlined noun to decide whether it should be singular possessive or plural possessive. Monitor students' work as they complete the sentences.

FLUENCY PRACTICE Have students choose a page from "Going Places" to read aloud.

Name _____

Draw pictures of three different kinds of transportation, or ways to travel. Label each picture.

TO THE TEACHER Brainstorm with students different kinds of transportation. Work with them to choose three kinds to illustrate.

The Cricket in Times Square/Going Places • **Lesson 13**   **79**

Use with "Two Lands, One Heart"

BEFORE
Building Background and Vocabulary

Build Background/Access Prior Knowledge

Tell students that many people move to America from other countries. Explain that these people are called immigrants. Ask: **Why do you think people leave their homes in other lands to come to America?** Record students' responses in an idea web like the one shown here.

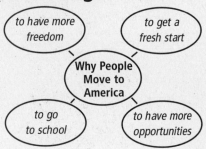

Selection Vocabulary

PRETEACH Display Teaching Transparency 130, and read the words aloud. Then point to the pictures as you read the following sentences:

1. The new girl does not speak English. The **interpreter** helps her understand what is being said.
2. The interpreter translates slowly. That way she will not **overwhelm** her friend.
3. The girls cry **hysterically**. They cannot stop crying.
4. **Occasionally** the girls stand in the sprinkler. Once in a while they have fun this way.
5. The sprinkler is part of the **irrigation** system. The water is used to water the lawn.
6. The food looks very **appetizing**. The girls know it will taste good.
7. The girls have an **equivalent** amount of food. They have the same amount.

AFTER
Building Background and Vocabulary

Selection Vocabulary

RETEACH Revisit Teaching Transparency 130. Have students answer questions such as: Does *occasionally* mean "once in a while" or "all the time"?

Read each sentence and ask students to choose a vocabulary word to complete it.

1. The farmer used an _____ system to water his crops. (*irrigation*)
2. The _____ translated English into German. (*interpreter*)
3. One hundred cents is _____ to one dollar. (*equivalent*)
4. Maya and her family go to the park _____. (*occasionally*)
5. Mr. Livingston made a dinner that looked _____. (*appetizing*)
6. Lin cried _____ during the sad movie. (*hysterically*)
7. A big school can _____ a new student. (*overwhelm*)

Have students write these words in their Language Dictionaries.

FLUENCY PRACTICE Encourage students to use vocabulary words to describe the illustrations on Teaching Transparency 130.

Build Background: "Two Lands, One Heart"

Have students look at the picture on *Pupil Edition* pages
352–353. Tell students that this is TJ and that he was born in
America. Explain that his mother moved to America from
Vietnam. She is an immigrant. Have students predict why TJ's
mother moved to America from Vietnam.

LEAD
THE
WAY

 ## Compare and Contrast

PRETEACH Tell students that to *compare* means to tell how things are
the same, and to *contrast* means to tell how things are different.

On the board, draw a chart like
this one to explain the concept.
Help students fill it in with story
information as they read the
selection.

United States	Both Countries	Vietnam
has tractors	farmers grow crops	has heavy carts pulled by water buffalo

Directed Reading: "Two Lands, One Heart"

RETEACH Use these bulleted sentences to walk students through the
story.

Pages 352–355
- Here is TJ. What is he holding in his hand? (*a fan*)
- Vietnam is in Southeast Asia. Point to Vietnam on the map.
- This map shows how far it is from TJ's home in Denver, Colorado to Ho Chi Minh City, Vietnam.

Pages 356–357
- TJ goes to the beach with his mother. He is standing in the ocean.
- TJ is excited. Why do you think he is excited? (*Responses will vary.*)

QUESTIONS:
pages 352–357
- Does TJ live in Vietnam? (*no*)
- Who is TJ going to visit in Vietnam? (*He is going to visit his grandparents.*)

Pages 358–361
- TJ's family is having a feast. A feast is a big dinner.
- The family is eating with chopsticks. Many people in Vietnam use chopsticks instead of forks.
- TJ's cousin is taking a shower. TJ helps dump water over his cousin's head.
- TJ's grandfather shows TJ how to get water from the well.
- TJ is looking at a silkworm. Silkworms make silk thread. Thread is used to make clothing.

Pages 362–363
- TJ finds a big jackfruit. The jackfruit is almost as big as TJ.
- TJ is riding a water buffalo. Water buffalo are used to plow fields.

Pages 364–366
- This type of field is called a rice paddy. TJ helps his aunt in the rice paddy.
- TJ and his uncle are in a canoe. A canoe is a kind of boat.
- TJ and his little cousin play in the river.

QUESTIONS:
pages 358–363
- Does TJ help his aunt in the rice paddy? (*yes*)
- What are the water buffalo used for? (*to plow fields*)

FLUENCY PRACTICE Ask a volunteer to read aloud a paragraph from *Pupil
Edition* page 354. Encourage students to describe the photographs on pages
358–359.

Build Background: "East Meets West"

PRETEACH Remind students that "Two Lands, One Heart" is about a boy who visits Vietnam. In "East Meets West" they will read about groups of immigrants who left their homes to move to America.

English-
Language
Learners
Book

Use the concept words in sentences that illustrate their meanings.

Concept Words

weather
maps
tools
dreamed
world
travel

- Min watched the **weather** to see if it was going to rain.
- Jen looked at the **maps** to help her find her way.
- **Tools** help people do things. Maps are useful tools for travelers.
- Ron **dreamed** about going to a far-away place.
- He imagined himself on the other side of the **world**.
- He could not wait to **travel** there.

Have students add these words to their Language Dictionaries.

Directed Reading: "East Meets West"

📖 **Summary** *Traders and explorers were among the first people to leave their homes to look for new places. Since then many people have left their homes to move to America. The immigrants came to America for different reasons.*

Use these sentences to walk students through the story.

Pages 2–5
- People use ships to travel the ocean.
- Compasses are used for finding directions. Point to North and South on the compass.
- This is a map. Maps show the land and the oceans.

Pages 6–7
- Christopher Columbus was an explorer. He discovered America.
- In the 1600s, many people came to America. They hoped for a better life.

QUESTIONS: pages 2–7
- Is a compass used for finding directions? (*yes*)
- Who was Christopher Columbus? (*the person who discovered America*)

Pages 8–11
- Clipper ships have many large sails. When gold was discovered in California, many people traveled there by clipper ship.
- In the 1800s, many immigrants came to America. Immigrants are people who move to a country from another country.

Pages 12–16
- Life was often hard for immigrants. It was hard to find work.
- Now people come to America by ships and by airplanes. Many enter the United States through New York, California, and Washington.

QUESTIONS: pages 8–16
- Do people from many other countries come to live in America? (*yes*)
- How do people come to America? (*by ship; by airplane*)

Compare and Contrast

RETEACH Review comparing and contrasting with students. Then draw on the board a Venn diagram. Ask students to revisit "East Meets West" to compare and contrast the immigrants who came to America in the 1600s with the immigrants who came to America in the 1960s. Fill in the Venn diagram with students' responses.

FLUENCY PRACTICE Have students choose a section of "East Meets West" to read aloud.

Interactive Writing: Definition Paragraph

PRETEACH Tell students that they are going to work with you to write a definition paragraph about what it means to be an *immigrant*. Explain that a definition paragraph or essay defines a word or a concept. Ask students to think about what it means to be an immigrant. Have them generate a concept web with the title *Being an Immigrant*. Then brainstorm with students what it means to be an immigrant.

Write the following sentence frames on the board or on chart paper. "Share the pen" with students by working with them to write the draft, using the information in the concept web.

speak another language

might not have many things, such as clothes

Being an immigrant

have different customs

might not have much money

Being an Immigrant

Immigrants are people who _____ . Immigrants come to America for a variety of reasons, including _____ . Life is hard for immigrants because _____ . However, immigrants feel they are better off in America because _____ .

Grammar: Abbreviations

PRETEACH Discuss with students the definition of an abbreviation. Point out the following:

- An *abbreviation* is a shortened form of a word.
- Use a *period* after most abbreviations.
- *Capitalize* abbreviations that stand for proper nouns.

Write the following sentences on the board:
- Dr. Hall was at the hospital.
- That car belongs to Mr. Delaney.
- Turn left on Green St.
- The bus arrives at 7 A.M.
- Today's date is Nov. 10.

Read aloud each sentence. Ask volunteers to circle the abbreviation in each sentence. Then make a two-column chart with the headings *Abbreviation* and *What It Means*. Under the heading *Abbreviations*, list the abbreviations from the board. Under the heading *What it Means*,

Abbreviation	What It Means
Dr.	doctor
Mr.	mister
St.	street
A.M.	morning; before noon
Nov.	November

write the meaning of each abbreviation.

FLUENCY PRACTICE Have volunteers read aloud the definition paragraph.

Interactive Writing: Definition Paragraph

RETEACH Display the completed paragraph from Preteach. Read it aloud with students. Ask them what they would like to change about it and why. Discuss students' suggestions for changing or adding to the paragraph. Write the revised paragraph using students' suggestions. Then have students copy the revised paragraph into their Language Journals.

Grammar-Writing Connection

RETEACH Review with students what abbreviations are. Then write the following sentences on the board.

1. Lorinda lives on Third Ave. (*Ave.; avenue*)
2. Martin Luther King, Jr., spoke about equality for all people. (*Jr.; junior*)
3. The movie starts at 7 P.M. (*P.M.; after noon*)
4. Many people move to the U.S. (*U.S.; United States*)
5. Please give the book to Ms. Carlton. (*Ms.; a woman*)
6. The meeting will be on Mon. night. (*Mon.; Monday*)

Have students copy the sentences in their notebooks, circling the abbreviations. Have students make a chart with the headings *Abbreviation* and *What It Means*. Have students complete the chart with the abbreviations from the sentences. Then write on the board the following abbreviations: *Mr, Mrs., Wed.* and *Ave.* Have students use each abbreviation in a sentence. Monitor students' work to make sure they use each abbreviation correctly.

FLUENCY PRACTICE Have students choose a page from "East Meets West" to read aloud.

Name _____

Draw a picture that shows a person moving from another country to America. Then write two or three sentences to describe your picture.

_____

_____

_____

_____

TO THE TEACHER Ask students to draw a picture of an immigrant moving from another country to America. Tell students that they can show the immigrant leaving the native country, traveling to America, or arriving in America. Then have each student write two or three sentences about his or her picture. Ask students to share their pictures and sentences with the class.

LESSON 15

Use with "Look to the North"

BEFORE

Building Background and Vocabulary

Build Background/Access Prior Knowledge

Have students look at the illustration on *Pupil Edition* pages 374–375. Point out the mother wolf and her pups. Tell students that wolves are wild animals that are related to dogs. Discuss with students the differences between wild animals and pets. Ask: **What wild animals can you name? What kinds of pets can you name?** Record students' responses in a chart like this one.

Wild Animals	Pets
wolves	dogs
tigers	cats
bears	rabbits

Selection Vocabulary

PRETEACH Display Teaching Transparency 139, and read aloud the words. Then point to the pictures as you read the following sentences:

1. Wolves live on the **tundra**. The tundra is very cold and has no trees.
2. There are lots of wolves. These animals are **abundant**.
3. The sad pup howls **piteously** so its mother will come to take care of it.
4. The pup **ceases** howling when its mother appears. It stops howling.
5. The pups are **bonding** as they play. They are becoming good friends.
6. One pup **surrenders**. It tells the other pup that it gives up.

AFTER

Building Background and Vocabulary

Selection Vocabulary

RETEACH Revisit Teaching Transparency 139. Read the words with students. Have students work in pairs to discuss the meanings of the words and to answer questions such as this: Does *ceases* mean "stops" or "starts"?

Write the following sentence frames on the board. Read each sentence and ask students to choose a vocabulary word to complete it. Write students' responses in the blanks.

1. The snow _____ falling when it is warm outside. (*ceases*)
2. The flowers are so _____ in this field. There are too many to count. (*abundant*)
3. The friends are _____ while on a camping trip. (*bonding*)
4. The child cried _____ when she was lost. (*piteously*)
5. If you _____, you give up the game. (*surrender*)
6. The Arctic fox ran across the frozen _____. (*tundra*)

Have students write these words in their Language Dictionaries.

FLUENCY PRACTICE Have students read the sentence frames aloud. Encourage them to describe the illustrations on Teaching Transparency 139, using the vocabulary words and any other words they know.

Build Background: "Look to the North"

LEAD THE WAY

Have students look at the pictures on *Pupil Edition* pages 378–379. Tell students that these wolves live on the tundra. Show students where the Arctic is on a map, and explain that the tundra is an Arctic region that does not have any trees. The ground is frozen all year. Ask students how they think the wolves might survive on the tundra.

Focus Skill

Summarize

Remind students that when they summarize a selection, they should tell the most important parts in a few words. Explain that to do this, students must select the most important ideas from the story, evaluate their importance, and then record the ideas in a summary.

Draw a chart like this one. As you read the selection with students, help them complete the chart with information from the story. Then ask students to write a short summary of the selection.

Important Facts to Include	Facts to Leave Out	Summary
Wolves live on the Arctic tundra.	Wolf pups have sharp teeth.	
Wolf pups grow and change.	Wolf pups play together.	
Wolf pups become part of a pack.	Wolf pups have a baby-sitter.	

Directed Reading: "Look to the North"

 RETEACH Use these sentences to walk students through the story.

Pages 374–375
- This mother wolf has just had pups. The mother and her pups are in the den.

Pages 376–377
- The wolf pups are playing.
- While her pups sleep, the mother wolf runs with the pack, or group.

Pages 378–381
- The pups can see, hear, and smell. They find their places in the pack.
- The rest of the pack returns from the hunt. The father wolf feeds the pups.

QUESTIONS: pages 374–381
- Are baby wolves called pups? (*yes*)
- Who brings food to the pups? (*the father wolf*)

Pages 382–385
- The wolves are going to their summer home.
- The pups are bonding with each other. They play together.
- Here, the pups are peeling hide, or skin, from a bone.

Pages 386–389
- When it snows, the wolves leave their summer homes.
- The pups practice hunting.
- When they are seven months old, the pups are full-grown.

QUESTIONS: pages 382–389
- Do wolves stay in their summer dens when snow falls? (*no*)
- When are pups full-grown? (*when they are seven months old*)

FLUENCY PRACTICE Invite students to describe their favorite illustration from the story. Encourage them to use vocabulary words in their descriptions.

Build Background: "A Place Called Home"

English-Language Learners Book

PRETEACH In "A Place Called Home" students will read about many different places that are on Earth. Discuss with students places they would like to visit.

Concept Words
land
ice
mountain
rocks
ocean
water

Use the concept words in sentences to illustrate their meanings.

- Mr. and Mrs. Dalton hiked across the **land**.
- The Daltons could see **ice** and snow on the top of the **mountain**.
- Some of the **rocks** from the mountain had fallen into the **ocean**.
- The rocks must have made a big splash in the **water**.

Have students add these words to their Language Dictionaries.

Directed Reading: "A Place Called Home"

📖 **Summary** *Earth has many different types of landforms and bodies of water. Maps and globes show places on Earth.*

Use these sentences to walk students through the story.

Pages 2–3
- Earth has many landforms and bodies of water. This is a desert.
- A continent is a large area of land.
- There are seven continents: Europe, Asia, Africa, Australia, North America, South America, and Antarctica.

Pages 4–7
- This is an ocean. There are five oceans: the Atlantic, the Pacific, the Indian, the Arctic, and the Antarctic Oceans.
- A peninsula is almost completely surrounded by water. An island is completely surrounded by water.
- This is an overview of Earth.

QUESTIONS: pages 2–7
- Is a continent a large area of land? (*yes*)
- How many oceans are there? (*five*)

Pages 8–9
- These are mountains. The low areas between mountains are called valleys.

Pages 10–13
- This is a river. The river is flowing into a lake.
- In the desert, it is very hot and dry. There is not much water.
- A prairie is a flat land that is covered with grass. Prairies have few trees.

Pages 14–16
- A map is a drawing of a region. Maps can show continents, oceans, countries, states, and landforms.
- A globe is a map that is printed on a sphere. It is round, like Earth's shape.

QUESTIONS: pages 8–16
- Is the desert cool and wet? (*no*)
- What does a prairie look like? (*Prairies are flat and grassy.*)

⭐ (Focus Skill) **Summarize**

RETEACH Review with students the steps for summarizing. Then ask students to write a few sentences summarizing "A Place Called Home."

FLUENCY PRACTICE Encourage students to describe an illustration from "A Place Called Home," using vocabulary words and concept words.

Interactive Writing: Explanatory Paragraph

PRETEACH Tell students that they are going to work with you to write a paragraph that explains why people use maps. Generate a concept web with the title *Why People Use Maps*.

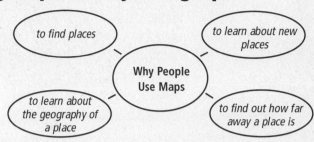

Then brainstorm with students reasons why people use maps and globes. Write their responses in the outer circles of the web.

Write the following sentence frames on the board. Have students work with you to fill in the blanks with words and phrases from the concept web.

Why People Use Maps

Maps are important tools. People use maps for many reasons. They use maps _____. Another reason people use maps is _____. In addition, people use maps _____.

Grammar: Pronouns and Antecedents

PRETEACH Discuss the definition of a pronoun and the antecedent with students. Point out the following:

- A **pronoun** is a word that takes the place of one or more nouns. Some common pronouns are *I*, *me*, *you*, *he*, *him*, *she*, *her*, *it*, *we*, *us*, *they*, and *them*.
- The **antecedent** of a pronoun is the noun or nouns to which the pronoun refers.
- A pronoun should agree with its antecedent. This means that the pronoun should show the same number as the antecedent (*one or more than one*) and the same gender as the antecedent (*masculine, feminine, or neuter*).

Write on the board the following sentences:

1. Boulder plays with his sister. (*pronoun: his; antecedent: Boulder*)
2. The mother wolf cannot leave the pups when they are very young. (*pronoun: they; antecedent: pups*)
3. The wolf moves fast as it runs across the tundra. (*pronoun: it; antecedent: wolf*)
4. The pack is on its way to hunt. (*pronoun: its; antecedent: pack*)
5. When the pups are young, the father wolf brings food to them. (*pronoun: them; antecedent: pups*)

Read aloud each sentence. Point out the pronoun by underlining it once. Point out the antecedent by underlining it twice. Remind students that a pronoun should show the same number as the antecedent (*one or more than one*) and show the same gender as the antecedent (*masculine, feminine, or neuter*).

FLUENCY PRACTICE Ask volunteers to read aloud the paragraph they completed in the writing activity.

Interactive Writing: Explanatory Paragraph

RETEACH Display the completed the paragraph from Preteach. Read it aloud with students. Ask them what they would like to change about it and why. Discuss students' suggestions for revising the paragraph. Work with them to add additional reasons and details. Write the revised paragraph based on students' suggestions. Then have students copy the revised paragraph into their Language Journals.

Grammar-Writing Connection

RETEACH Review with students what pronouns and antecedents are. Write the following sentences on the board.

1. The pups have not left their mother. (*pronoun: their; antecedent: pups*)
2. The mother wolf sleeps with her pups. (*pronoun: her; antecedent: mother wolf*)
3. Talus says, "Come play with me." (*pronoun: me; antecedent: Talus*)
4. The wolf howls to say, "I am lonely." (*pronoun: I; antecedent: wolf*)
5. The people went across the lake in their boat. (*pronoun: their; antecedent: people*)
6. The mountain has snow on its peaks. (*pronoun: its; antecedent: mountain*)

Draw on the board a two-column chart with the headings *Pronouns* and *Antecedents*. Have students copy the chart into their notebooks. Then have them complete the chart by writing in the appropriate columns the pronouns and antecedents from the sentences. Monitor students' work as they complete the chart. Then write these sentences on the board, underlining as shown. Have students rewrite each sentence, replacing the underlined word or words with a pronoun.

1. <u>Anna</u> made cupcakes. (*She*)
2. <u>Al and Joe</u> ran in the race. (*They*)
3. Josh forgot <u>Josh's</u> backpack. (*his*)

FLUENCY PRACTICE Have students choose a page from "A Place Called Home" to read aloud.

Name _____

Draw a picture of the word in each box. Then write a sentence about each picture.

island	mountain
_____ _____	_____ _____
river	lake
_____ _____	_____ _____

TO THE TEACHER Explain to students that they are to draw a picture in each of the four boxes on the page. Depending on the label in the box, students should draw an island, a mountain, a river, or a lake. When all have completed the exercise, ask volunteers to share their pictures with the class.

Look to the North/A Place Called Home • **Lesson 15**   **91**

Use with "The Kids' Invention Book"

Build Background/Access Prior Knowledge

Point out objects in the classroom, such as a clock, a chalkboard, and a pen. Tell students that someone invented all of these things. Explain that inventors, or people who invent things, see a problem and try to make something to solve that problem. Ask students to name inventions that they find helpful in their daily lives. Ask: **What inventions do you use a lot?** Record students' responses in an idea web like this:

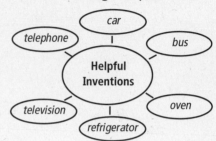

Selection Vocabulary

PRETEACH Display Teaching Transparency 149 and read the words aloud. Then point to the pictures as you read the following sentences:

1. This girl has a **prosthetic** leg to replace the leg she is missing.
2. This special **device** is built to help people like this girl.
3. The girl's **disabilities** make it harder for her to do certain things.
4. The teacher will **modify** or change the tennis game.
5. The girl pulls a **document** out of the envelope. It is an important paper.
6. There is a large **circular** seal on the envelope. The seal is shaped like a circle.
7. The award is for a **scholarship** because she does a good job in school.

Selection Vocabulary

RETEACH Revisit Teaching Transparency 149. Have students work in pairs to discuss the meanings of the words and to answer questions such as: **Is a document an important paper or a worthless paper? Does** *modify* **mean to keep the same or to change?**

Write the following sentence frames on the board. Read each sentence and ask students to choose a vocabulary word to complete it. Write students' responses in the blanks.

1. The vet invented a _____ wing for injured birds. (*prosthetic*)
2. A person with _____ has difficulty doing some things. (*disabilities*)
3. The boy earned the _____ by studying hard. (*scholarship*)
4. He made a _____ driveway so visitors could drive in a circle. (*circular*)
5. The inventor made a _____ to solve a problem. (*device*)
6. Jenna signed the _____ and gave the paper to the doctor. (*document*)
7. The teacher had to _____ the rules so everyone could play. (*modify*)

Have students write these vocabulary words in their Language Dictionaries.

FLUENCY PRACTICE Have students read the sentence frames aloud. Encourage them to describe the illustrations on Teaching Transparency 149 using the vocabulary words and any other words they know.

BEFORE

**Reading
"The Kids'
Invention Book"**
pages 402–416

Build Background: "The Kids' Invention Book"

Have students look at the picture on *Pupil Edition* pages 402 and 403. Tell students that the things on these pages are inventions. Explain that inventions are made to solve a particular problem. Point out that inventors, or people who create inventions, are sometimes children just like them.

LEAD
THE
WAY

★ Focus Skill **Main Idea and Details**

PRETEACH Tell students the main idea is what the story is mostly about. Details in a story give information that explains or supports the main idea. On the board, draw a two column chart with the headings *Main Idea* and *Supporting Details* to help explain the concept. Then have students copy the chart into their notebooks, and help them fill it in with information from the story as they read the selection.

AFTER

**Reading
"The Kids'
Invention Book"**

Pages 402–405

Pages 406–409

Pages 410–411

 QUESTIONS:
pages 402–411

Pages 412–413

Pages 414–416

 QUESTIONS:
pages 412–416

Directed Reading: "The Kids' Invention Book"

RETEACH Use these sentences to walk students through the story.

- All of these items were invented by someone.
- This girl is wearing earmuffs. What do earmuffs do? (*keep ears warm*)
- This is Chester Greenwood. He invented earmuffs.
- Josh Parsons invented something to help David play baseball.
- This is David. What sport is he playing? (*baseball*)
- This is Reeba Daniel. She invented a washer and dryer that work together.
- This is a round sprinkler. It is used to water trees.
- This is Larry Villella. He invented the round sprinkler.
- Do children ever invent things? (*yes*)
- What did Chester Greenwood invent? (*earmuffs*)
- What does Josh's invention do? (*It helps David catch and throw baseballs.*)
- This girl has a pencil and paper. She is thinking. What do you think she is thinking about? (*Responses will vary.*)
- This is the girl's notebook. She makes a list of problems and solutions.
- The girl draws diagrams to show her invention. A diagram is a picture with labels. What is the girl's invention? (*a totally adjustable sunhat*)
- This girl is wearing the invention.
- Does an inventor make a model first? (*no*)
- What is a diagram? (*a picture with labels*)
- What is the first step in inventing something? (*Think of a problem that needs to be solved.*)

FLUENCY PRACTICE Ask volunteers to read aloud a paragraph from their favorite page in the story. Encourage students to describe the illustrations on *Pupil Edition* page 414 using as many vocabulary words as they can.

Build Background: "Observe, Think, Try!"

PRETEACH Remind students that "The Kids' Invention Book" is about inventions developed by children. In "Observe, Think, Try" they will read about some inventors. Ask students to describe an invention that they would like to make.

Write the concept words on the board. Use them in sentences to illustrate their meanings.

Concept Words
large
small
people
today
good
school

- Some inventions, like an airplane, are **large**.
- Some inventions, like a wristwatch, are **small**.
- **People** who make inventions are called inventors.
- **Today**, you might see a problem that needs to be solved.
- You will need to think of a **good** idea for how to solve it.
- You can show your invention to other students at **school**.

Have students add these words to their Language Dictionaries

Directed Reading: "Observe, Think, Try!"

📖 **Summary** *An invention is something new made to address an old problem. You can also invent new ways to speak and live. These inventions are equally important.*

Use these sentences to walk students through the story.

Pages 2–5
- What do you think this boy is thinking about? (*Responses will vary.*)
- This is a list of inventions that use brakes. Brakes help moving things stop.
- These carts in a grocery store are used to carry groceries.
- What do you think will happen next? (*The carts will run into each other.*)
- The boy is modifying a cart by adding a brake.

Pages 6–9
- Look at all these shoes. Name as many different kinds of shoes as you can.
- This boy is looking at his shoes.
- Why do you think he has a pad and paper next to him? (*Responses will vary.*)
- This is Thomas Edison. This is Edison with a device that he invented. What is Edison's invention? (*a light bulb*)

❓ QUESTIONS:
pages 2–9
- Do brakes stop things? (*yes*)
- Who invented the light bulb? (*Thomas Edison*)

Pages 10–13
- This boy and his family are getting off an airplane.
- Where do you think the boy has traveled to? (*Responses will vary.*)
- These children are in the cafeteria. The boy is new to the school.
- This is a page in a notebook. Read the words on the page.
- The students in this class are observing, or watching, the teacher.

Pages 14–16
- These people are gathered around a flagpole, raising an American flag.
- This boy is reading to the class a list of things he has written. He is smiling.

❓ QUESTIONS:
pages 10–16
- Is an airport a place for trains to come and go? (*no*)
- What does *observing* mean? (*watching*)

⭐ **Focus Skill** ## Main Idea and Details

RETEACH Review main idea and details with students. Ask students to revisit the story to complete a *Main Idea and Supporting Details* chart like the one on page 93.

FLUENCY PRACTICE Have students use their favorite illustration from the story to retell part of "Observe, Think, Try!" Encourage them to use as many vocabulary words and concept words as possible.

Interactive Writing: Paragraphs that Contrast

PRETEACH Tell students that they are going to work with you to write paragraphs that contrast. Then brainstorm with students the differences between earmuffs and the all-in-one washer/dryer described on *Pupil Edition* pages 404–405 and 408–409 in the selection "The Kids' Invention Book."

Write the following sentence frames on the board or on chart paper. "Share the pen" with students by working with them to write the draft, using the information in the concept web.

Different Inventions

Earmuffs and the all-in-one washer/dryer are two different inventions. Earmuffs were invented by _____ . They were invented to _____ . People could see how earmuffs worked because _____ . The washer/dryer was invented by _____ . It was invented to _____ . People who wanted to know how the washer/dryer worked had to look at diagrams because _____ .

Grammar: Subject and Object Pronouns

PRETEACH Discuss the following with students:

- A **subject pronoun** takes the place of one or more nouns in the subject of a sentence.
- The words I, you, he, she, it, we, and they are subject pronouns. Always capitalize the pronoun I.
- An **object pronoun** follows an action verb, such as see or tell, or a word called a preposition, such as at, for, to, or with.
- The object pronouns are me, you, him, her, it, us, and them.
- The pronouns I and me sometimes come after other pronouns or nouns.

Write the following sentences on the board:

- Caitlin asked me to help her solve a problem. (*object pronouns: me, her*)
- We thought of ways to solve the problem. (*subject pronoun: we*)
- She gave me an idea. (*subject pronoun: she; object pronoun: me*)
- She and I made the invention. (*subject pronouns: she, I*)
- We showed it to the class. (*subject pronoun: we; object pronoun: it*)

Read aloud each sentence. Call students' attention to the pronouns. Point out that subject pronouns take the place of one or more nouns in the subject of a sentence and that object pronouns follow an action verb or a preposition.

FLUENCY PRACTICE Have volunteers read aloud the paragraphs they completed in the writing activity.

Interactive Writing: Paragraphs that Contrast

RETEACH Display the completed paragraphs from Preteach. Read them aloud with students. Ask students what they would like to change about the paragraphs and why. Discuss students' suggestions for changing or adding to the paragraphs. Write the revised paragraphs based on students' suggestions. Then have students copy the revised paragraphs into their Language Journals.

Grammar-Writing Connection

RETEACH Review with students subject and object pronouns. Then write the following sentences on the board.

1. Bob told some friends, "I want to invent a new light bulb." (*subject pronoun: I*)
2. They thought he was joking. (*subject pronoun: they; object pronoun: he*)
3. Dora asked, "Can you tell us about it?" (*subject pronoun: you; object pronoun: us, it*)
4. He looked at her. (*subject pronoun: he; object pronoun: her*)
5. "Sure. Just listen to me," Bob said. (*object pronoun: me*)
6. Then Bob told them about the light bulb. (*object pronoun: them*)
7. Bob's friends thought it was a good idea. (*object pronoun: it*)
8. Bob said, "Someday we will use these light bulbs." (*subject pronoun: we*)

Have students copy the sentences in their notebooks, circling the subject pronouns and underlining any object pronouns. Remind students to pay close attention to whether each pronoun is a subject or object. Monitor students' work as they complete the sentences.

FLUENCY PRACTICE Have students read aloud their revised paragraphs.

Name _____

Think of an invention that you would like to make. The invention should solve a problem. Draw a diagram of your invention.

My invention is: _____

TO THE TEACHER Read aloud the directions with students. You may want to brainstorm invention ideas with them. Encourage students to tell what problem their inventions solve.

The Kids' Invention Book/Observe, Think, Try! • Lesson 16   97

© Harcourt

Use with "The Case of Pablo's Nose"

Build Background/Access Prior Knowledge

Write the word *mystery* on the board.
Tell students that a mystery is a puzzling
problem that needs to be solved.
In real life, a detective or police officer
often solves a mystery. Ask: **What kind
of mysteries have you tried to solve?**
Record students' responses in a concept web.

Selection Vocabulary

PRETEACH Display Teaching Transparency 158 and read the words aloud.
Then point to the pictures as you read the following sentences:

1. Jake ran to the police **straightaway**. He went directly to the police.
2. The police were **strengthening** their case. They were building a case
   against the person who stole the statue.
3. Jake had been in school all day. He told the police his **alibi** to prove
   that he could not have stolen the statue.
4. The policeman **retorted**, "Well, who took it?"
5. Jake quietly **muttered**, "I have solved the case."
6. The policeman returned the statue to the **sculptor** who had made it.

Selection Vocabulary

RETEACH Revisit Teaching Transparency 158. Read the words with students. Have students work in pairs to discuss the meanings of the words
and to answer questions such as: If you do something **straightaway**, do
you do it *right away* or *later*? If you **muttered**, would it be *easy* or *hard*
for people to hear you?

Write the following sentence frames on the board. Read each sentence
and ask students to choose a vocabulary word to complete it. Write students' responses in the blanks.

1. Martin went to the bank _____ with his paycheck. (*straightaway*)
2. The _____ made a statue of a dog. (*sculptor*)
3. Fran's _____ was that she was asleep when the bicycle was stolen.
   (*alibi*)
4. The angry man _____ to himself quietly. (*muttered*)
5. Xavier was _____ his muscles by lifting weights. (*strengthening*)
6. The angry thief loudly _____, "You can't catch me!" (*retorted*)

Have students write these words in their Language Dictionaries.

FLUENCY PRACTICE Have students read the sentence frames aloud.
Encourage them to describe the illustrations on Teaching Transparency 158 using
the vocabulary words and any other words they know.

Build Background: "The Case of Pablo's Nose"

Have students look at the picture on *Pupil Edition* page 426. Tell students that Pablo, the boy wearing the yellow shirt, has come to tell his friends, Encyclopedia Brown and Sally, that a piece of his artwork was stolen. Pablo wants his friends to help him solve this mystery.

 LEAD THE WAY

 Focus Skill ## Sequence

PRETEACH Tell students that understanding the sequence of events will help them better understand the story. Explain that *sequence* refers to the order in which events take place. Tell students that sometimes an author may use signal words like *first*, *next*, *last*, or *finally* to show sequence.

On the board, draw a sequence chain with four or five boxes entitled Event 1, Event 2, and so on. Write the title "How the Case Was Solved" over the sequence chain. Then have students copy the chart into their notebooks. Help them fill in the chart with information from the story as they read the selection.

Directed Reading: "The Case of Pablo's Nose"

Use these sentences to walk students through the story.

- Someone is riding a bicycle away from a house.
- The house belongs to Pablo.
- Pablo tells his friends Sally and Encyclopedia about what happened. They are detectives. Pablo hopes that they will be able to find the missing nose.
- Encyclopedia and Sally are asking Pablo questions about his stolen sculpture.

 QUESTIONS:
pages 424–427

- Was Pablo's bicycle stolen? (*no*)
- What was stolen from Pablo? (*a nose made of stone*)
- How did the thief get away? (*The thief rode away on a purple bicycle.*)

Pages 428–430

- Desmoana says that she never rides her bike.
- Desmoana is riding her bicycle. It is a purple bicycle.
- Encyclopedia, Sally, and Pablo watch Desmoana ride her bike. She rides well. She can even do tricks on her bike.
- Pablo, Sally, and Encyclopedia think that Desmoana is the thief.

 QUESTIONS:
pages 428–430

- Does Desmoana have a purple bicycle? (*yes*)
- Why do Encyclopedia Brown, Sally, and Pablo think Desmoana is the thief? (*because she has a purple bicycle and is good at riding it*)
- Why do you think Desmoana stole the nose? (*Responses will vary.*)

FLUENCY PRACTICE Ask a volunteer to read aloud the solution to the case on page 430. Encourage students to describe the illustration on *Pupil Edition* page 429. Encourage students to use as many vocabulary words as they can in their descriptions.

Build Background: "The Case of the Red Bicycle"

PRETEACH Remind students that "The Case of Pablo's Nose" is about three children trying to solve the mystery of who stole a piece of art. In "The Case of the Red Bicycle," students will read another mystery. Ask students what they would do if something were stolen from them.

English-
Language
Learners
Book

Concept Words
loved
moved
looked
said
turned
pushed

Write these words on the board.

- Betina **loved** to solve mysteries.
- She **moved** things around as she searched for her mother's missing car keys.
- She **looked** at a small hair through a magnifying glass.
- Betina **said**, "I know whose hair this is!"
- Then she **turned** to her mother.
- Betina smiled, "You **pushed** the keys into the trash while cleaning the table."

Have students add these words to their Language Dictionaries.

Directed Reading: "The Case of the Red Bicycle"

📖 **Summary** *Sam rides a red bike with a bell. Cliff is new in Sam's neighborhood. Sam accidentally rides over Cliff's foot. When Sam goes to get help for Cliff, someone takes Sam's bike. Cliff's mother and sister come to take him home. Cliff gets a new bike and becomes Sam's friend.*

Use these sentences to walk students through the story.

Pages 2–5
- This is Sam. He likes to ride his red bike in his neighborhood.
- Sam rings his bell when someone is standing in his way on the sidewalk.
- This is Cliff. He is unhappy. He misses his old neighborhood.

Pages 6–9
- Sam rides his bike by the blue house on the street.
- Sam likes to pretend that his bike is a racehorse. He rides very fast.
- Sam sees Cliff on the sidewalk. Sam accidentally rides over Cliff's foot.

**QUESTIONS:
pages 2–9**
- Is Cliff riding his bicycle? (*no*)
- What color is Sam's bike? (*red*)

Pages 10–13
- Cliff sits on the curb. Sam runs to get help.
- A boy and a man put the bike in the trunk of a car and drive away.
- Cliff worries that Sam's bike has been stolen.
- This is Cliff's mother and sister. They have come in their van to pick up Cliff.

Pages 14–16
- Cliff's mom bought new bikes for him and his sister. Cliff is happy.
- Sam calls Cliff to see if he is feeling better. Sam says that his father and brother picked up his bike for him.

**QUESTIONS:
pages 10–16**
- Does Sam ride his bike home? (*no*)
- How did Sam get his bike back? (*His father and brother picked it up.*)

Focus Skill **Sequence**

Review sequence with the students. Then draw a sequence chain with five boxes on the board. Ask students to copy the chart and fill the boxes with five events that happened in the story.

FLUENCY PRACTICE Have students use the illustrations on pages 10 and 11 to retell part of "The Case of the Red Bicycle." Encourage them to use as many vocabulary and concept words as possible.

Interactive Writing: Persuasive Letter

PRETEACH Tell students that they are going to work with you to write a persuasive letter to the local police department. Remind students that Encyclopedia Brown and Sally did a good job solving the mystery in "The Case of Pablo's Nose." Then brainstorm a list of reasons why children should be allowed to solve mysteries.

Write the following sentence frames on the board or on chart paper. Share the pen with students by working with them to write the draft, using the information from the list.

Grammar: Possessive Pronouns

PRETEACH Review possessive pronouns with students. Point out the following:

- A **possessive pronoun** shows ownership and takes the place of a possessive noun.
- One kind of possessive pronoun is used before a noun. These pronouns are *my, your, his, her, its, our,* and *their.*
- The other kind of possessive pronoun stands alone. These pronouns are *mine, yours, his, hers, its, ours,* and *theirs.*

> Dear Police Department,
>
>   Children should be allowed to help solve mysteries because they are good at it. One reason they are good at solving mysteries is _____. For example, _____. Another reason children make great detectives is _____. We know this is true because _____. One last reason children should be allowed to solve mysteries is that _____. For example, _____.
>
>   Sincerely,
>
>   _____

Then write the following sentences on the board.

- *Cliff was riding his bike.*
- *Sam's bike is older than his.*

Point out the possessive pronouns in these sentences. (*his, his*) Write the following sentences on the board and instruct students to copy them and circle all possessive pronouns.

1. This is my bicycle. (*my; comes before a noun*)
2. Are you sure it is yours? (*yours; stands alone*)
3. Kenny thinks it is his bike. (*his; comes before a noun*)
4. No, it is mine. (*mine; stands alone*)
5. My bike has yellow stripes on its tires. (*my, its; both before nouns*)

When students are done writing, have them reread the sentences. Ask them to identify which possessive pronouns come before a noun and which ones stand alone.

FLUENCY PRACTICE Have volunteers read aloud the persuasive letter they completed in the writing activity.

Interactive Writing: Persuasive Letter

RETEACH Display the completed the persuasive letter from Preteach. Read it aloud with students. Ask students what they would like to change about it and why. Discuss students' suggestions for changing or adding to the persuasive letter. Write the revised persuasive letter based on students' suggestions. Then have students copy the revised persuasive letter into their Language Journals. Students should personalize their paragraphs.

Grammar-Writing Connection

RETEACH Have students work in pairs or small groups to discuss special possessions that they own. Have students draw pictures of two of their favorite possessions. Then work with them to write a sentence or two to describe those possessions. Students should use possessive pronouns in their sentences. Check students' writing and make corrections as necessary.

FLUENCY PRACTICE Have students share their pictures and sentences orally with the class.

Name _____

Your friend's toy is missing. You must solve the mystery of where it is. Fill in the sequence chain below to show the steps you will take to solve the mystery. Then share your plan with the class.

_____ was sad because his toy _____ was missing.

↓

↓

↓

I found his toy _____ under the table next to the _____.

TO THE TEACHER Ask students to fill in the sequence chain to solve the mystery of the missing toy. Have students read their sequence chains aloud for sense. Then have them copy the sequence into their Language Journals. The Case of Pablo's Nose/The Case of the Red Bicycle • **Lesson 17** **103**

Use with "In the Days of King Adobe"

Build Background/Access Prior Knowledge

Tell students that people need money to buy necessary things, such as food, clothing, electricity, and water. People also need money to buy fun things, such as books and music. Ask volunteers to tell what they would buy if they had extra money. Record students' responses in a concept web like this one.

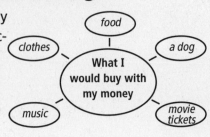

Selection Vocabulary

PRETEACH Display Teaching Transparency 168, and read the words aloud. Then point to the pictures as you read the following sentences:

1. Jerry is **fascinated** by the bike. He is amazed at how shiny it looks.
2. The **roguish** boy takes things that don't belong to him. He is behaving badly.
3. The **rascally** boy is being naughty.
4. This boy is **thrifty** and saves all his money in his piggy bank.
5. The boy gives the clerk a **generous** amount of money for the bike. The bike costs a lot of money.

Selection Vocabulary

RETEACH Revisit Teaching Transparency 168. Read the words with students. Have students work in pairs to discuss the meanings of the words and to answer questions such as this: Does *generous* mean "a lot" or "a little"?

Write the following sentence frames on the board. Read each sentence and ask students to choose a vocabulary word to complete it. Write students' responses in the blanks.

1. The _____ old woman saved all of her pennies in a jar. (*thrifty*)
2. Her grandmother gave her a _____ amount of money for her birthday. (*generous*)
3. The _____ men stole from the old woman. (*rascally; roguish*)
4. The children were _____ by the clown. (*fascinated*)
5. The _____ girl did not tell the truth to her mother. (*roguish; rascally*)

Have students write these words in their Language Dictionaries.

FLUENCY PRACTICE Have students read the completed sentences aloud. Encourage them to describe the illustrations on Teaching Transparency 168, using the vocabulary words and any other words they know.

Build Background: "In the Days of King Adobe"

Have students look at the picture on *Pupil Edition* pages 442–443. Tell them that the old woman gives two strangers food and a place to stay. Have students predict how the strangers will repay the old woman's kindness.

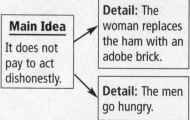

LEAD
THE
WAY

 ## Main Idea and Details

PRETEACH Tell students that the main idea is what the selection is mainly about. Explain that details provide information that supports the main idea. When the main idea is not directly stated, students must use details to figure out the main idea.

On the board, draw a graphic organizer like this one to illustrate the concept. As students read the selection, have them identify the main idea and the details that support it.

Main Idea
It does not pay to act dishonestly.

→ **Detail:** The woman replaces the ham with an adobe brick.

→ **Detail:** The men go hungry.

AFTER

Reading
"In the Days of
King Adobe"

Pages 440–441

Pages 442–443

❓ **QUESTIONS:**
pages 440–443

Pages 444–448

❓ **QUESTIONS:**
pages 444–448

Directed Reading: "In the Days of King Adobe"

RETEACH Use these sentences to walk students through the story.

- This is the old woman. She is very poor.
- Two young men are traveling and need a place to stay. The old woman lets them stay with her.

- The woman makes dinner for her guests. She shares part of her special ham.
- The two men are whispering. They are planning to steal the ham.

- Did the old woman make dinner for the men? (*yes*)
- What did the young men plan to do? (*They planned to steal the ham.*)

- The woman does not trust the men because they seem rascally.
- She sees the men put the ham in their bag. When they are asleep, she replaces the ham with a brick.
- When the men leave, they think the ham is in the bag.
- They open the bag and find a brick instead of the ham.
- They learn not to play any more tricks.

- Does the old woman trust the two men? (*no*)
- What do the men find in their bag instead of the ham? (*a brick*)

FLUENCY PRACTICE Encourage students to describe the illustration on *Pupil Edition* pages 444–445, using as many vocabulary words as they can in their descriptions.

Build Background: "Money, Money"

PRETEACH Remind students that "In the Days of King Adobe" is about a poor woman who is generous even though she doesn't have a lot of money. In "Money, Money," students will read about different kinds of coins and paper money. Have students name different units of money.

English-
Language
Learners
Book

Use the concept words in sentences that illustrate their meanings.

- You eat **food** for breakfast, lunch, and dinner.
- You **trade money** for the things you want to buy.
- Abraham Lincoln is on the **front** of a penny.
- The Lincoln Memorial is on the **back** of a penny.

Have students add these words to their Language Dictionaries.

Concept Words
food
money
trade
front
back

Directed Reading: "Money, Money"

📖 **Summary** *In "Money, Money" students will read about different kinds of money and their values.*

Use these sentences to walk students through the story.

Pages 2–5
- This is Peter Minuit. He traded with Native Americans to purchase land. A long time ago, people did not use money.
- These old coins are from ancient Rome and ancient Greece.
- Different countries use different kinds of money.
- This is a penny. It is a coin. It is worth one cent.

Pages 6–9
- This is a nickel. It is worth five cents. Important people are pictured on coins and bills. This is Thomas Jefferson. He was a President.
- This is a dime. It is worth ten cents.
- This is a quarter. It is worth twenty-five cents.

QUESTIONS: pages 2–9
- Were coins invented before paper money? (*yes*)
- How much is a quarter worth? (*twenty-five cents*)

Pages 10–13
- This is a scale. One side has ten dollars in coins. The other side has ten dollars in paper money. The coins weigh more than the paper money.
- This is a one-dollar bill. It is equal to 100 pennies.

Pages 14–16
- This is a five-dollar bill. Abraham Lincoln is on the front.
- Other units of money used in the United States are the ten, twenty, fifty, and one hundred dollar bills.

QUESTIONS: pages 10–16
- Are dollar bills heavier than coins? (*no*)
- What are coins made from? (*metal*)

★ (Focus Skill) **Main Idea and Details**

RETEACH Review main idea and details with students. Then draw a main idea graphic organizer on the board. Ask students to revisit "Money, Money" to find the main idea and details to complete the graphic organizer.

FLUENCY PRACTICE Have students choose a kind of money and reread aloud the section that tells about it.

Interactive Writing: Response to Literature

PRETEACH Tell students that they are going to work with you to write a response to literature paragraph about "Money, Money." Explain to students that when they write a response to literature, they will be asked to demonstrate an understanding of what they have read and support their response with details from the story.

Write on the board this prompt: *What was the most interesting thing you learned from reading "Money, Money"? How did the author make the information about money interesting?* Then brainstorm with students a list of interesting things they read about in "Money, Money." Organize their responses in a web like this one.

The first coins were made thousands of years ago.

Quarters have different backs.

Interesting Information in "Money, Money"

Every country has its own money.

Paper money is made from cloth.

Write the following frames on the board. Share the pen with students by working with them to write the draft, using the information in the web. Responses will vary.

> *"Money, Money" gives interesting information about _____. One of the most interesting things I learned was _____. I thought this was interesting because _____. The author of this selection made the information about money interesting by _____ and _____. I _____ reading this book.*

Grammar: Adjectives and Articles

PRETEACH Discuss the definitions of adjectives and articles with students. Point out the following:

- An **adjective** is a word that describes a noun or pronoun. Adjectives tell *what kind, how many,* or *which one.* An adjective can come before the noun it describes, or it can follow a verb such as *is, seems,* or *appears.*
- The adjectives *a, an,* and *the* are called **articles**. Use *a* before a word that begins with a consonant sound. Use *an* before a word that begins with a vowel sound.

Write the following sentences on the board and read them aloud. Work with students to identify the adjectives and articles in each one.

- The girl saved her money in a glass jar. *(adjective: glass; articles: the, a)*
- She counted the shiny coins. *(adjective: shiny; article: the)*
- The girl noticed her favorite coin was missing. *(adjective: favorite; article: the)*
- An unhappy girl cried. *(adjective: unhappy; article: an)*
- A generous man gave us food. *(adjective: generous; article: a)*
- They live in a tiny country. *(adjective: tiny; article: a)*

FLUENCY PRACTICE Have students read aloud the paragraph they completed in the writing activity.

Interactive Writing: Response to Literature

RETEACH Display the completed paragraph from Preteach. Read it aloud with students. Ask them what they would like to change about it and why. Discuss students' suggestions for changing or adding to the paragraph. Work with students to add additional selection details to support their responses. Write the revised paragraph based on students' suggestions. Then have students copy the revised essay into their Language Journals. Students should personalize their paragraphs by using precise adjectives.

Grammar-Writing Connection

RETEACH Show students a variety of coins. Point out that each coin looks different. Have students choose three coins to draw. Tell students to write a descriptive sentence below each drawing. Have them underline the articles and circle the adjectives they used in their sentences. Remind students to use the article *a* before a word that begins with a consonant sound and *an* before a word that begins with a vowel sound. Encourage students to share their work with the class. Check students' writing and suggest any corrections they need to make.

FLUENCY PRACTICE Have students choose a page from "Money, Money" to read aloud.

Name _____

A Complete the sentences by putting the correct number in the blank.

1. A dollar is the same as _____ pennies.

2. A dime is the same as _____ pennies.

3. A nickel is the same as _____ pennies.

4. A quarter is the same as _____ pennies.

5. A quarter and a dime are the same as _____ pennies.

B Choose a word from the box and write it under the correct picture.

penny	nickel	dime	quarter

1. _____

3. _____

2. _____

4. _____

TO THE TEACHER Read aloud the directions. Before students complete the activities, review with them the value of a dollar, a dime, a nickel, and a quarter.

Use with "Red Writing Hood"

Build Background/Access Prior Knowledge

Show students a storybook and a newspaper. Tell students that the stories in storybooks may be real or make-believe. The stories in the newspaper are real. Ask: **What is your favorite type of story?** Record students' responses in an idea web:

Selection Vocabulary

PRETEACH Display Teaching Transparency 177 and read the words aloud. Then point to the pictures as you read the following sentences:

1. The director has a **script** that shows the lines the actors say.
2. The director **desperately** needs the actors to remember their lines.
3. The play is about **injustice**. It shows how a man was unfairly accused of a crime.
4. The director tells the actor to look **repentant** or sorry.
5. The actor gives an **acceptable** performance. The director is satisfied.
6. The director **discards** his coat by throwing it on the stage.
7. The play will not be delayed under any **circumstances**. Nothing will stop this play from opening.
8. The actor stands **triumphantly** on the stage. He is very proud.

Selection Vocabulary

RETEACH Revisit Teaching Transparency 177. Have students work in pairs to discuss the meanings of the words and to answer questions such as: If someone is **repentant**, does that person feel *sorry* or *not sorry*?

Write the following sentence frames on the board. Read each sentence and ask students to choose a vocabulary word to complete it. Write students' responses in the blanks.

1. Chloe _____ the soda can in the recycling bin. (*discards*)
2. The _____ was forty pages long. (*script*)
3. The winning team walked _____ off the field. (*triumphantly*)
4. The _____ of the accident were in the report. (*circumstances*)
5. The boy was _____ after he broke the toy. (*repentant*)
6. Tyler spoke out against _____ because he thinks all people should be treated fairly. (*injustice*)
7. We _____ need more help in the office. (*desperately*)
8. The child gave the teacher an _____ answer in class. (*acceptable*)

Have students write these words in their Language Dictionaries.

FLUENCY PRACTICE Have students read the sentence frames aloud. Encourage them to describe the illustrations on Teaching Transparency 177 using the vocabulary words and any other words they know.

Build Background: "Red Writing Hood"

PRETEACH Have students look at the picture on *Pupil Edition* pages 456–457. Tell students that this selection is a play. Explain that a play is a story that can be performed in front of an audience. Point out that the picture shows characters from many fairy tales. Have students identify as many of the characters as they can.

LEAD
THE
WAY

 ## Sequence

PRETEACH Tell students that events in a story follow a sequence, or order, that makes sense. The sequence tells the reader what happens first, next, and last in the story.

Directed Reading: "Red Writing Hood"

RETEACH Use these sentences to walk students through the story.

Pages 456–459

- These are all the characters from "Red Writing Hood."
- This is Red. Red is on the way to her grandmother's house.
- Red takes out her notepad. She does not want the wolf to hurt her or her grandmother. She writes a new ending and makes the wolf turn into a dancer.

Pages 460–461

- Red does not want Miss Muffet to be scared by a spider, so she changes that fairy tale.
- Prince Charming joins Miss Muffet.

**QUESTIONS:
pages 456–461**

- Does the wolf eat Red? (*no*)
- Who joins Miss Muffet? (*Prince Charming*)
- What special power does Red Writing Hood have? (*She can change the endings of fairy tales by writing new endings in her notepad.*)

Pages 462–463

- This is Cinderella. She is looking for Prince Charming.
- Red creates another Prince Charming so that Cinderella will not be alone.

Pages 464–467

- Bo Peep has too many sheep and cannot control them.
- Everyone is angry with Red. Her changes confused all of the characters in the fairy tales.
- The FBI shows up to help Red. The FBI stands for Fairytale Believers, Incorporated.
- They take Red's notebook and fix all of her changes.
- However, the FBI allows the wolf to live happily ever after.

**QUESTIONS:
pages 462–467**

- Is Cinderella in this play? (*yes*)
- What does FBI stand for? (*Fairytale Believers, Incorporated*)

FLUENCY PRACTICE Assign parts to two volunteers. Then have volunteers read aloud *Pupil Edition* page 458. Encourage students to describe the illustration on *Pupil Edition* pages 464–465 using as many vocabulary words as they can in their descriptions.

BEFORE

Making Connections
pages 468–469

Build Background: "Read All About It"

PRETEACH Remind students that "Red Writing Hood" is about a girl who rewrites stories to change the endings. In "Read All About It," students will learn about newspapers. Remind students that newspapers contain real stories. Ask: **What kinds of stories might you find in a newspaper?**

English-Language Learners Book

Concept Words
who
what
when
where
why
how

Write these words on the board. Use them in sentences to illustrate their meanings.

- Mr. Nelson asked, "**Who** wrote this terrific story?"
- He said to Gina, "I would like to know **what** happens next."
- Gina told Mr. Nelson **where** the characters would go for their next adventure.
- Mr. Nelson said, "**Why** don't you write the next part of the story?"
- **When** Gina was done writing, she told her story to the class.
- Another student asked **how** Gina had thought of such a great story.

Have students add these words to their Language Dictionaries.

AFTER

Skill Review
pages 470–471

Directed Reading: "Read All About It"

 Summary *Newspapers help people learn about their world. There are three main kinds of newspapers—daily, weekly, and special-interest. It takes many people to produce a newspaper.*

Use these sentences to walk students through the story.

Pages 2–5
- Newspapers are full of information.
- A newspaper is produced in a busy place called a newsroom.
- The publisher is the person in charge of the newspaper.

Pages 6–9
- An editor decides what the stories and photos in a newspaper will be about.
- Reporters find out who, what, when, where, why, and how about stories.
- Photographers are also reporters. They tell stories through pictures.
- Readers can tell their opinions by writing a letter to the editor.

 QUESTIONS: pages 2–9
- Are reporters in charge of newspapers? (*no*)
- Where is a newspaper produced? (*a newsroom*)

Pages 10–13
- This is a letter to the editor written by a boy named Ari.
- Features are stories that are not news.
- This person is looking for a job. Newspapers also tell readers about jobs.

Pages 14–16
- Many things must happen before a newspaper is ready to read.
- Proofreaders must make sure that there are no mistakes in the newspaper.
- The circulation department sends newspapers to homes and newsstands.

 QUESTIONS: pages 10–16
- Does Ari write to ask for a new school in his town? (*no*)
- What is a proofreader's job? (*They make sure there are no mistakes.*)

 Sequence

Review sequence with students. Draw a sequence chain with five blank boxes and instruct students to copy it. Ask students to revisit the story to complete the chart.

> **FLUENCY PRACTICE** Have students use the illustrations on pages 14 and 15 to retell part of "Read All About It." Encourage them to use as many vocabulary words and concept words as possible.

Interactive Writing: Compare and Contrast Paragraph

PRETEACH Tell students that they are going to work with you to write a compare and contrast paragraph. Generate a Venn diagram with the title *Compare and Contrast*. Then brainstorm with students how the two stories "Red Writing Hood" and "Read All About It" are alike and different.

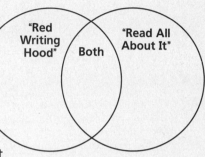

Compare and Contrast

The stories "Red Writing Hood" and "Read All About It" are alike and different. They are alike because they both _____. However, "Red Writing Hood" is different than "Read All About It" because it _____. "Read All About It" is different than "Red Writing Hood" because _____.

Write the following sentence frames on the board or on chart paper. Share the pen with students by working with them to write the draft. Use the information from the Venn diagram.

Grammar: Comparing Using Adjectives

PRETEACH Discuss how to compare using adjectives.

- **Adjectives** describe by comparing people, places, or things.
- Add *-er* to short adjectives that compare two things. Add *-est* to short adjectives that compare three or more things.
- *More* and *most* are used with longer adjectives to make comparisons.

Write the following sentences on the board:

1. I enjoy reading the (shorter, most shortest) articles in the newspaper.
2. Of all the areas of the newspaper, the circulation department is the (busiest, busier).
3. The editor has the position of (greatest, most greatest) importance.
4. Proofreading is (easier, more easier) than writing.
5. The sports section is the (more, most) interesting part of the newspaper.

Tell students to copy the sentences into their notebooks and circle the correct answer for each. Monitor students' work as they complete the sentences. Read each sentence aloud.

FLUENCY PRACTICE Have volunteers read aloud the essay they completed in the writing activity.

Interactive Writing: Compare and Contrast Paragraph

`RETEACH` Display the completed compare and contrast paragraph from Preteach. Read it aloud with students. Ask them what they would like to change about it and why. Discuss students' suggestions for changing or adding to the essay. Write the revised essay based on students' suggestions. Then have students copy the revised essay into their Language Journals. Students should personalize their essays.

Grammar-Writing Connection

`RETEACH` Review how to compare using adjectives. Then write the following sentences on the board. Direct students to fill in the blanks using the correct form of the word provided. Circulate to offer assistance.

1. hungry—Papa Bear was the _____ of the three bears. (*hungriest*)
2. hard—Goldilocks thought Mama Bear's bed was _____ than Baby Bear's bed. (*harder*)
3. frightening—Miss Muffet thought the spider was _____ than a Prince Charming. (*more frightening*)
4. beautiful—Cinderella wanted to be the _____ of all the girls at the ball. (*most beautiful*)
5. loud—Agent Andersen complained the _____. (*loudest*)

After students have completed their work, read each sentence aloud.

FLUENCY PRACTICE Have students read their revised and personalized essays out loud.

Name _____

A **Pretend that you are a reporter. Think about an event at your school that would make a good news story. Answer the following questions to plan your news story.**

Who is the story about?

_____

What happens at the event?

_____

Where does the event happen?

_____

When does the event happen?

_____

Why does the event take place?

_____

How was the event planned or organized?

_____

B **Draw a picture to go with your news story. Label the picture.**

TO THE TEACHER Read aloud the directions with students. You may want to brainstorm story ideas with them before they begin. When students finish planning their news stories, you may choose to have them write the news stories.

Red Writing Hood/Read All About It • Lesson 19   **115**

LESSON 20

Use with "One Grain of Rice"

Build Background/Access Prior Knowledge

Show students a math textbook. Tell them that people use math every day. Ask students to share how they use math in their everyday lives. Ask: **How do you use math?** Record students' responses in a web like the one shown here.

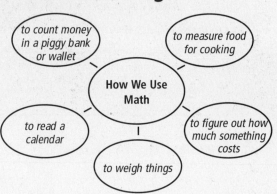

Selection Vocabulary

PRETEACH Display Teaching Transparency 186, and read the words aloud. Then point to the pictures as you read the following sentences:

1. Rice grew **plentifully** in the fields. The farmers were pleased because there was so much rice.
2. The rain started to **trickle** down on the crops. The thin stream of water refreshed the rice plants.
3. The starving children told the king there was a **famine**. The king did not realize there was not enough food for his people.
4. The children **implored** the king to give them some food. After the children begged, the king gave them some rice.
5. The king **decreed** that all his people would have rice to eat. He ordered that the people be given rice.

Selection Vocabulary

RETEACH Revisit Teaching Transparency 186. Read the words with students. Have students work in pairs to discuss the meanings of the words and to answer questions such as: In a **famine**, do people have too much to eat or too little to eat? Is a **trickle** a thin stream or a downpour?

Write the following sentence frames on the board. Read each frame aloud, and ask students to choose a vocabulary word to complete it. Write students' responses in the blanks.

1. The student _____ the teacher to let her retake the test. (*implored*)
2. Many people were starving because of the _____. (*famine*)
3. It rained _____ on the fields. (*plentifully*)
4. Kayla could hear a _____ of water coming from the faucet. (*trickle*)
5. The queen _____ that her people work together. (*decreed*)

Have students write these words in their Language Dictionaries.

FLUENCY PRACTICE Encourage students to describe the illustrations on Teaching Transparency 186, using the vocabulary words and other words they know.

Build Background: "One Grain of Rice"

**LEAD
THE
WAY**

Have students look at the picture on *Pupil Edition* pages
486–487. Tell students that all these elephants are carrying
grains of rice. Have students predict why the elephants are carrying the rice. Ask them to guess how much rice is there.

 ## Compare and Contrast

PRETEACH Tell students that to compare means to tell how things are
alike, or the same, and to contrast means to tell how things are different.

On the board, draw a Venn diagram like the one below. Have students
copy the chart, and help them fill it in with information from the story as
they read.

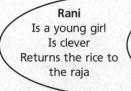

Rani
Is a young girl
Is clever
Returns the rice to
the raja

Both
Live in India
Eat rice

The Raja
Is like a king
Is foolish
Takes rice from
the farmers

Directed Reading: "One Grain of Rice"

RETEACH Use these sentences to walk students through the story.

■ This is Rani. She lives in India.
■ The raja orders that all the rice be saved for him.

Pages 474–477

■ The raja is the man riding the elephant. The raja is a king in India.

Pages 478–481

■ The elephant is taking rice to the raja for the feast.
■ Rani collects rice that is spilling and takes it to the raja.
■ The raja wants to reward Rani. He agrees to give her one grain of rice and,
for the next 30 days, double the amount from the previous day.

 QUESTIONS:
pages 474–481

■ Does the raja take all the rice? (*yes*)
■ How is the rice carried to the palace? (*by elephants*)

Pages 482–487

■ Each day, Rani gets more rice from the raja.
■ The raja sends so much rice that he has to transport it by Brahma bulls.
■ On the thirtieth day, the raja has to send the rice using 256 elephants.

Pages 488–492

■ Rani gives her rice to all the hungry people.
■ The people are very happy. There is plenty of rice for everyone.
■ The raja learns a lesson to be fair and share the rice.

QUESTIONS:
pages 482–492

■ Does Rani get less rice from the raja each day? (*no*)
■ In what way do you think Rani was clever? (*Responses will vary.*)

FLUENCY PRACTICE Ask volunteers to read aloud a paragraph from their
favorite page in the story. Encourage students to describe their favorite illustration, using as many vocabulary words as they can in their descriptions.

Concept Words
math
numbers
clocks
measure
count
fingers

Build Background: "Numbers"

PRETEACH Remind students that "One Grain of Rice" is about a young girl who uses math to outsmart the raja. In "Numbers" they will read about some of the many uses of numbers.

English-
Language
Learners
Book

Write the concept words on the board. Use them in sentences.

- The students learned to add and subtract in their **math** books.
- They learned how to read **numbers**.
- They used that skill to learn how to read the time on **clocks**.
- We used a ruler to **measure** the room.
- To tell time, the children had to learn to **count** by fives.
- Some students counted on their **fingers**, while others counted in their heads.

Have students add these words to their Language Dictionaries.

Directed Reading: "Numbers"

Summary *Throughout history, people have had different ways of writing numbers. There are many different kinds of numbers.*

Use these sentences to walk students through the story.

Pages 2–3
- Look at the things that have numbers on them—a cake, a ruler, a scoreboard, a street sign, and sheet music.
- People started to use numbers a long time ago.

Pages 4–5
- Some people count using their fingers.
- This is an abacus. It is an early counting machine.
- Roman numerals look like letters. Some clocks have Roman numerals on them.

Pages 6–9
- This chart shows the Roman numerals from 1–30.
- These are Arabic numerals. These are the types of numbers we use today.

**QUESTIONS:
pages 2–9**
- Is an abacus an early counting machine? (*yes*)
- What is the name of the numbers we use today? (*Arabic*)

Pages 10–13
- The symbol for zero was invented in India.
- There are ten symbols used to write numbers: 0, 1, 2, 3, 4, 5, 6, 7, 8, 9.

Pages 14–16
- Numbers can be even or odd.
- A prime number can be divided only by itself and 1.
- This chart shows how to count from one to ten in different languages.

**QUESTIONS:
pages 10–16**
- Do people around the world all use the same numerals? (*no*)
- How many symbols are used to write Arabic numbers? (*ten*)

(Focus Skill) Compare and Contrast

Review the concept of compare and contrast with students. Then draw a three-column chart on the board with the headings *Arabic Numerals*, *Word*, and *Roman Numerals*. Write the Arabic numbers 1–10 in the left column. Then have students use the selection to fill in the other columns.

FLUENCY PRACTICE Have students choose an illustration to retell part of "Numbers." Encourage them to use vocabulary words and concept words.

Interactive Writing: Compare-and-Contrast Essay

PRETEACH Tell students that they are going to work with you to write a compare-and-contrast essay. Draw a Venn diagram on the board. Then brainstorm with students how "One Grain of Rice" and "Numbers" are alike and different.

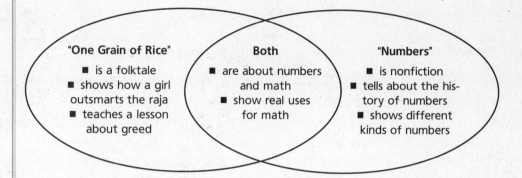

"One Grain of Rice"
- is a folktale
- shows how a girl outsmarts the raja
- teaches a lesson about greed

Both
- are about numbers and math
- show real uses for math

"Numbers"
- is nonfiction
- tells about the history of numbers
- shows different kinds of numbers

Write the following sentence frames on the board or on chart paper. Share the pen with students by working with them to write the draft, using the information from the Venn diagram.

> *In some ways, the stories "One Grain of Rice" and "Numbers" are both alike and different. They are alike because they both _____. However, "One Grain of Rice" is different because it _____. "Numbers" is different because it _____.*

Give students the opportunity to add more sentences.

Grammar: Verbs

PRETEACH Discuss the definition of a verb with students. Point out the following:

- A **verb** is the main word in the predicate of a sentence.
- A verb expresses action (what something *does*) or being (what something *is*).
- Sometimes a verb is a pair or group of words that work together.
- A sentence with a compound predicate has two or more verbs.

Write the following sentences on the board:

1. Early people drew marks on cave walls. (*drew*)
2. They counted and recorded numbers of animals. (*counted; recorded*)
3. Tallies are also marks. (*are*)
4. Numbers made math easier. (*made*)

Underline the verbs in each sentence. Point out that sentences 1, 2, and 4 have verbs that express action. Tell students that sentence 2 has a compound predicate with two verbs. Call students' attention to the verb in sentence 3. Explain that *are* is a verb that tells what something is.

FLUENCY PRACTICE Have volunteers read aloud the completed essay from the writing activity.

Interactive Writing: Compare-and-Contrast Essay

RETEACH Display the completed compare-and-contrast essay from Preteach. Read it aloud with students. Ask them what they would like to change about it and why. Discuss students' suggestions for changing or adding to the essay. Write the revised essay, based on students' suggestions. Then have students copy the revised essay into their Language Journals.

Grammar-Writing Connection

RETEACH Review with students the definition of a verb. Then write the following sentences on the board.

1. The raja _____ the rice from the farmers. (*Suggested response: took*)
2. He said that he _____ the rice for the future. (*Suggested response: would store*)
3. One year there _____ a famine. (*Suggested response: was*)
4. The raja _____ all the rice for himself. (*Suggested response: kept*)
5. One day some rice _____ from a basket. (*Suggested response: fell*)
6. Rani _____ the rice and _____ it to the palace. (*Suggested responses: collected; carried*)
7. She _____ it to the raja. (*Suggested response: gave*)
8. The raja _____ Rani for her good deed. (*Suggested response: rewarded*)

Have students copy the sentences into their notebooks, filling in each blank with a verb. Remind students to pay close attention to whether the verb is a pair or group of words that work together or whether the sentence has two or more verbs that make up a compound predicate. Monitor students' work as they complete the sentences.

FLUENCY PRACTICE Have students choose a page from "Numbers" to read aloud.

Name _____

Draw pictures to show four ways that you use numbers. Write a sentence to describe each picture.

```
┌─────────────────────────────────────────────────────────┐
│                                                         │
│                                                         │
│                                                         │
│                                                         │
└─────────────────────────────────────────────────────────┘
```

_____

```
┌─────────────────────────────────────────────────────────┐
│                                                         │
│                                                         │
│                                                         │
│                                                         │
└─────────────────────────────────────────────────────────┘
```

_____

```
┌─────────────────────────────────────────────────────────┐
│                                                         │
│                                                         │
│                                                         │
│                                                         │
└─────────────────────────────────────────────────────────┘
```

_____

```
┌─────────────────────────────────────────────────────────┐
│                                                         │
│                                                         │
│                                                         │
│                                                         │
└─────────────────────────────────────────────────────────┘
```

_____

TO THE TEACHER Have students draw one picture in each box to show how they use numbers. Then ask students to write a sentence about each picture. You may want to model how to write a sentence such as *I use numbers to tell time.*

Use with **"Fire!"**

Build Background/Access Prior Knowledge

Write the word *Careers* on the board, and
explain its meaning. Discuss with students
various careers with which they are familiar.
Record students' responses in a web like the
one shown.

You may wish to discuss with students what
they know about each of the careers you have listed in the web.

Selection Vocabulary

PRETEACH Display Teaching Transparency 196 and read the words aloud.
Then point to the pictures as you read the following sentences:

1. The **brigade** of firefighters was organized to put out the fire.
2. The **billowing** smoke made it hard to see.
3. Blowing air will **ventilate** the building.
4. The curtains caught on fire right away. They were very **flammable**.
5. With **dedication**, the firefighters were able to stop the fire.
6. The **curfew** tells when people must be inside.

Selection Vocabulary

RETEACH Revisit Teaching Transparency 196. Have students work in pairs
to discuss the meanings of the words and to answer questions such as: If
something is **billowing**, is it rising or falling in big waves? If something is
flammable, is it easy or hard to catch on fire?

Write the following sentence frames on the board. Read each frame and
ask students to choose a vocabulary word to complete it.

1. The police ordered a midnight _____ in the summer. (*curfew*)
2. When Mia uses strong cleansers, she is sure to _____ the room.
   (*ventilate*)
3. Some fabrics are _____ and burn easily. (*flammable*)
4. A fire _____ arrived at the burning building. (*brigade*)
5. Smoke was _____ up from the burning trees. (*billowing*)
6. It took _____ for us to climb to the top of the mountain.
   (*dedication*)

Have students write these words in their Language Dictionaries.

FLUENCY PRACTICE Have students read the completed sentence frames
aloud. Encourage them to describe the illustrations on Teaching Transparency
196 by using the vocabulary words.

Build Background: "Fire!"

Display and discuss with students the photographs on *Pupil Edition* pages 510–511. Tell students that firefighting is one type of career. Point out that fighting fires is a dangerous but important job. Have students predict what dangers firefighters might face.

LEAD THE WAY

Elements of Nonfiction: Text Structure

PRETEACH Tell students that the authors of nonfiction text like "Fire!" may organize their information in various ways. One way is by main idea and details.

Main idea	Supporting Details
Firefighters do an important job.	People count on firefighters to help them.
	Firefighters stop fires from destroying buildings and other property.

On the board, draw a chart like the one below to explain the concept. Then have students copy the chart into their notebooks, and help them fill it in with information from the story as they read the selection.

Directed Reading: "Fire!"

RETEACH Use these sentences to walk students through the story.

Pages 504–507
- Some firefighters get paid while others are volunteers.
- Firefighters must be ready at all times.
- They may work in big cities or in small towns.
- The firefighters drive the fire engine to the scene of a fire.

Pages 508–509
- Pants and boots are ready for the firefighter to jump into them.
- The firefighters use masks so they can fight the fire safely.

 QUESTIONS:
pages 504–509
- Are firefighters ready at all times? (*yes*)
- Why do firefighters wear masks? (*to protect themselves*)

Pages 510–513
- Firefighters must work together so no one gets hurt.
- In 1608 Jamestown, Virginia, burned to the ground.
- The houses were made from flammable materials—wood, straw, and grasses.
- Long ago, all the people in town would help put out a fire.
- The firefighters filled and passed buckets of water to put out the fire.

Pages 514–516
- This is an all-woman firefighting crew from the early 1900s.
- Benjamin Franklin started the first fire department.
- This diagram shows the equipment of a modern firefighter.

QUESTIONS:
pages 510–516
- Did Benjamin Franklin start the first fire department? (*yes*)
- How did people get the water to fires long ago? (*in buckets*)

FLUENCY PRACTICE Ask students to read aloud a section from the selection.

Build Background: "Two Fridas"

PRETEACH Remind students of the career they read about, firefighting. Then tell them that in "Two Fridas" they will read about a girl who is named after a famous artist. Point out that being an artist is also a career.

English-
Language
Learners
Book

Write the concept words on the board. Use them in sentences to illustrate their meanings.

Concept Words
name
born
young
mother
right

- My **name** is Manuel.
- I was **born** in Peru.
- My family moved here when I was very **young**.
- My **mother** and father know they made the **right** decision.

Have students add these words to their Language Dictionaries.

Directed Reading: "Two Fridas"

Summary *Frida was named after Frida Kahlo, a famous artist. After she learns about Frida Kahlo's traffic accident, Frida befriends Eric, a class-mate who uses a wheelchair.*

Use these sentences to walk students through the story.

Pages 2–5
- Frida was named after the Mexican artist, Frida Kahlo.
- Frida Kahlo was married to another famous Mexican artist, Diego Rivera.
- Frida likes to paint. She sends her paintings to her grandparents in Mexico.

Pages 6–9
- Frida wants to see Casa Azul in Mexico City. Frida Kahlo once lived there.
- Frida and her parents are walking through Casa Azul.
- Frida buys postcards to send home.
- Back at school, Frida eats lunch with her new friends Carmela and Mu Lan.
- Eric is in a wheelchair. Frida wonders whether he is lonely.

**QUESTIONS:
pages 2–9**
- Was Frida Kahlo an artist? (*yes*)
- Where do Frida's grandparents live? (*Mexico*)

Pages 10–13
- Frida tells her mother about Eric.
- Frida's mother tells Frida to talk to Eric.
- Frida goes to the school library to learn more about Frida Kahlo.
- Frida Kahlo was injured in a bus accident. She was in pain for the rest of her life.

Pages 14–16
- Frida wants to make friends with Eric.
- Eric says he was in a car accident.
- Frida learns that Eric plays the violin.

**QUESTIONS:
pages 10–16**
- Do Eric and Frida become friends? (*yes*)
- What does Frida learn about Eric? (*He plays the violin.*)

(Focus Skill) Elements of Nonfiction: Text Structure

RETEACH Discuss with students the charts they completed after reading "Fire!"

> **FLUENCY PRACTICE** Have students use their favorite illustrations to retell part of "Two Fridas." Encourage them to use as many vocabulary words and concept words as possible.

Independent Writing: Report (Organization)

PRETEACH Tell students that they will prewrite a research report on a career. Explain to students that before they begin writing, they must choose a topic, research it, and organize their notes in a logical order. Brainstorm with students a list of careers and have them each choose one for their reports. Then direct students to various resources for their research. Have them take notes on their topic, listing only the most important information they find. Tell students to restate the information they find in their own words, rather than copying it exactly. Finally, have students organize their notes in a logical order.

Grammar: Main and Helping Verbs

PRETEACH Discuss with students the following:

- A **helping verb** works with the **main verb** to tell about an action.
- The **helping verb** always comes before the **main verb**.
- Sometimes another word comes between the **helping verb** and the **main verb.**

Write the following sentences on the board. Read aloud each sentence. Help students identify the main verbs and the helping verbs. Point out that sentence 2 has another word (*to*) that comes between the main and helping verb.

- Firefighters are putting out fires every day. (*helping verb: are; main verb: putting*)
- At the station, they have to listen for the bells and buzzers. (*helping verb: have; main verb: listen*)
- Firefighters must be ready at all times. (*helping verb: must; main verb: be*)
- They will arrive at a fire as quickly as possible. (*helping verb: will; main verb: arrive*)
- Then the real work will begin. (*helping verb: will; main verb: begin*)

FLUENCY PRACTICE Have volunteers read aloud the report they drafted.

Independent Writing: Report (Organization)

RETEACH Have students reread their drafts from page 125. Ask them what they would like to change about them and why. Discuss students' suggestions for changing the organization of the report or adding details to it. Then have students rewrite their reports in their Language Journals.

Grammar-Writing Connection

RETEACH Review with students what main and helping verbs are. Then write the following sentences on the board. Have students identify the main verbs and the helping verbs. Monitor students' work as they analyze the sentences.

  1. Frida was born in Mexico. (*helping verb: was; main verb: born*)
  2. She was named after a Mexican artist. (*helping verb: was; main verb: named*)
  3. Frida and her family have moved to the United States. (*helping verb: have; main verb: moved*)
  4. Today Frida is taking an art class after school. (*helping verb: is; main verb: taking*)
  5. She is enjoying the class. (*helping verb: is; main verb: enjoying*)
  6. Frida will tell her friends about the class. (*helping verb: will; main verb: tell*)
  7. Then maybe they will join too. (*helping verb: will; main verb: join*)
  8. Frida would like that. (*helping verb: would; main verb: like*)

FLUENCY PRACTICE Have students read aloud the sentences on the board.

Name _____

Think of a career that you would like to have. Draw a picture to show yourself working in that career. Then write a few sentences to tell about your picture.

_____

_____

_____

_____

TO THE TEACHER Discuss careers with students. as necessary. Invite students to share their pictures and sentences with the class.

Fire!/Two Fridas • **Lesson 21** **127**

Use with "A Very Important Day"

Build Background/Access Prior Knowledge

Tell students that many people who are new to this country settle in big cities. Ask students why they think this occurs. Record students' responses in a concept web like this:

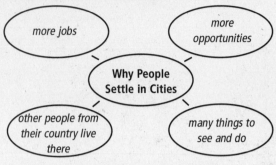

Selection Vocabulary

PRETEACH Display Teaching Transparency 206, and read the words aloud. Then point to the pictures as you read the following sentences:

1. The **petitioners** officially requested to become American citizens.
2. The **examiner** asked the immigrant some questions about America.
3. The judge **apologized** to the family. She said she was sorry.
4. The judge asked everyone to sit. Everyone **obliged** her by sitting.
5. The family got a **certificate**. The document said they were American citizens.
6. The cheers **resounded** in the courtroom. They echoed through the room.
7. New citizens **enrich** our country. They make it better.

Selection Vocabulary

RETEACH Revisit Teaching Transparency 206. Have students answer questions such as: Does *enrich* mean "to make better" or "make worse"?

Write the following sentence frames on the board. Read each sentence and ask students to choose a vocabulary word to complete it.

1. Ann _____ me by doing what I asked. (*obliged*)
2. The _____ asked the governor to clean up the city. (*petitioners*)
3. Tony got a _____ for making good grades. (*certificate*)
4. The applause _____ from one end of the building to the other. (*resounded*)
5. Nicole _____ when she made a mistake. (*apologized*)
6. Some students _____ their lives by taking after-school classes. (*enrich*)
7. The _____ asked the immigrants questions. (*examiner*)

Have students write these words in their Language Dictionaries.

FLUENCY PRACTICE Encourage students to use vocabulary words to describe the illustrations on Teaching Transparency 206.

Build Background: "A Very Important Day"

Have students look at the picture on *Pupil Edition* page 535.
Explain that the people in the picture are immigrants. They
are celebrating a very important day. Ask volunteers to tell
about some special days in their lives.

LEAD
THE
WAY

 ## Author's Purpose

PRETEACH Tell students that authors have purposes, or
reasons, for writing. An author may want to *entertain*, *inform*, or
persuade. Explain to students that they can use details from the story to
help them determine the author's purpose. Explain that sometimes an
author may have more than one reason for writing.

On the board, draw a chart like
this one to explain the concept.
Work with students to add to
the chart as they read
the selection.

Author's Purpose	Supporting Examples
Inform readers about how and why people become citizens	describes how the immigrants prepare on the day that they will become citizens describes what happens at the courthouse

Directed Reading: "A Very Important Day"

RETEACH Use these sentences to walk students through the story.

- This girl is on a ferryboat in New York Harbor. Point to the Statue of Liberty.
- This is the Huerta family. They are from Mexico.
- What does the family see outside the window? (*snow*) What season is it?
- Families from different countries are getting ready to go downtown.

- This family is also going downtown. The boy's friend tosses him a gift.
- Where do you think the families are going? (*Responses will vary.*)

- Are all the families from the same country? (*no*)
- Do these people live in a city or the country? (*the city*)

- The Idris family is at a restaurant. They are eating breakfast.

- Look at all the people in this courtroom. All these people are immigrants. This means they moved to America from another country.
- The judge stands in front of the group. He is in charge of the courtroom.
- The families take an oath. An oath is a promise. They promise to be good American citizens.
- The judge tells the people that they are now United States citizens.
- The people leave the courthouse to celebrate their special day.

- Do the people become citizens? (*yes*)
- Why is the day important? (*The families become citizens.*)

FLUENCY PRACTICE Ask students to choose a section of "A Very Important
Day" to read aloud.

Build Background: "Big Town"

PRETEACH Remind students that "A Very Important Day" is about immigrant families who live in New York City. In "Big Town," students will read about what it is like in a big city. Ask volunteers to tell what they know about cities.

English-Language Learners Book

Write the concept words on the board. Use them in sentences to illustrate their meanings.

- **Most** people live in cities.
- **Other** people live in the country.
- **Many** people work in the city.
- **Some** people work in the country.
- You can **still** work in a city if you live in the country.
- Cities are **always** busy.

Have students add these words to their Language Dictionaries.

Concept Words
most
other
many
some
still
always

Directed Reading: "Big Town"

Summary *Many people live in cities. There are many things to do and see in cities.*

Use these sentences to walk students through the story.

Pages 2–9
- Cities have businesses and neighborhoods. Businesses are where people work. Neighborhoods are where people live.
- These tall buildings are called skyscrapers.
- This is a restaurant.
- These people are going to ride a subway. A subway is an underground train.
- Cities are very busy. There are people and signs everywhere.
- This is a theater. People see plays, stage shows, or movies at the theater.
- Look at the taxi. People pay the taxi driver to take them places.

QUESTIONS: pages 2–9
- Are skyscrapers tall buildings? (*yes*)
- What is the name of the underground train? (*the subway*)

Pages 10–16
- This is an apartment building. Many people live in apartments.
- These people are firefighters and police officers. They keep people safe.
- Look at the chart. Which city has the most people?
- In the city, people can visit museums or go to parks.
- A ferry is a special boat that takes people and cars across a body of water.

QUESTIONS: pages 10–16
- Do many people live in cities? (*yes*)
- What is a ferry? (*a special boat that transports people and cars*)

Focus Skill Author's Purpose

RETEACH Review author's purpose. Work with students to identify the author's purpose for writing "Big Town."

FLUENCY PRACTICE Have students describe the photograph on page 4 of "Big Town."

Independent Writing: Outline

PRETEACH Tell students that they are going to outline the information in "Big Town." Brainstorm with students a list of the main topics in "Big Town."

Write the following outline frame on the board or on chart paper. Model how to complete the first part of the outline. Then have students complete the outline independently, using the information on the list to help them.

Grammar: Action and Linking Verbs

PRETEACH Discuss the definitions of action and linking verbs. Point out that:

- An *action verb* tells what the subject of a sentence does.
- A *linking verb* connects the subject of a sentence to a noun, a pronoun, or an adjective in the predicate.
- The most common *linking verb*s are forms of *be*: *am*, *is*, *are*, *was*, and *were*.

Write the following sentences on the board and read them aloud:

1. Alvaro runs around the track. (action verb: *runs*)
2. Maria sings in the show. (*action verb: sings*)
3. Don is an American. (*linking verb: is*)

Point out the action verbs in sentences 1 and 2. Explain that *runs* and *sings* tell what Alvaro and Maria are doing. Then point out the linking verb in sentence 3. Explain that *is* links *Don* to *American*. Write on the board the following sentence: *Paul was sick*. Ask a volunteer to underline the verb and tell whether it is an action verb or a linking verb.

Big Cities

I. How Big Cities Look
   A. Have businesses uptown and downtown
   B. Have old neighborhoods
   C. Always adding new buildings

II. _____
   A. _____
   B. _____
   C. _____

III. _____
   A. _____
   B. _____
   C. _____

IV. _____
   A. _____
   B. _____
   C. _____

FLUENCY PRACTICE Have students choose a section of "Big Town" to read aloud.

Independent Writing: Outline

RETEACH Have students return to the outlines they drafted during Preteach. Work with students to revise their outlines. Encourage them to look again at "Big Town" to add details to their outlines. Check students' outlines to make sure they are in the correct format. Then have students copy their revised outlines into their Language Journals.

Grammar-Writing Connection

RETEACH Review action verbs and linking verbs with students. Then write the following sentences:

1. City life is fast paced. (*linking verb: is*)
2. People rush here and there. (*action verb: rush*)
3. Some people like city life. (*action verb: like*)
4. They are comfortable with the crowds and noise. (*linking verb: are*)
5. They eat at different restaurants. (*action verb: eat*)
6. These people feel bored in the country. (*linking verb: feel*)

Have students copy the sentences into their notebooks, circling the action verbs and underlining the linking verbs. Remind students that action verbs tell what the subject of a sentence does. Linking verbs connect the subject of a sentence to a noun, a pronoun, or an adjective in the predicate. Then ask students to think about some things they would like to do on a trip to the city. Have each student draw a picture to show his or her ideas. Tell students to write two or three sentences describing their pictures. Have them use at least one action verb and one linking verb.

FLUENCY PRACTICE Have students read aloud the sentences they wrote to describe their pictures.

Name _____

Look again at "Big Town." Choose four words from the story that are new to you. Write one of the words on each short line below. Draw a picture in the box that will help you remember the word. Then write a sentence using the word.

1. Word: _____

   Sentence: _____

   _____

   _____

2. Word: _____

   Sentence: _____

   _____

   _____

3. Word: _____

   Sentence: _____

   _____

   _____

4. Word: _____

   Sentence: _____

   _____

   _____

TO THE TEACHER Brainstorm with students a list of words that may be new to them. After students have completed the activity, have them add their words to their Language Dictionaries.

Use with "Saguaro Cactus"

BEFORE

Building
Background
and Vocabulary

Build Background/Access Prior Knowledge

Display *Pupil Edition* pages 546–547 and discuss deserts with students. Ask students to share what they know about deserts. Ask: **What is the weather like in the desert? What kinds of animals live there?** Record students' responses in a web like this.

Selection Vocabulary

PRETEACH Display Teaching Transparency 215 and read the words and phrases aloud. Then point to the pictures as you read the following sentences:

1. The saguaro cactus is a **habitat** for many animals.
2. So many animals live in the cactus that it is **teeming** with life.
3. The birds sip sweet-tasting **nectar** from the cactus flowers.
4. The saguaro is covered with **spiny** needles that protect it.
5. The birds **perch** on the very top of the cactus.
6. Small animals hide in the **brush** at the bottom of the cactus.
7. Very strong winds can **topple** an old cactus over onto its side.
8. As the dead cactus **decomposes** it adds nutrients to the soil.

AFTER

Building
Background
and Vocabulary

Selection Vocabulary

RETEACH Revisit Teaching Transparency 215. Have students work in pairs to discuss the meanings of the words and to answer questions such as: *If something is* **teeming** *with life is it full of living things or have few living things? Does* perch *mean "to sit" or "to fly"?*

Write the following sentence frames on the board. Read each frame aloud and ask students to choose a vocabulary word to complete it. Write students' responses in the blanks.

1. As the apple _____, it turns brown and smells bad. (*decomposes*)
2. The bird sat on its _____ in the cage. (*perch*)
3. The pond is _____ with plants and fish. (*teeming*)
4. We learned about what lives in a desert _____. (*habitat*)
5. Ramón watched the old saguaro _____ to the ground. (*topple*)
6. Ms. Winn cut some _____ to start her campfire. (*brush*)
7. "The _____ cactus is very sharp," warned Mr. Chang. (*spiny*)
8. The butterfly drank the sweet _____ from the flowers. (*nectar*)

Have students write these words in their Language Dictionaries.

FLUENCY PRACTICE Have students read the completed sentence frames aloud. Encourage them to describe the illustrations on Teaching Transparency 215 by using the vocabulary words and any other words they know.

Build Background: "Saguaro Cactus"

Point out the photograph of the Saguaro Cactus on *Pupil Edition* page 548. Tell students that this desert plant provides food, water, and shelter for different kinds of animals, such as birds, lizards, mice, and insects.

LEAD
THE
WAY

 ## Elements of Nonfiction

PRETEACH Tell students that nonfiction selections can be organized in different ways. Explain that "Saguaro Cactus" is organized according to the sequence of events in the life of a saguaro cactus.

On the board, draw a timeline like this. Have students copy the timeline, and help them fill it in with information from the story.

Life of a Saguaro Cactus	
0 Years	fruit falls to ground; some seeds take root
10 years	
50 years	
60 years	
75 years	
150 years	

Directed Reading: "Saguaro Cactus"

RETEACH Use these sentences to walk students through the story.

- The tiny elf owl makes its home in the saguaro cactus.
- The fruit of the saguaro is bright red inside. It is food for insects, mice, and birds.
- Birds, bats, and insects drink the nectar of the cactus flower.
- A gila woodpecker drills a hole in the cactus to make its home.
- The gila woodpecker is feeding its baby.

QUESTIONS:
pages 546–553

- Do saguaros grow in forests? (*no*)
- What animals drink the nectar of the cactus flowers? (*birds, bats, and insects*)
- What kind of bird makes holes in the saguaro? (*the gila woodpecker*)

Pages 554–555

- At 60 years old, the cactus is almost 18 feet tall.
- More birds build their nests in the saguaro.

Pages 556–557

- Lizards and insects live in the holes of the saguaro.
- A coyote and a bobcat hunt for animals near the cactus.

Pages 558–559

- This saguaro is more than 150 years old.
- After it dies, the cactus is a home for scorpions, horned lizards, and javelinas.

QUESTIONS:
pages 554–559

- Do some lizards live in saguaros? (*yes*)
- What kinds of animals live in a saguaro? (*birds, insects, lizards*)

FLUENCY PRACTICE Ask volunteers to read aloud one of the captions in the selection. Encourage them to describe orally one or more of the photographs.

Concept Words
travel
photographer
magazine
camera
zoom lens

Build Background: "Desert Night"

PRETEACH Discuss with students what they learned about deserts in "Saguaro Cactus." Tell students that in "Desert Night," they will read about a family's trip to the desert.

English-
Language
Learners
Book

Write the Concept Words on the board and use them in sentences.

- I like to **travel** to a different place every year.
- The **photographer** asked us to smile before he took the picture.
- My favorite **magazine** has articles about science in it.
- Pedro got a new **camera** for his birthday.
- Pedro used the **zoom lens** to take a picture of an animal in the distance.

Have students add these words to their Language Dictionaries.

Directed Reading: "Desert Night"

📖 **Summary** *Lela and Aunt Doli visit Uncle Gil in the desert, where Lela has some interesting experiences.*

Use these sentences to walk students through the story.

Pages 2–5
- Lela and her Aunt Doli ride a bus to the desert to visit Uncle Gil.
- Aunt Doli is a photographer. She has brought her camera to take pictures in the desert.
- Uncle Gil meets Lela and Aunt Doli at the bus station. He is carrying a king snake.

Pages 6–9
- Uncle Gil is a scientist who studies reptiles such as snakes, lizards, and alligators.
- Lela finds a rock called a geode.
- There is a rattlesnake skin next to the geode.
- Lela finds a tarantula in a tank in her room.

❓ QUESTIONS:
pages 2–9
- Does Uncle Gil live in the desert? (*yes*)
- Why has Aunt Doli brought her camera with her? (*She will take photographs in the desert.*)

Pages 10–13
- Aunt Doli wants to take pictures at night.
- Lela hears a coyote howling and sees bats flying.
- When they get to Uncle Gil's house, Lela thinks she hear a rattlesnake.

Pages 14–16
- Uncle Gil uses a stick with a big hook to catch the snake.
- Uncle Gil says it is a gopher snake and is not dangerous.
- Lela is safe in her bed. She says she likes the desert.

❓ QUESTIONS:
pages 10–16
- Does Lela really hear a rattlesnake? (*no*)
- What does Uncle Gil use to catch the snake? (*a long stick with a hook*)

(Focus Skill) Elements of Nonfiction: Text Structure

RETEACH Review with students the sequential organization of nonfiction text. Then ask students to display the timelines they created after reading "Saguaro Cactus."

FLUENCY PRACTICE Have students choose an illustration to retell part of "Desert Night." Encourage them to use as many vocabulary words and concept words as possible.

Independent Writing: Report

PRETEACH Tell students that they are going to begin to write a report about a desert animal. Have students look back at the selections they read in this lesson to find a topic for their report. Write students' ideas on the board and have each student choose one animal. Then work with students to research their topics. Encourage them to use several sources to find at least three interesting facts about the animal they chose. Help students write interesting, attention-grabbing introductory sentences. Then have them write about the information they found to support their introductions.

Grammar: Present Tense Verbs

PRETEACH Discuss the following with students:

- The **tense** of a verb shows the time of the action.
- A **present tense verb** shows action that is happening now.
- Add -*s* or -*es* to most present-tense verbs when the subject of the sentence is *he, she, it*, or a singular noun.
- Do not add -*s* or -*es* to a present-tense verb when the subject is *I, you, we*, or *they* or when it is plural.

Write the following sentences on the board:

1. The saguaro cactus lives in the desert. (*lives*)
2. Many animals use the saguaro for food and shelter. (*use*)
3. Birds, bats, and insects drink nectar from the saguaro flowers. (*drink*)
4. A gila woodpecker drills a hole with its beak. (*drills*)
5. The baby woodpeckers live in the nest. (*live*)

Read aloud each sentence. Work with students to identify the present-tense verb in each one.

FLUENCY PRACTICE Have volunteers read aloud the draft of the report they wrote on a desert animal.

Independent Writing: Report

RETEACH Have students reread the drafts they wrote on page 137. Ask them what they would like to change about it and why. Ask: **Is your introduction interesting? Will it grab the reader's attention? Do your facts support the introduction?** Discuss students' suggestions for changing or adding to their reports. Work with students to revise their reports. Have students check their work for errors in grammar and spelling, including the use of present-tense verbs. Then have students copy the revised essay into their Language Journals.

Grammar-Writing Connection

RETEACH Review with students present-tense verbs. Then write the following sentence frames on the board.

1. Lela and Aunt Doli _____ the bus to the desert. [ride/rides]
2. Aunt Doli _____ her camera. [take/takes]
3. She _____ to take pictures of desert animals. [plan/plans]
4. Lela _____ what it will be like in the desert. [wonder/wonders]
5. She _____ out the window and _____ for some animals. [stare/stares; watch/watches]
6. Lela and Aunt Doli _____ Uncle Gil at the bus station. [meet/meets]
7. Uncle Gil _____ a variety of snakes and lizards in his office. [keep/keeps]

(1. ride; 2. takes; 3. plans; 4. wonders; 5. stares, watches; 6. meet; 7. keeps)

Have students read the frames aloud. Then have them choose the correct verb tense and write it in the blank. Have the group read each completed sentence aloud. Remind students to pay close attention to the subject in each sentence to decide whether to add -s or -es to the verbs. Monitor students' work as they complete the sentences.

FLUENCY PRACTICE Have volunteers read their revised reports aloud to the class. Encourage listeners to ask questions about the report and have the author answer them.

Name _____

Draw a picture of an adventure you might have in the desert. Write a few sentences to tell about your picture.

_____
_____
_____
_____
_____

TO THE TEACHER Read aloud the directions with students. Encourage students to make their drawings and sentences as interesting and exciting as possible.

Saguaro Cactus/Desert Night • **Lesson 23** **139**

BEFORE

Building Background and Vocabulary

Build Background/Access Prior Knowledge

Display a world map or a map of the United States. Ask students to share their travel experiences, pointing out on the map places they have been. Record students' responses in a web like this one.

California — Texas

Places We Have Been

New Mexico — Florida

Selection Vocabulary

PRETEACH Display Teaching Transparency 225 and read the words aloud. Then point to the pictures as you read the following sentences:

1. Kent **sulkily** looked at the unfamiliar dish his mother had prepared.
2. "Try it. You'll like it," Kent's mother said with **certainty**.
3. Kent's lip **protruded** as he pouted.
4. Kent's mother was **indifferent**. She was used to Kent's moods.
5. Kent thought, "This is **undoubtedly** going to taste awful."
6. Kent was sure he would **loathe** this new dish.
7. Kent's mother was right—Kent liked the food and ate it **heartily**.

AFTER

Building Background and Vocabulary

Selection Vocabulary

RETEACH Revisit Teaching Transparency 225. Have students work in pairs to discuss the meanings of the words and to answer questions such as: *If something is said with* **certainty** *are you sure or unsure about it? When you do something* **heartily**, *do you do it with enthusiasm or caution?*

Write the following sentence frames on the board. Read each frame and ask students to choose a vocabulary word to complete it.

1. Elise felt _____ because she did not care who won the game. (*indifferent*)
2. The traveler nodded with _____ because she was sure she had made a reservation. (*certainty*)
3. Dan walked away _____ when he heard the bad news. (*sulkily*)
4. Some people _____ airports because of the crowds. (*loathe*)
5. The children laughed _____ at the joke. (*heartily*)
6. A bump _____ from Alex's head where he had hit it. (*protruded*)
7. The sun is shining and it will _____ be a good day. (*undoubtedly*)

Have students write these words in their Language Dictionaries.

FLUENCY PRACTICE Have students read the sentence frames aloud. Encourage them to describe the illustrations on Teaching Transparency 225 by using the vocabulary words and other words they know.

Build Background: "Blue Willow"

Have students look at the picture on *Pupil Edition* pages 570 and 571. Tell students that this story takes place in the 1940s. The girl in the picture is Janey. Explain that Janey's father is a migrant worker and the family has to travel a lot to find work.

LEAD THE WAY

 Author's Purpose

PRETEACH Tell students that authors have purposes, or reasons, for writing. An author may want to entertain, inform, or persuade. Explain to students that an author's perspective is the way he or she feels about a topic. Tell students that they can use details from the story to determine the author's perspective.

Have students determine the author's purpose for writing "Blue Willow." Then have them look for details as they read to determine the author's perspective.

Directed Reading: "Blue Willow"

RETEACH Use these sentences to walk students through the story.

- Janey and her father are driving to the cotton fields. Janey will be going to a camp school.
- A camp school is for the children of migrant workers.
- The migrant workers pick cotton.

- Does Janey go to school? (*yes*)
- What does Janey's dad do for a living? (*picks cotton*)
- What is a camp school? (*a school for the children of migrant workers*)

- Janey is waiting for school to open.
- She finds a small horned toad in the dust.
- Janey shows her teacher the horned toad.

- The teacher's name is Miss Peterson.
- They name the horned toad Fafnir.
- Janey thinks Miss Peterson is the most wonderful teacher in the world.
- This is a plate that once belonged to Janey's grandmother. It is a blue willow plate.

- Does Janey catch a turtle? (*no*)
- What is the teacher's name? (*Miss Peterson*)
- Where does the story title come from? (*the blue willow plate*)

FLUENCY PRACTICE Ask a volunteer to read aloud a paragraph from *Pupil Edition* pages 580–581. Encourage students to describe the illustration on *Pupil Edition* page 576.

BEFORE

Making
Connections
pages 586–587

Build Background: "Time Keepers"

PRETEACH Tell students that in "Time Keepers" they will read about ways to tell time.

Write the Concept Words on the board and use them in these sentences:

English-
Language
Learners
Book

Concept Words
year
day
moon
sun
night
stars

- Last **year** Commander Zapata traveled through space.
- One **day** he got in his rocket and blasted off.
- He gazed at the **moon** as he flew by it.
- Before long the **sun** looked like just a tiny speck in the distance.
- In space it always looked like **night** because it was so dark.
- Commander Zapata was amazed by all the **stars** twinkling in the darkness.

Have students add these words to their Language Dictionaries.

AFTER

Skill Review
pages 588–589

Directed Reading: "Time Keepers"

Summary *Throughout history, people have found many ways to tell time, from using the sun, moon, and stars to using clocks.*

Use these sentences to walk students through the story.

Pages 2–5
- People long ago watched the sun, stars, and moon to mark time.
- The phases of the moon mark one month.
- The ancient Egyptians used the cycles of the sun to measure time.

Pages 6–9
- The longest night is in December. The longest day occurs in June.
- The length of a shadow on a sundial can be used to tell time.
- This is one of the first mechanical clocks. It was put in a tower.

 QUESTIONS:
pages 2–9
- What did the ancient Egyptians use to tell time? (*the sun*)
- In what month is the longest day of the year? (June)

Pages 10–16
- These are two types of watches—a pocket watch and a wristwatch.
- This map shows the four time zones in the United States.
- This is a compass rose. It shows the directions north, south, east, and west on maps.
- You can use a timer to find out exactly how long something takes.
- A telescope is used to see objects in space.

 QUESTIONS:
pages 10–16
- What is a compass rose used for? (*showing north, south, east, and west*)
- What might you use a timer for? (*Responses will vary.*)

(Focus Skill) Author's Purpose

RETEACH Ask students to revisit "Time Keepers" to determine the author's purpose.

FLUENCY PRACTICE Have students use the illustration on pages 4 and 5 to retell part of "Time Keepers." Encourage them to use as many concept words as possible.

Independent Writing: Informative Paragraph

PRETEACH Tell students that they are going to write a paragraph on travel tips. Brainstorm with students the steps that they might follow to take a trip.

Help students organize their ideas according to what they would do to plan their trip, where they would go and when, and what they would pack. Encourage students to use sequence words as they write to keep their ideas in a logical sequence.

Grammar: Past and Future Tenses

PRETEACH Discuss the following with students:

- A verb in the **past tense** shows that the action happened in the past.
- Add *-ed* to regular verbs to form the **past tense**.
- A verb in the **future tense** shows that the action will happen in the future.
- To form the **future tense** of a verb, use the helping verb *will* with the main verb.

Write the following sentences on the board and read them aloud with students. Identify the past tense verbs and the future tense verbs. Point out that -ed is added to regular verbs to form the past tense.

1. Vincent glanced at the clock. (*past tense verb: glanced*)
2. He looked unhappy. (*past tense verb: looked*)
3. He remarked, "I will be late for my soccer practice." (*past: remarked; future: will be*)
4. Vincent hurried out the door. (*past: hurried*)
5. "Next time I will leave earlier," he sighed. (*past: sighed; future: will leave*)

FLUENCY PRACTICE Have volunteers read aloud the travel paragraphs they wrote.

Independent Writing: Informative Paragraph

RETEACH Have students reread the paragraphs they wrote on page 143. Ask them what they would like to change about them and why. Discuss students' suggestions for changing or adding to their work. Have them write the revised paragraphs in their Language Journals.

Grammar-Writing Connection

RETEACH Review with students past and future verb tenses. Then write the following sentence frames and bracketed verbs on the board.

1. Yesterday Gina _____ for her watch. [search]
2. She _____ everywhere for it. [look]
3. She _____ if she _____ it at school. [wonder; drop]
4. Gina _____ in the lost and found box. [check]
5. Gina _____, "What _____ to my watch?" [ask; happen]
6. Then she _____ into her pocket and _____ her watch. [reach; discover]
7. Gina _____, "Next time I _____ in my pockets first!" [laugh; look]
8. Gina's mother said, "If you lose your watch again, I _____ you if you are wearing clothes with pockets." [ask]

Have students come to the board and fill in the blanks with the regular past-tense or future-tense forms of the bracketed verbs. Remind students to pay close attention to when the action is happening to determine the tense. Monitor students' work as they complete the sentences.

FLUENCY PRACTICE Encourage students to explain how they formed the tenses of the verbs in the Grammar-Writing Connection.

Name _____

Choose a place that you would like to visit or live in. Draw the front page of a travel brochure about that place. Write a few sentences about the place you chose.

_____

_____

_____

_____

© Harcourt

TO THE TEACHER Encourage students to share their pictures and sentences with the class.

Blue Willow/Time Keepers • **Lesson 24** **145**

Build Background/Access Prior Knowledge

Display pages 12–13 of "Party." Tell students that people have parties for many different reasons. Ask students to share what they know about parties. Ask: **What do you know about having a party?** Record students' responses in a web.

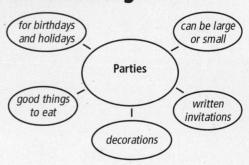

Selection Vocabulary

PRETEACH Display Teaching Transparency 233, and read the words aloud. Then point to the pictures as you read the following sentences:

1. Ms. Vasquez wants to season the meat with a **chile**. Her family loves the hot flavor of these peppers.
2. The **barbecue** is hot. Ms. Vasquez puts on the meat to cook it.
3. Ms. Vasquez cooks the meat over charcoal made from **mesquite** trees.
4. Aunt Trudi is playing an **accordion**. Many people like the music.
5. Jackson can decorate the table with **confetti**. When the party is over, he will have to clean up these tiny pieces of paper.
6. These people celebrate birthdays as part of their **culture**. Birthday parties are one of their customs.

Selection Vocabulary

RETEACH Revisit Teaching Transparency 233. Read the words with students. Have students discuss the meanings of the words and answer questions such as this: Is *mesquite* a type of tree or a flower?

Write the following sentence frames on the board. Read each sentence frame aloud, and ask students to choose a vocabulary word to complete it.

1. Shaniqua cut tiny pieces of paper to use as _____. (*confetti*)
2. Mr. Henderson chopped down the _____ tree. (*mesquite*)
3. In our _____, we have special dances for holidays. (*culture*)
4. We could smell the meat as it cooked on the _____. (*barbecue*)
5. Phillip could not believe how hot the _____ peppers were. (*chile*)
6. Margarite took music lessons to learn how to play the _____. (*accordion*)

Have students write these words in their Language Dictionaries.

FLUENCY PRACTICE Have students read the sentence frames aloud. Tell them to describe the illustrations on Teaching Transparency 233, using the vocabulary words and any other words they know.

Build Background: "In My Family"

Have students look at the picture on *Pupil Edition* page 598. Tell students that the people in this picture are at a birthday party. Have students predict what kind of food will be served at the party.

LEAD
THE
WAY

Sequence

PRETEACH Tell students that events in a story follow a sequence, or order, that makes sense. Explain that signal words, such as *first, next, then,* and *finally* help identify the sequence of events.

On the board, draw a flowchart like this one to explain the concept. Then have students copy the flowchart into their notebooks, and help them fill it in with information from the selection.

First
The author tells the story about horned toads.

⬇

Next
The author tells the story about her grandfather cleaning nopalitos.

⬇

| **Then** |

⬇

| **Finally** |

Directed Reading: "In My Family"

RETEACH Use these sentences to walk students through the story.

Pages 592–595
- This is the author, Carmen Lomas Garza, and her family.
- This is Carmen and her brother, Arturo. Arturo is trying to feed a fire ant to a horned toad. A horned toad is a type of lizard.

Pages 596–597
- Carmen's grandfather and her sister Margie are on the porch. Grandfather is taking the thorns off a cactus pad. The cactus pads are cooked and eaten.
- Carmen's aunt and uncle are making turnovers called empanadas.
- Carmen is wearing a blue dress. Point to Carmen.

**QUESTIONS:
pages 592–597**
- Is Carmen the author of this story? (*yes*)
- What kind of lizard does Arturo try to feed? (*horned toad*)

Pages 598–599
- This is a birthday party for Carmen's sister, Mary Jane. The family is having a barbecue to celebrate Mary Jane's birthday.
- Carmen's father is cooking at the barbecue. Point to Carmen's father.
- Carmen's grandfather is shoveling in the coals and mesquite wood.
- The family is sitting at a table. Everyone is decorating eggshells for Easter. The eggshells are filled with confetti. Confetti is little pieces of paper.

Page 600
- On Saturday nights, everyone in the neighborhood goes to a restaurant to dance. The band is playing music.

**QUESTIONS:
pages 598–600**
- Does Carmen's mother cook food at the barbecue? (*no*)
- Why is the family having a barbecue? (*to celebrate Mary Jane's birthday*)

FLUENCY PRACTICE Ask volunteers to read aloud a paragraph from their favorite page in the story. Encourage students to describe the illustrations on *Pupil Edition* pages 596–597, using as many vocabulary words as they can.

Build Background: "Party"

PRETEACH Remind students that "In My Family" is about an author who recalls events from her childhood, including parties. In "Party" they will read about how to plan and have a party. Ask: **What kind of party would you like to have? What activities would you have at the party?**

Use the concept words in sentences to illustrate their meanings.

Concept Words
need
eat
want
can
will
use

- Jeremy said, "I **need** to plan before I have my party."
- Mother asked, "What kinds of food would you like to **eat** at the party?"
- "I **want** hamburgers," Jeremy responded.
- "We **can** cook them outside on the barbecue," Mother said.
- "Let's **use** the mesquite charcoal," added Mother.
- Jeremy smiled and said, "I hope it **will** be a great party."

Have students add these words to their Language Dictionaries.

Directed Reading: "Party"

Summary *There are many kinds of parties. There are different things that need to be done. You learn how to make the invitations, plan the food, and plan the entertainment.*

Use these sentences to walk students through the story.

Pages 2–5
- These people are having a street party.
- Parties have people, food, and entertainment.
- This girl is making a list of people to invite to her party.

Pages 6–9
- Some people use the telephone to invite people to their party.
- The girl is making invitations.
- This is a copy of an invitation. RSVP means "Please reply."
- The girl is mailing the invitations to her party.

QUESTIONS: pages 2–9
- Can you use the telephone to invite people to a party? (*yes*)
- What goes on a party invitation? (*information about the party*)

Pages 10–13
- Planning a party includes knowing what kind of food to have.
- Children like to play games at a party.
- The girl and her brother are decorating for the girl's party.

Pages 14–16
- The children are eating pizza and drinking soda. They are having fun at the party.
- The girl and boy are saying good-bye to the guests.
- The last part of giving a party is cleaning up.

QUESTIONS: pages 10–16
- Did the girl mail her invitations? (*yes*)
- What is the last part of giving a party? (*cleaning up*)

Focus Skill Sequence

RETEACH Review sequence with students. Then draw on the board a flowchart with the headings *First, Next, Then,* and *Finally*. Ask students to revisit the story to complete the chart.

FLUENCY PRACTICE Have students choose their favorite illustration to retell part of "Party." Encourage them to use as many vocabulary words and concept words as possible.

Independent Writing: Expository Writing

PRETEACH Tell students that they are going to write an essay that tells the steps in a process. Generate a flowchart with the title *How to Plan a Party*. Then brainstorm with students the steps needed to plan a party.

Have students write their drafts independently, using the information in the flowchart. Tell students to elaborate on each step by explaining the step or providing details or examples.

```
How to Plan a Party
        │
      First
        │
      Next
        │
      Then
        │
     Finally
```

Grammar: Irregular Verbs

PRETEACH Discuss the definition of irregular verbs with students. Point out the following:

- An **irregular verb** does not end in *-ed* in the past tense.
- Some irregular verbs show a past tense by using a different form of the main verb with the helping verb *have*, *has*, or *had*.

Write the following sentences on the board:

1. My grandparents came over to my house. (*irregular verb: came*)
2. They brought some empanadas. (*irregular verb: brought*)
3. I have eaten empanadas. (*irregular verb: eaten; helping verb: have*)
4. We drank milk with the empanadas. (*irregular verb: drank*)
5. It was a very good snack. (*irregular verb: was*)

Read aloud each sentence. Circle the irregular verbs in each sentence. Underline the helping verb in sentence 3. Remind students that irregular verbs do not end with *-ed*.

FLUENCY PRACTICE Have volunteers read aloud the essays they completed in the writing activity.

Independent Writing: Expository Writing

RETEACH Have students revisit their essays from Preteach. Ask them what they would like to change about their essays and why. Discuss students' ideas for changing or adding to their essays. Then have students revise their essays and copy them into their Language Journals. Finally, have students publish their essays by presenting them to the class.

Grammar-Writing Connection

RETEACH Review with students the definition of irregular verb. Then write the following sentences on the board.

1. Quentin wrote five invitations for his party. (*irregular verb: wrote*)
2. He drew a picture on the front of each invitation. (*irregular verb: drew*)
3. He put the invitations in the envelopes. (*irregular verb: put*)
4. He took the invitations outside and stood by the mailbox. (*irregular verbs: took, stood*)
5. Soon he saw the mail carrier as she drove down his street. (*irregular verbs: saw, drove*)
6. He gave the invitations to the mail carrier. (*irregular verb: gave*)
7. Then he went back inside the house. (*irregular verb: went*)
8. He said to his mom, "I have given the invitations to the mail carrier." (*irregular verb: said, given; helping verb: have*)

Have students copy the sentences into their notebooks, circling the irregular verbs and underlining the helping verbs. Remind students that irregular verbs do not end with -*ed*. Point out that a sentence might have more than one irregular verb. Monitor students' work as they write the sentences.

FLUENCY PRACTICE Have students choose a page from "Party" to read aloud.

Name _____

Draw a picture in each box that shows steps that would have to be completed to have a party. Write a sentence to describe each step.

Step 1

_____

Step 2

_____

Step 3

_____

Step 4

_____

© Harcourt

TO THE TEACHER Have students pick four things that would have to be completed to have a party. Have students write a sentence to describe each step. Ask students to share their pictures and sentences with the class.

Use with "The Gold Rush"

BEFORE
Building Background and Vocabulary

Build Background/Access Prior Knowledge

Have students look at the picture on *Pupil Edition* pages 614–615. Tell students that this man is looking for gold. Ask students to share what they know about gold. Ask: **What does gold look like? What is it used for?** Record students' responses in a concept web like the one shown here.

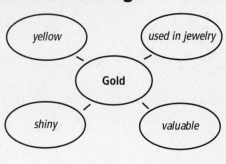

Selection Vocabulary

PRETEACH Display Teaching Transparency 243, and read the words aloud. Then point to the pictures as you read the following sentences:

1. City life **beckons** to the man. The noise and excitement attract him.
2. People **abandoned** their homes. They left them behind.
3. The road was **rugged.** It had a rough surface.
4. People pay **fares** to ride the train. It costs money to take the train.
5. The settlers who moved west were a **multicultural** group of people. They came from many different countries and backgrounds.
6. The man's job is very **profitable**. He makes a lot of money.

AFTER
Building Background and Vocabulary

Selection Vocabulary

RETEACH Revisit Teaching Transparency 243. Have students answer questions such as: Does *rugged* mean "rough" or "smooth"?

Write the following sentence frames on the board. Read each sentence and ask students to choose a vocabulary word to complete it.

1. The _____ land was rough and uneven. (*rugged*)
2. Grandma and Grandpa paid their _____ to ride the bus. (*fares*)
3. The _____ group in Ben's class talked about their different customs. (*multicultural*)
4. A business that makes a lot of money is _____. (*profitable*)
5. Settlers _____ one town and moved to the next. (*abandoned*)
6. The smell of cookies _____ us to the kitchen. (*beckons*)

Have students write these words in their Language Dictionaries.

> **FLUENCY PRACTICE** Have students read the completed sentences aloud. Encourage them to describe the illustrations on Teaching Transparency 243 by using the vocabulary words and any other words they know.

Build Background: "The Gold Rush"

Revisit the picture on *Pupil Edition* pages 614–615. Tell students that this man is a prospector. His job is to look for gold. Discuss with students why people would want to look for gold.

LEAD
THE
WAY

★ Focus Skill Fact and Opinion

PRETEACH Tell students that a fact is a statement that can be proved. An opinion is a statement that tells what someone thinks, feels, or believes. It cannot be proved. Explain to students that looking for signal words such as *should* and *I think* will help them identify opinions.

On the board, draw a two-column chart with the headings *Fact* and *Opinion*. Work with students to fill in each column with examples of facts and opinions from the selection.

Directed Reading: "The Gold Rush"

RETEACH Use these sentences to walk students through the story.

Pages 614–617

- This man is a gold prospector. Prospectors are people who look for gold.
- The first gold rush in North America took place in California.
- The man in the photograph is James Marshall. He was the first settler to find gold.

Pages 618–619

- Another gold rush was the Klondike gold rush. This man is a miner in the Klondike.
- People traveled to the gold rush by land and by sea. This map shows the routes that they used.

Pages 620–623

- People also traveled west in covered wagons.
- This woman is a prospector. She is staking a claim. This tells other miners that any gold found in the area belongs to her.
- Prospectors use pans to separate gold from dirt.

QUESTIONS:
pages 614–623

- Is a prospector someone who looks for gold? (*yes*)
- Who was the first settler to find gold? (*James Marshall*)

Pages 624–627

- These are the tools the prospectors used. Point to the pan.
- Hydraulic mining, or mining that uses water, is another way to find gold.

Pages 628–632

- A boomtown is a small town that grows quickly into a large city.
- Look at this home. People who found a lot of gold built homes like this one.
- This city is San Francisco. It started as a boomtown. Now it is a large city.

QUESTIONS:
pages 624–632

- Were prospectors looking for silver? (*no*)
- What is an example of a boomtown? (*San Francisco*)

FLUENCY PRACTICE Ask students to choose a section of "The Gold Rush" to read aloud.

Build Background: "What Should I Be?"

PRETEACH Remind students that "The Gold Rush" is about prospectors, people whose job it was to look for gold. In "What Should I Be?" they will read about other kinds of jobs. Discuss with students jobs they would like to have when they grow up.

English-
Language
Learners
Book

Concept Words
report
work
ideas
dinner
food
song

Use the concept words in sentences that illustrate their meanings.
- Nadia had to write a **report** about different kinds of jobs.
- She found books in the library to help her with the **work**.
- She wrote down several **ideas** from the books.
- Then she helped her mother prepare **dinner**.
- Everyone enjoyed the **food** they prepared.
- After dinner, Nadia's mother played the piano and they all sang a **song**.

Have students add these words to their Language Dictionaries.

Directed Reading: "What Should I Be?"

 Summary *The boy telling the story imagines what kind of job he will have when he grows up. He sees himself doing many different jobs.*

Use these sentences to walk students through the story.

Pages 2–5
- This is Mr. Moore. He is the teacher.
- Mr. Moore asks students to think about careers they would like to have. He writes their ideas on the board.
- The boy is imagining being an astronaut. Astronauts travel into space.

Pages 6–9
- Now the boy is imagining that he is a chef. Chefs prepare food.
- Next, the boy imagines that he is a doctor. A doctor helps sick and injured people.

QUESTIONS: pages 2–9
- Does the boy imagine being an astronaut? (*yes*)
- What other careers does the boy think about? (*chef; doctor*)

Pages 10–13
- The boy thinks about becoming a firefighter. What do firefighters do?
- The boy thinks about becoming a sound engineer. A sound engineer knows how to make a song sound better.

Pages 14–16
- The boy thinks about becoming a teacher. Teachers help students learn.
- There are so many careers to choose from that the boy is not sure what to write his report about.

QUESTIONS: pages 10–16
- Does the boy think about becoming a teacher? (*yes*)
- What do sound engineers do? (*They make music sound better.*)

 Focus Skill # Fact and Opinion

RETEACH Review fact and opinion with students. Then draw on the board a Fact and Opinion chart like the one you created for "The Gold Rush." Ask students to revisit "What Should I Be?" to complete the chart.

FLUENCY PRACTICE Have students choose a career that is discussed in "What Should I Be?" and read that section aloud.

Independent Writing: Descriptive Paragraph

PRETEACH Tell students that they are going to write a descriptive paragraph about their classroom. Brainstorm with students a list of vivid words to describe the classroom. Help them choose words that appeal to the senses. You may want to organize their responses into a chart like the one shown here. Have students write the draft independently, using the information in the chart to help them.

My Classroom		
Smells	**Sights**	**Sounds**
chalk	colorful bulletin boards	teacher's voice

Grammar: Contractions and Negatives

PRETEACH Discuss with students the definition of contractions and negatives. Point out the following:

- A *contraction* is a short way to write two words. One of the words is always a verb. An *apostrophe* (') takes the place of one or more letters.
- A word that has *no* in its meaning is called a *negative*. The words *never*, *no*, *nobody*, *none*, *not*, *nothing*, and *nowhere* are negatives.
- Do not use two negatives in a sentence.
- Do not confuse a possessive adjective such as *its* with a contraction such as *it's*.

Write the following sentences on the board:

1. He'd like a new bike.
2. I'll go to the store.
3. I do not want to miss the bus.

Read aloud each sentence. Circle the contractions in the first and second sentences. Ask volunteers to tell what words make up each contraction. Then call students' attention to the negative word *not* in sentence 3. Have students write *do not* as a contraction.

FLUENCY PRACTICE Have students read aloud their descriptive paragraphs.

Independent Writing: Descriptive Paragraph

RETEACH Have students return to the paragraphs they drafted during Preteach. Ask what they would like to change about their paragraphs and why. Help them identify places where they could add descriptive language. Work with students to revise their paragraphs. Remind them to check their spelling and punctuation. Then have students copy their revised paragraphs into their Language Journals.

Grammar-Writing Connection

RETEACH Review contractions and negatives with students. Then write on the board the following sentences.

- I never have no money.
- I'm not going to eat no spinach.
- I can't never get up early.

Read each sentence aloud. Ask students to identify the double negative in each sentence. Work with them to rewrite each sentence correctly. Then write these word pairs on the board: *I will*, *do not*, *I would*, and *would not*. Ask students to write each pair of words as a contraction. Have them use each contraction in a sentence. Check students' writing and point out any corrections they need to make.

FLUENCY PRACTICE Have students read aloud their descriptive paragraphs.

Imagine that you are a prospector during the gold rush. Draw a picture of yourself prospecting. Then write a short diary entry telling what happened on a particular day.

_____

_____

_____

_____

_____

_____

TO THE TEACHER Have students draw a picture of themselves looking for gold. You may want to model writing a diary entry: *Today I dug for gold. I dug for hours. However, I didn't find any gold.* Invite students to share their pictures and diary entries with the class.

BEFORE

Building
Background
and Vocabulary

Build Background/Access Prior Knowledge

Write the word *wilderness* on the board. Explain to students that there are no towns in the wilderness, only a lot of trees and wildlife. Tell students that many years ago in the United States people traveled West to the

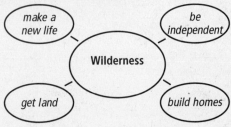

wilderness to live. Ask students why they think people traveled there. Record their responses in a web like the one shown.

Selection Vocabulary

PRETEACH Display Teaching Transparency 253 and point to the pictures as you read the following sentences:

1. This **pioneer** family settled in the West.
2. The farmer dreams of the **possibilities** of a good crop.
3. The farmer knows the corn would grow well in the **fertile** soil.
4. The woman is picking grapes from the **arbor**.
5. The birds sing lovely sounds in **harmony**.

AFTER

Building
Background
and Vocabulary

Selection Vocabulary

RETEACH Revisit Teaching Transparency 253. Have students work in pairs to answer questions such as: *If soil is **fertile**, is it good for growing crops or poor for growing crops? Is a **pioneer** a person who settles an area or a person who has always lived in that area?*

Write the following sentence frames on the board. Read each frame aloud and ask students to choose a vocabulary word to complete it.

1. The twins sang their favorite song in _____. (*harmony*)
2. Jimmy built the _____ to grow tomato plants in his garden. (*arbor*)
3. The _____ soil was good for growing crops. (*fertile*)
4. There are many _____ if you like to try new things. (*possibilities*)
5. Life was not easy for the _____ families who settled the West. (*pioneer*)

Have students write these words in their Language Dictionaries.

> **FLUENCY PRACTICE** Have students read the completed sentence frames aloud. Encourage them to describe the illustrations on Teaching Transparency 253 by using the vocabulary words and other words they know.

Build Background: "I Have Heard of a Land"

Have students look at the picture on *Pupil Edition* pages
642–643. Tell students that these people are pioneers. Explain
that pioneers were people who settled the western part of the
United States.

LEAD
THE
WAY

 Word Relationships

PRETEACH Tell students that when they read an unfamiliar word,
they can use context, or the words around that word, to figure out its
meaning. Explain that knowing how words are related can help unlock
meaning.

Discuss with students the following:

How Words Are Related	Examples
Synonyms are words that have similar meanings.	They <u>lift</u> the logs. They <u>hoist</u> the logs.
Antonyms are words that have opposite meanings.	I <u>catch</u> the ball. I <u>throw</u> the ball.
Homophones are words that sound the same but have different meanings and spellings.	There is <u>no</u> need for an umbrella. I <u>know</u> it won't rain.
Homographs are words that are spelled the same but have different meanings and pronunciations.	The pioneer family <u>lives</u> in the wilderness. The pioneers had difficult <u>lives</u>.
Multiple-meaning words are words that have more than one meaning.	The pioneer <u>plants</u> her crops. There are many <u>plants</u> in the field.

Directed Reading: "I Have Heard of a Land"

RETEACH Use these sentences to walk students through the story.

Pages 640–645

- This story is a poem. The poet tells about the land out west.
- The pioneer family travels across the country in a covered wagon.
- This woman hammers a post into the ground to show that the land is hers.

Pages 646–649

- The pioneer family built this home.
- It is cold outside. The family is eating flapjacks, or pancakes.

 QUESTIONS:
pages 640–649

- Does the pioneer family build their own home? (*yes*)
- How does the woman claim her land? (*She hammers a post into the ground.*)

Pages 650–655

- The woman walks across the snow-covered ground.
- It is springtime. The girl is on a homemade swing.
- The pioneer woman sleeps on the floor of her home.

Pages 656–661

- The neighbors work together to build a log cabin.
- This pioneer woman lives in the log cabin. She writes about her life in her journal.
- The pioneer family is standing outside the log cabin.

QUESTIONS:
pages 650–661

- Does the woman sleep on the floor of her home? (*yes*)
- Who helps build the log cabin? (*the neighbors*)

FLUENCY PRACTICE Encourage students to describe the illustration on *Pupil
Edition* pages 646–647 and read the text aloud.

Build Background: "Wagon Wheels"

PRETEACH Remind students that "I Have Heard of a Land" is about a pioneer woman and her family. Tell students that they will read more about pioneers in "Wagon Wheels." Ask: **What would you like most about being a pioneer? What would you like least about being a pioneer?**

English-
Language
Learners
Book

Write the concept words on the board. Use the words in these sentences.

Concept Words
walked
picked
rolled
crossed
stopped
saved

- The children **walked** onto the field.
- Antonio **picked** up the ball.
- He **rolled** the ball toward Michelle.
- The ball **crossed** in front of Michelle.
- Edgar **stopped** the ball before it went down the hill.
- Edgar **saved** the ball from going into the stream.

Have students add these words to their Language Dictionaries.

AFTER

Skill Review
pages 666–667

Directed Reading: "Wagon Wheels"

Summary *The Clark family and Emily Walker travel to a new settlement in the West. Emily is reunited with her family and adjusts to her new life.*

Use these sentences to walk students through the story.

Pages 2–5
- The pioneers traveled across America in covered wagons.
- Emily's parents moved West two years ago. Now she will join them.
- The pioneers arrive at the settlement.

Pages 6–9
- Emily arrives at her parents' cabin.
- Emily greets her mother and meets her new brother, William.

**QUESTIONS:
pages 2–9**
- Does Emily travel across the prairie with her parents? (*no*)
- How long has it been since Emily has seen her family? (*two years*)

Pages 10–13
- Emily's father and her brother John arrive.
- Emily and Hope search for food, feed the chickens, and look for eggs.
- The men plow the field. They use rocks to build walls.
- They try to catch fish in the river.

Pages 14–16
- The families eat their biggest meal at noon.
- There was so much work to do all day long.

**QUESTIONS:
pages 10–16**
- Do the men make walls from rocks in the field? (*yes*)
- When do the families eat the biggest meal? (*noon*)

 Word Relationships

RETEACH Review word relationships with students. Then ask students to reread "Wagon Wheels" and look for synonyms, antonyms, and multiple-meaning words.

FLUENCY PRACTICE Have students choose an illustration to retell part of "Wagon Wheels."

Independent Writing: Poem

PRETEACH Tell students that they are going to write an unrhymed poem. Explain that they should make their feelings clear in their poems and that the words they use should help the reader imagine what the poem is about. Then have students think of something they feel strongly about. Have them brainstorm vivid words to express their feelings. Guide students to introduce the topic of their poem and use the vivid words they brainstormed to write the poem. Tell students to conclude their poems with a strong image.

Grammar: Adverbs

PRETEACH Discuss the definition of adverbs with students. Point out the following:

- An **adverb** is a word that describes a verb.
- An adverb may tell *where*, *when*, or *how* an action happens.
- Adverbs that tell *how* often end with *-ly*.

Write the sentences below on the board. Read them aloud and identify the adverb in each one. Point out that sentences 1 and 5 have adverbs that tell *how*, sentences 2 and 4 have adverbs that tell *where*, and sentences 3 and 5 have adverbs that tell *when*.

1. The mules moved carefully across the prairie. (*carefully; tells how*)
2. They pulled the wagon up and down the hills. (*up, down; tell where*)
3. It was often difficult for pioneers to make the long trip. (*often; tells when*)
4. At night, the family slept inside the wagon or outside on the ground. (*inside, outside; tell where*)
5. The next morning, the family anxiously got an early start. (*anxiously; tells how; early; tells when*)

FLUENCY PRACTICE Have volunteers read aloud the poems they completed in the writing activity.

Independent Writing: Poem

RETEACH Have students reread the poems they wrote on page 161. Ask students what they would like to change about their poems and why. Discuss students' suggestions for changing or adding to their poems. Have students revise and rewrite the poems in their Language Journals. Encourage students to illustrate their poems.

Grammar-Writing Connection

RETEACH Review adverbs with students. Then write the sentences below on the board. Have students come to the board and identify the adverbs. Then ask the group whether the adverb tells where, when, or how.

1. Mother carefully lit the lantern. (*carefully; tells how*)
2. The light cast shadows on the inside of the cabin. (*inside; tells where*)
3. Mother quickly looked at the sleeping baby. (*quickly; tells how*)
4. Suddenly the baby started to cry softly. (*suddenly, tells when; softly, tells how*)
5. Mother gently rocked the cradle. (*gently; tells how*)
6. Then Mother began to knit. (*then; tells when*)
7. She worked quietly while the family slept. (*quietly; tells how*)
8. Later, she sleepily went to bed. (*later, tells when; sleepily, tells how*)

Have students look back at their poems to make sure they used adverbs correctly.

FLUENCY PRACTICE Have students read the sentences on the board aloud. Encourage them to explain how they determined whether the adverbs told where, when, or how.

Name _____

Use each of the following adverbs in a sentence.

Tells How	Tells When	Tells Where
quickly suddenly	today always	there outside

1. _____

   _____

2. _____

   _____

3. _____

   _____

4. _____

   _____

5. _____

   _____

6. _____

   _____

TO THE TEACHER Review the adverbs in the chart with students. You may want to model writing this sentence: *The boy finished his homework quickly.* Then invite students to share their sentences with classmates.

I Have Heard of a Land/Wagon Wheels • Lesson 27   **163**

BEFORE

Building
Background
and Vocabulary

Build Background/Access Prior Knowledge

If possible, take students outside. Point out the natural surroundings, such as the soil and trees. Explain that some people have jobs that use the land or other things in nature. Ask students to name jobs that use the land or things in nature. Record students' responses in a concept web like the one shown.

farmer — Living Off the Land — miner

rancher — logger

Selection Vocabulary

PRETEACH Display Teaching Transparency 262, and read the words aloud. Then point to the pictures as you read the following sentences:

1. Paul Bunyan is **softhearted**. He is kind and gentle.
2. Babe is ready for his **ration** of food. His daily portion is more than a regular ox would eat.
3. Babe is **bellowing** because he is hungry. He makes a loud, deep roaring sound to ask for his food.
4. The lumberjack uses **gadgets** to cut down the trees. The small machines make his job easier.
5. On this **fateful** day, Babe fell into a ditch. Babe hurt his leg in this accident.
6. Paul said, "Please fill in the ditch. We do not need another **tragedy**."

AFTER

Building
Background
and Vocabulary

Selection Vocabulary

RETEACH Revisit Teaching Transparency 262. Have students answer questions such as: If someone is softhearted, is that person *kind* or *mean*?

Write the following sentence frames on the board. Read each sentence aloud and ask students to choose a vocabulary word to complete it.

1. The child fed the horse its _____ of hay. (*ration*)
2. One _____ day a tornado destroyed the wheat crops. (*fateful*)
3. The _____ rancher picked up the crying calf. (*softhearted*)
4. The bad accident was a _____. (*tragedy*)
5. The animals were _____ for their food. (*bellowing*)
6. Our family uses a variety of kitchen _____, such as a can opener and a blender. (*gadgets*)

Have students write these words in their Language Dictionaries.

FLUENCY PRACTICE Have students read the sentence frames aloud. Encourage them to describe the illustrations on Teaching Transparency 262, using the vocabulary words and any other words they know.

BEFORE

Reading
"Paul Bunyan and
Babe the Blue Ox"
pages 670–683

Build Background: "Paul Bunyan and Babe the Blue Ox"

Have students look at the picture on *Pupil Edition* pages 670–671. Point out the giant man and the blue ox. Tell students that this story is a tall tale. Tall tales have unrealistic characters and events. Discuss with students the ways in which Babe is different from a real ox.

 Fact and Opinion

PRETEACH Tell students that a fact is a statement that can be proved. An opinion expresses what someone thinks or feels. It cannot be proved.

On the board, draw a chart like this one to explain the concept. As students read, have them look for words and phrases, such as *I think* and *I believe*, that signal opinions.

Facts	Opinions
"Paul Bunyan" is an American tall tale.	Paul Bunyan was the greatest logger of all time.

AFTER

Reading
"Paul Bunyan and
Babe the Blue Ox"

Pages 670–673

Pages 674–675

QUESTIONS:
pages 670–675

Pages 676–679

Pages 680–681

QUESTIONS:
pages 676–681

Directed Reading: "Paul Bunyan and Babe the Blue Ox"

RETEACH Use these sentences to walk students through the story.

- Paul Bunyan is a giant. He is a logger. His job is to cut down trees.
- This is Babe the Blue Ox. Babe is Paul Bunyan's pet. Paul rescued Babe from a frozen river.
- Babe grows so large that he does not fit in the barn anymore.

- Babe helps Paul Bunyan's crew.
- Was Paul Bunyan a logger? (*yes*)
- Who is Babe? (*the blue ox*)

- Paul is moving his logging camp to North Dakota.
- Paul ties the bunkhouses together, and Babe pulls them.
- Paul cuts down too many trees in the Dakotas. He feels very sad.
- Paul has some bad luck. His men are attacked by insects that are half mosquito, half bee. He also has an accident with some oxen.

- Paul and Babe are retired. When someone is retired, that person does not work anymore. They enjoy their life in the woods.

- Do Paul and Babe decide to retire? (*yes*)
- What attacks the loggers as they cut down trees? (*giant insects*)

FLUENCY PRACTICE Ask students to read aloud a paragraph from their favorite page in the story. Encourage students to describe their favorite illustration.

Build Background: "County Fair"

PRETEACH Remind students that "Paul Bunyan and Babe the Blue Ox" is about people who are loggers, or earn money by chopping down trees. Tell students that in "County Fair," they will read about ways that farmers and ranchers earn money and win prizes.

English-Language Learners Book

Concept Words
vegetables
fruits
food
jam
jelly
prize

Use the concept words in sentences that illustrate their meanings.

- Peas and green beans are **vegetables**.
- Apples and bananas are **fruits**.
- Celia decided to enter some homemade **food** in the county fair.
- She used fresh strawberries in her strawberry **jam**.
- Then she used grape juice to make grape **jelly**.
- Celia hoped to win first **prize** for one of her entries.

Have students add these words to their Language Dictionaries.

Directed Reading: "County Fair"

📖 **Summary** *A county fair is a fun way to spend a summer day. There are many things to see, and many things to do. People enjoy the games, rides, and contests.*

Use these sentences to walk students through the story.

Pages 2–5
- County fairs are fun and exciting.
- There are many contests at fairs. There are contests for foods, animals, crafts, and skills.
- This girl's goat has won a blue ribbon. This means it won first prize.

Pages 6–9
- Farmers try to grow the largest vegetables and fruits.
- These people are in a contest to see who can eat the most watermelon.
- In a tractor pull, farmers compete to see how much their tractors can pull.

❓ QUESTIONS: pages 2–9
- Is the county fair during the summer? (*yes*)
- Why do farmers bring fruits and vegetables to the fair? (*to win a prize*)

Pages 10–16
- This is a cowboy in a rodeo. People ride bulls and horses in rodeos.
- The midway is where the rides and games are. People ride roller coasters, carousels, and Ferris wheels.
- People play games to win prizes, such as stuffed animals, at the county fair.

❓ QUESTIONS: pages 10–16
- Are there games and rides at the fair? (*yes*)
- What are some things to do at a county fair? (*Responses will vary.*)

⭐(Focus Skill) Fact and Opinion

RETEACH Review fact and opinion with students. Ask students to write two facts and two opinions from "County Fair."

FLUENCY PRACTICE Have students use their favorite illustration to retell part of "County Fair."

Independent Writing: Persuasive Essay

PRETEACH Tell students that they are going to write a persuasive essay. Tell students that in a persuasive essay, the writer tries to convince an audience of his or her opinion on a particular topic. Draw on the board a concept web entitled

"Why We Should Save Trees." Then brainstorm with students reasons to save trees and write them in the surrounding ovals.

Have students write the draft independently, using the information in the web to help them.

Grammar: Comparing with Adverbs

PRETEACH Discuss comparing with adverbs with students. Point out the following:

- **Adverbs** can be used to compare two or more actions.
- To compare one action with another action, add *-er* to most short adverbs.
- To compare one action with two or more other actions, add *-est* to most short adverbs.
- Use *more* or *less*, or *most* or *least* before most adverbs of two or more syllables, such as *angrily* or *happily*.
- There are a few irregular adverbs, such as *good*, *better*, *best* and *badly*, *worse*, *worst*.

Write the following sentences on the board and read each one aloud. Circle the adverbs that compare. Point out that sentences 1, 2, and 5 have adverbs that compare two actions. Call students' attention to the use of *more* in sentences 2 and 5. Point out that sentences 3 and 4 have adverbs that compare more than two actions.

1. Some plants bloom sooner than others. (*sooner*)
2. The small plants grow more densely than the larger plants. (*more densely*)
3. This tree loses its leaves the fastest. (*fastest*)
4. These new seeds do best with plenty of water. (*best*)
5. The children worked more excitedly on their garden than on their homework. (*more excitedly*)

FLUENCY PRACTICE Have volunteers read aloud their persuasive essays.

Independent Writing: Persuasive Essay

RETEACH Have students return to the essays they drafted during Preteach. Point out that every reason they give should be supported with specific examples and details. Work with students to add specific examples and details to their writing. Point out places where they should add words. Help them identify and correct errors in spelling, punctuation, and grammar. Have students copy their revised essays into their Language Journals.

Grammar-Writing Connection

Review with students adverbs that compare. Then write the following sentences on the board. Have students copy the sentences in their notebooks, correcting the adverbs that compare. Remind students to pay close attention to the sentence to determine whether two or more actions are being compared. Monitor students' work as they complete the sentences.

1. This year the county fair started more early than last year. (*earlier*)
2. Some children prepared their animals carefullier than other children. (*more carefully*)
3. Patrick thought his pig looked most best of all. (*best*)
4. Jared's pony was fastest than Misty's donkey. (*faster*)
5. The rodeo cowboys worked hard of all. (*hardest*)

Then have students write two sentences comparing themselves to other members of the class. For example, students might write *I am taller than Joey. I am the tallest boy in the class.* Check students' work to make sure they correctly used the comparing forms of the adverbs.

FLUENCY PRACTICE Have students read aloud their revised essays.

In the boxes below, write three sentences that express facts and three sentences that express opinions. Then cut out the sentence strips, mix them up, and give them to a partner. Have your partner read the sentences and say which three are facts and which three are opinions.

Facts

(blank box)

(blank box)

(blank box)

Opinions

(blank box)

(blank box)

(blank box)

TO THE TEACHER Review the concept of fact and opinion with students. Then ask students to write three sentences that express a fact and three sentences that express an opinion. Have students write their sentences on a separate sheet of paper first. Monitor their writing to ensure they have understood the concept. Then ask them to copy their sentences into the appropriate boxes. Have students cut out their sentences and exchange them with a partner, who will identify them as facts or opinions.

Use with "Fly Traps! Plants that Bite Back"

Build Background/Access Prior Knowledge

Discuss with students what they know about plants. Ask: **What kinds of plants do you know about? What do you need to live and grow?** Record students' responses in a web like this.

sun   air

What Plants Need to Live and Grow

water   food

Selection Vocabulary

PRETEACH Display Teaching Transparency 271 and read the sentences aloud. Then point to the pictures as you read the following sentences:

1. This watery place is the **boggiest** part of the mountain.
2. We did not plan to look for the plants; we discovered them **accidentally**.
3. **Fertilizer** helps some plants to grow big.
4. **Carnivorous** plants eat animals such as bugs and insects.
5. Special **chemicals** in the plants turn parts of the bugs into a liquid.
6. Plants eat the soft, **dissolved** parts of the bugs.
7. With so many insects in the water, plants have a lot of **victims** to eat.

Selection Vocabulary

RETEACH Revisit Teaching Transparency 271. Have students work in pairs to discuss the meanings of the words and to answer questions such as: *If something is **carnivorous**, does it eat meat or plants? Is **fertilizer** food for plants or people?*

Write the following sentence frames on the board. Read each frame aloud and ask students to choose a vocabulary word to complete it. Write students' responses in the blanks.

1. Mr. Hawkins used different _____ for the science experiment. (*chemicals*)
2. We saw many plants as we walked through the _____ part of the mountain. (*boggiest*)
3. Ms. Jennings put _____ on her lawn to help her grass grow. (*fertilizer*)
4. Marta _____ forgot to water her plant, so it died. (*accidentally*)
5. The plant waited for its next _____ to land on it. (*victim*)
6. Some plants and animals are _____ and eat meat. (*carnivorous*)
7. Does sugar _____ faster in hot water or cold water? (*dissolve*)

Have students write these words in their Language Dictionaries.

FLUENCY PRACTICE Have students read the sentence frames aloud. Encourage them to describe the illustrations on Teaching Transparency 271 using the vocabulary words and any other words they know.

BEFORE

Reading
"Fly Traps! Plants
that Bite Back"
pages 692–707

Build Background: "Fly Traps! Plants that Bite Back"

Point out the picture on *Pupil Edition* page 693. Tell students that these plants are carnivorous and eat animals such as bugs and insects.

LEAD
THE
WAY

 Word Relationships

PRETEACH Tell students that paying attention to the way words are related can help them understand what they read. Discuss with students word relationships such as synonyms, antonyms, homonyms, and multiple-meaning words.

On the board, draw a chart like this. Have students copy the chart and help them fill it in with words from the story.

Word Relationships	Words From Story
synonyms	little/tiny
antonyms	opens/shuts
homophones	no/know
multiple-meaning words	neat

AFTER

Reading
"Fly Traps! Plants
that Bite Back"

Pages 692–696
Pages 697–699

Questions:
pages 692–699

Pages 700–703

Pages 704–707

Questions:
pages 700–707

Directed Reading: "Fly Traps! Plants that Bite Back"

RETEACH Use these sentences to walk students through the story.

- These are carnivorous plants. They eat bugs.
- Bladderwort plants grow in ponds. They use water to trap and eat bugs.
- These fly traps are called sundews. They live on mountains.
- Bugs stick to the leaves and the plant eats them.
- These are butterworts. They are fly traps that live in the same areas as sundews.
- Sundew and butterwort plants eat the bugs that stick to their leaves.
- The Venus flytrap catches insects by trapping them inside its leaves.
- What do carnivorous plants eat? (*animals*)
- How does the Venus fly trap catch insects? (*It traps them inside its leaves.*)
- Ants are small enough to escape the Venus fly trap. Flies and wasps cannot escape.
- Insects crawl inside the cobra lily. They fall into a pool inside the plant and cannot get out.
- Pitcher plants catch insects the same way that cobra lilies do. Some animals, such as spiders and small tree frogs, live in the pitchers.
- Can ants escape from the Venus fly trap? (*yes*)
- How do cobra lilies and pitcher plants catch bugs? (*The bugs fall into a pool inside the plants and cannot get out.*)

FLUENCY PRACTICE Invite volunteers to read one of the captions in the selection. Challenge them to choose one of the plants illustrated and to describe orally how it catches bugs.

Build Background: "The Food on Your Plate"

BEFORE

Making Connections pages 710–711

Concept Words
grow
farmer
store
eat
cooking
meal

PRETEACH Discuss with students what they learned about plants in "Fly Traps." Tell them that in "The Food on Your Plate" they will read about plants that we eat.

> **English-Language Learners Book**

Write the Concept Words on the board and use them in sentences.

- Janie wants to **grow** her own vegetables.
- She likes the idea of being a **farmer**.
- She will not buy vegetables at the **store** any more.
- She wants to **eat** only fresh vegetables from her garden.
- Janie uses different recipes when **cooking** her vegetables.
- She will eat her vegetables at almost every **meal**.

Have students add these words to their Language Dictionaries.

Directed Reading: "The Food on Your Plate"

AFTER

Skill Review pages 712–713

Summary *Much of the food we eat comes from plants — grains, fruits, and vegetables. Most plant foods are grown on farms by farmers who then sell the food to large companies that process and ship it to the stores where we buy it.*

Use these sentences to walk students through the story.

Pages 2–5
- Food is important for everyone.
- Bread, pasta, and cereal come from plants called grains.
- Rice is the most popular grain. People around the world eat rice every day.

Pages 6–9
- Other grains, such as wheat, rye, and corn are used to make bread.
- Fruits and vegetables come from plants, too.
- Most plant foods are grown on farms. The United States has a lot of farms.

 QUESTIONS: pages 2–9
- Where do bread, pasta, and cereal come from? (*plants called grains*)
- Where are most plant foods grown? (*on farms*)
- Why do you think the United States has a lot of farms? (*Responses will vary.*)

Pages 10–13
- Certain types of food are grown in different regions of the United States.
- Here a harvester gathers wheat.

Pages 14–16
- Farmers sell the food they grow to companies that process it.
- The food is sent to factories where it can become applesauce, bread, or another kind of food we buy at the supermarket. Some food is put in cans.

QUESTIONS: pages 10–16
- Is all food grown in the same region in the United States? (*no*)
- What do farmers do with the food they grow? (*They sell it to large companies that process it.*)
- What would you like about being a farmer? (*Responses will vary.*)

(Focus Skill) Word Relationships

RETEACH Review word relationships with students. Then draw on the board a two-column chart with the headings **Selection Words** and **Relationship to Other Words**. Ask students to revisit the story to complete the chart.

> **FLUENCY PRACTICE** Have students use their favorite illustration to retell part of "The Food on Your Plate." Encourage them to use as many vocabulary words and concept words as possible.

Independent Writing: Descriptive Paragraph

PRETEACH Tell students that they are going to begin to write a descriptive paragraph. Have students look back at the selections they read in this lesson to find a topic for their paragraph. Guide students to choose topics that lend themselves easily to descriptive writing. Write students' ideas on the board and have each student choose one. Work with students to write engaging introductions for their paragraphs. Encourage them to use lively, colorful verbs and as many sensory details as possible to fully describe their topics.

Grammar: Prepositions

PRETEACH Discuss the following with students:

■ A **preposition** is a word that shows how a noun or pronoun is related to another word in the sentence.

■ The **object of a preposition** is the noun or pronoun that follows the preposition.

Write the sentences below on the board and read them aloud. Circle the preposition in each sentence and underline the object of the preposition.

1. A bladderwort grows in a pond. (*preposition: in; object of the preposition: pond*)

2. The flowers are above the water. (*preposition: above; object of the preposition: water*)

3. The stems are under the water. (*preposition: under; object of the preposition: water*)

4. The stems have tiny bubbles on them. (*preposition: on; object of the preposition: them*)

5. Bugs get trapped inside the bubbles. (*preposition: inside; object of the preposition: bubbles*)

FLUENCY PRACTICE Have volunteers read aloud the descriptive paragraphs they wrote on plants and plant life.

Independent Writing: Descriptive Paragraph

RETEACH Have students read the drafts they wrote on page 173. Ask them what they would like to change about it and why. Ask: **Is your introduction interesting? Will it attract the reader's attention? Are your verbs lively and colorful? Do your details fully describe what you are writing about?** Discuss students' suggestions for changing or adding to their paragraphs. Work with students to revise their paragraphs. Monitor their work for errors in grammar and spelling, including their use of prepositions. Then have students copy the revised essay into their Language Journals.

Grammar-Writing Connection

RETEACH Review prepositions with students. Then write the following sentences on the board.

1. We eat many different kinds of plants. (*preposition: of; object of the preposition: plants*)
2. People depend on farmers for most foods. (*preposition: on; object of the preposition: farmer; preposition: for; object of the preposition: foods*)
3. People go to the store to buy foods. (*preposition: to; object of the preposition: store*)
4. Grains are made into many kinds of foods. (*preposition: into; object of the preposition: kinds; preposition: of; object of the preposition: foods*)
5. Grains come from grass plants. (*preposition: from; object of the preposition: grass plants*)
6. Many people eat grains at every meal. (*preposition: at; object of the preposition: meal*)
7. Wheat is another grain that is grown around the world. (*preposition: around; object of the preposition: world*)
8. Wheat is often ground into flour for bread. (*preposition: into; object of the preposition: flour; preposition: for; object of the preposition: bread*)

Have volunteers read the sentences aloud. Then have them circle the prepositions and underline their objects. Point out that some sentences have more than one preposition.

FLUENCY PRACTICE Have volunteers read their revised paragraphs aloud. Encourage listeners to pay attention to the details they hear and to ask the reader to clarify any that they do not understand.

Name _____

A Write a synonym for each of the following words.

1. big _____

2. shut _____

3. tale _____

Write an antonym for each of the following words.

4. stop _____

5. right _____

6. first _____

B Draw a picture of a carnivorous plant. Then write a few sentences to tell how the plant catches the bugs it eats.

_____

_____

_____

_____

TO THE TEACHER Review synonyms and antonyms with students. Then read the directions for part A aloud with students and have them complete the activity. For part B, read the directions aloud and encourage students to make their drawings and sentences as accurate and descriptive as possible.

LESSON 30

Use with "The Down and Up Fall"

Building Background and Vocabulary

Build Background/Access Prior Knowledge

Discuss with students the topic of pets and the importance of taking care of them. Prompt discussion by asking: **How many of you have a pet? What kind of pet do you have? What are some things you do to take care of your pet?** Record the responses on a concept web like this one.

Selection Vocabulary

PRETEACH Display Teaching Transparency 280, and read the words aloud. Then point to the pictures as you read the following sentences:

1. Tim sneaks down the **corridor**. He walks quietly down the hallway.
2. He is going to **investigate** a noise. He wants to find out what is causing it.
3. Toby welcomes Tim **enthusiastically**. He is very happy that Tim has come.
4. Toby has **transformed** his room. He has made many changes to it.
5. The new **decor** makes the room look like a cave. This painting is part of Toby's plan of decoration.
6. "**Apparently**, you worked hard on this. I can see all of the changes you made," Tim said.

AFTER

Building Background and Vocabulary

Selection Vocabulary

RETEACH Revisit Teaching Transparency 280. Read the words aloud with students. Have students work in pairs to discuss the meanings of the words and to answer questions such as: Does investigate mean "to find out about" or "to quiet down"?

Write the following sentence frames on the board. Read each frame, and ask students to choose a vocabulary word to complete it.

1. Candles are part of our holiday _____. (*decor*)
2. Our living room is _____ by the glowing lights. (*transformed*)
3. We put candles in the _____, too. (*corridor*)
4. Our cat, Felix, likes to _____ them. (*investigate*)
5. He plays _____ with the shadows they make. (*enthusiastically*)
6. _____, he thinks they are alive! (*Apparently*)

Have students write these words in their Language Dictionaries.

> **FLUENCY PRACTICE** Have students read the sentence frames aloud. Encourage them to describe the illustrations on Teaching Transparency 280, using the vocabulary words and any other words they know.

BEFORE
Reading "The Down and Up Fall" pages 716–729

Build Background: "The Down and Up Fall"

Have students look at the pictures on *Pupil Edition* pages 716–717. Tell students that the girl is Bolivia and that the bird is Bolivia's pet, a parrot named Lucette. Ask students where they think Bolivia and Lucette are. Then ask: **Does this look like a good place for a parrot? Does Lucette look happy?**

LEAD THE WAY

(Focus Skill) Author's Purpose

PRETEACH Tell students that an author's purpose is his or her reason for writing about a subject. Explain that the most common purposes are to inform, to entertain, and to persuade. Explain that the details and language an author uses are clues to his or her purposes. On the board draw a two-column chart with the headings Author's Purpose and Details. As students read, ask them to think about the author's purpose. Then complete the chart with students after they have read the story.

AFTER
Reading "The Down and Up Fall"

Directed Reading: "The Down and Up Fall"

RETEACH Use these sentences to walk students through the story.

Pages 716–719

? QUESTIONS: pages 716–719

Pages 720–723

- This is Bolivia and her pet parrot, Lucette.
- The nature club at Bolivia's school has made their classroom look and feel like a rain forest.
- Mr. Peters, the science teacher, has invited Bolivia to bring Lucette to visit the rainforest.
- Does Lucette visit a real rain forest? (*no*)
- What kind of bird is Lucette? (*a parrot*)
- This is Bolivia in the rain forest room with Kenny. The rain forest room looks and feels like a real rain forest.
- Kenny, Bolivia's classmate, has brought two pet snakes.
- The room starts to get very warm.

Pages 724–728

- Dr. Osborne, the assistant principal, visits the room. She doesn't like snakes.
- The sprinkler system goes on because it is too hot in the classroom.
- Dr. Osborne tells Mr. Peters that it's time for the nature club to study something else.

? QUESTIONS: pages 720–728

- Does the classroom look and feel like a real rain forest? (*yes*)
- Why does the sprinkler system go on? (*The room is very hot.*)

FLUENCY PRACTICE Ask students to read aloud their favorite part of the story.

Build Background: "Zoo-ology"

PRETEACH Discuss with students what they learned about pet care in "The Down and Up Fall." In "Zoo-ology" students will read about how zoologists and other scientists protect and care for animals, especially endangered animals.

English-
Language
Learners
Book

Concept Words
extinct
endangered
protect
natural
zoologist
aquarium

Write the concept words on the board and use them in sentences.

- Dinosaurs are **extinct**. They do not live on Earth anymore.
- Many **endangered** animals are in danger of becoming extinct.
- People need to **protect** animals so that they are safe.
- Wild animals live in **natural** homes, such as forests, mountains, and rivers.
- A **zoologist** is a scientist who studies animals.
- An **aquarium** is a home for animals that live in water.

Have students add these words to their Language Dictionaries.

Directed Reading: "Zoo-ology"

 Summary *A zoo is a place where wild animals are protected and studied. Zoos help endangered animals, and today zoo animals live in natural surroundings. Aquariums are zoos for animals that live in water.*

Use these sentences to walk students through the story.

Pages 2–3
- People keep animals such as fish, birds, lizards, or hamsters in their homes as pets.
- Most animals in the zoo are wild animals. The zoo protects and studies them.

Pages 4–7
- Some animals, like the dinosaur, are extinct. They no longer live on the earth.
- Animals that are almost extinct are called endangered. Zoos try to protect endangered animals. The Bronx Zoo saved the buffalo from extinction.

QUESTIONS: pages 2–7
- Are dinosaurs extinct? (*yes*)
- What animal did the Bronx Zoo save from extinction? (*the buffalo*)
- Why are zoos important? (*They protect and study animals, and they help save endangered animals from extinction.*)

Pages 8–11
- More than 500 kinds of animals are endangered.
- Zoologists and other scientists work hard to save endangered animals.
- Animal doctors called vets help keep the zoo animals healthy.

Pages 12–13
- Zoos used to keep animals in cages. Now zoo animals live in more natural settings.

Pages 14–15
- An aquarium is a zoo for animals that live in water.
- Scientists help these animals, too.

QUESTIONS: pages 8–15
- Is a zoologist a kind of animal? (*no*)
- What is an animal doctor called? (*a vet*)
- What is an aquarium? (*a zoo for animals that live in water*)

★ Focus Skill Author's Purpose

RETEACH Review author's purpose with students. Have them display the charts they completed after reading "The Down and Up Fall."

FLUENCY PRACTICE Have volunteers read a page from the selection or choose an illustration to describe.

Independent Writing: Story

PRETEACH Tell students that they are going to write a story about a character who helps an endangered animal. Tell students that they may want to write about one of the animals they read about in "Zoo-ology." Remind students that every story has characters, a setting, a problem, and a solution. Draw on the board a story map. Ask students to copy the story map, and work with them to fill it in. Have students use their completed story maps to draft their stories.

Characters	Setting

Problem

Important Events

Solution

Grammar: Prepositional Phrases

PRETEACH Discuss prepositional phrases with students. Point out the following:

■ A **prepositional phrase** is made up of a preposition, the object of the preposition, and any words in between.

Write the following sentences on the board, and read them aloud:

■ *Whales live in the ocean.*
■ *They cannot live on land.*
■ *Yet they cannot breathe under the water.*

Circle the prepositional phrase in each sentence, pointing out the preposition and the object of the preposition.

Write the following sentences on the board and read them aloud. Have students circle the prepositional phrase in each sentence, naming the preposition and its object.

1. Felipe went to a real rain forest.
2. It is in Canada.
3. Felipe took a hike through the rain forest.
4. He waded across a stream.
5. He took pictures of the animals.

FLUENCY PRACTICE Have volunteers read aloud the stories they completed in the writing activity.

Independent Writing: Story

RETEACH Have students return to the stories they drafted during Preteach. Have students work in pairs to revise their stories. Tell students to look for places where story events aren't clear or the word choice could be clearer. Help them identify and correct errors in spelling, grammar, and punctuation. Have students copy their revised stories into their Language Journals.

Grammar-Writing Connection

RETEACH Write these sentences on the board, and read them aloud with students: *"The Down and Up Fall" tells about a pet parrot and how the parrot's owner protects her. "Zoo-ology" tells how zoos and scientists protect animals.*

Ask students if they can identify the one prepositional phrase in the sentences above. (*about a pet parrot*) Ask students to name the preposition and its object. (*about, parrot*)

Have students work in pairs or in small groups to discuss why it is important for people to protect and care for animals. Then have each student draw a picture to show his or her ideas. Have students write paragraphs describing their pictures. Tell students to use prepositional phrases in some of their sentences. Ask them to underline the phrases. Check students' writing and point out any corrections they need to make.

FLUENCY PRACTICE Have students read aloud the paragraphs that describe their pictures.

Name _____

Think about the wild animals that you know. Draw a picture showing the animals in their natural homes. Label your picture with the names of the animals that you draw.

TO THE TEACHER Have students think about wild animals, either those that live in a zoo or those that live in the wild. Ask students to draw pictures showing some of these animals in their natural habitats. Have students label their pictures with the names of the animals they have drawn.